ORPHANLAND

Advance Praise for *Orphanland*

"*Orphanland* is a heartwarming novel that explores the impact of the opioid epidemic on children and their families. The story includes meaningful friendships between kids who come from a variety of challenging circumstances, an adorable kitten, and a page-turning mystery involving Willa's caretaker—along with the discovery of old diaries that may contain clues. Willa is easy to root for."

—**Sydney Dunlap,** award-winning author of
Racing the Clouds and *It Happened on Saturday*

"As an advocate for depictions of belonging in children's books, I can say that *Orphanland* delivers. It is a hopeful story that at its heart is about people's desire and right to be seen in all of their fullness. Through beautiful storytelling, Lauren Fischer effortlessly tackles topics that, while important to discuss, can be difficult to talk about in an age-appropriate way. Kudos."

—**Clothilde Ewing,** author of *Stella Keeps the Sun Up*

"Lauren Fischer should be applauded for bringing a nonbinary teen character into the fold as well as a character with Down syndrome who is written as just another person in the house who is loved. *Orphanland* has strong messages about the differences each of us has, and the benefits those differences bring."

—**Rob Snow,** executive producer, The Improvaneers
documentary series (*Burn the Script*), and
CEO/creator, The Improvaneer Method

"*Orphanland* is an equally heartwarming and heartbreaking novel about young people's resilience in the face of tragedy. As a physician and someone whose family has been affected by the opioid crisis, I consider *Orphanland* an essential read."

—**Juliet Bradley,** MD, family physician

"With the perfect mix of secret library shelves, new friendships, and a potentially haunted school, *Orphanland* keeps readers turning pages while falling in love with Willa and her friends."

—**Lynn Leitch,** children's author

ORPHANLAND

Lauren Fischer

M·P·P
www.MissionPointPress.com

Published by Mission Point Press
www.MissionPointPress.com

Cover Design: Jeff Bane

 Mission Point Press

Hardcover ISBN: 978-1-965278-76-5
Softcover ISBN: 978-1-965278-77-2

LoC Control Number: 2025910679

Printed in the United States of America

CONTENTS

Chapter 1. Hardly Used — 1

Chapter 2. The Southern Ohio Children's Home — 11

Chapter 3. Forgetting What Came Before — 27

Chapter 4. The Midlands Christian Academy for (Bad) Boys — 43

Chapter 5. Helpless Creatures — 59

Chapter 6. Secrets and Ghosts — 73

Chapter 7. Sanctuary in the Woods — 87

Chapter 8. To the Letter — 105

Chapter 9. The Ties of Kinship — 121

Chapter 10. Secrets to the Grave — 135

Chapter 11. Sometimes You Have to Be Nosy — 149

Chapter 12. Curling Up With the Moon — 161

Chapter 13. Past Meets Present — 171

Chapter 14. The School Revisited — 187

Chapter 15. What We Don't Talk About — 201

Chapter 16. Changing a System — 215

Chapter 17. The Remembering Ceremony — 225

Chapter 18. Hope Isn't Always Enough — 241

Chapter 19. How Do You Say Goodbye? — 253

Chapter 20. Making the World Your Home as You Would Like to See It — 267

Acknowledgments — 281

Discussion Questions — 285

For J and A
I am forever grateful I get to be your mom.

or·phan \'or-fən\ n
1. a child deprived by death of one or usually both parents
2. a young animal that has lost its mother
3. one deprived of some protection or advantage

The Merriam-Webster Dictionary, 11th ed

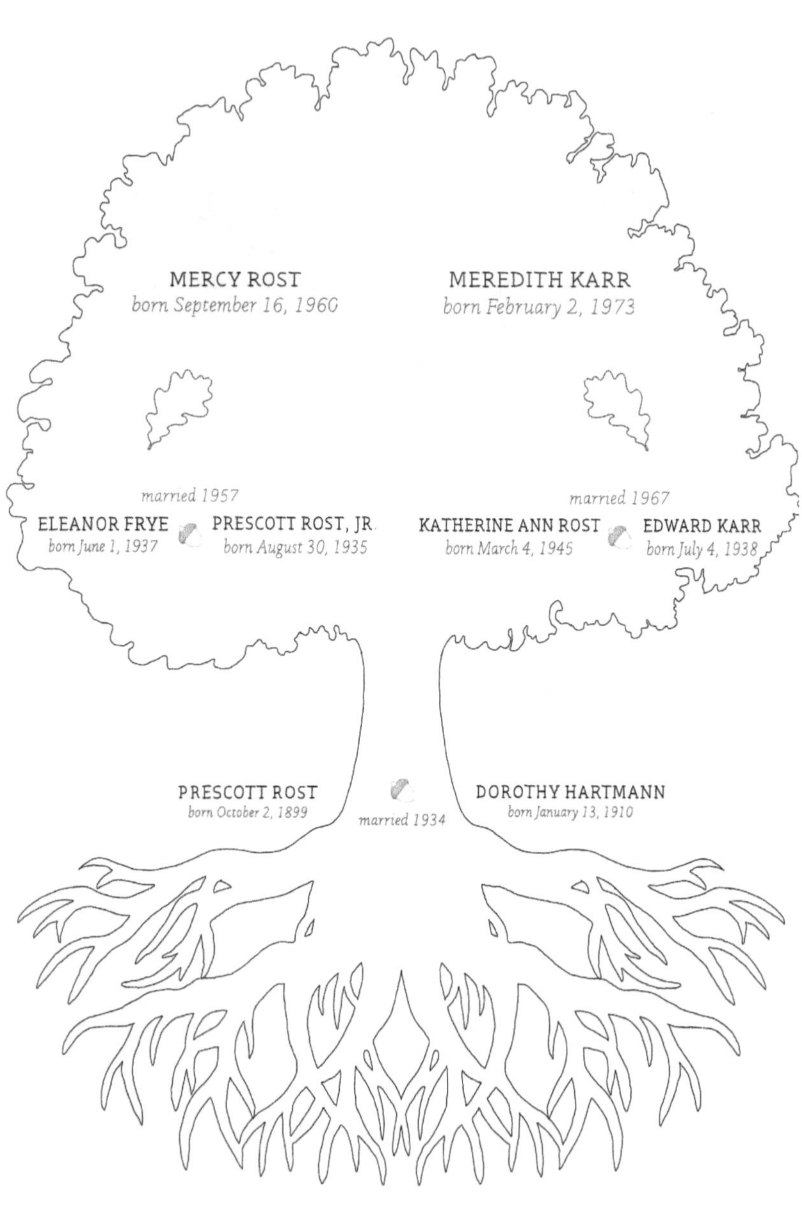

MERCY ROST
born September 16, 1960

MEREDITH KARR
born February 2, 1973

married 1957
ELEANOR FRYE
born June 1, 1937
PRESCOTT ROST, JR.
born August 30, 1935

married 1967
KATHERINE ANN ROST
born March 4, 1945
EDWARD KARR
born July 4, 1938

PRESCOTT ROST
born October 2, 1899
married 1934
DOROTHY HARTMANN
born January 13, 1910

June 2, 1976

Dear Mercy,

It might not come as a big surprise that I have to leave Shawneeville. It's better if I disappear. I want you to know I am not sorry for meeting you. I'm pinning my hope on seeing you again someday. You are the only good thing that happened to me here.

Love,
Jack

2019

Hardly Used

IN MY LIFE, THERE'S NO such thing as happy-happiness. Everything happy has a sad part attached. I am always sad when a new orphan comes to the Southern Ohio Children's Home, because every new kid brings another sad story. Each story has some happiness too, like having a soft landing with Mercy. She is the kindest grown-up I've ever met. We don't call her Miss Mercy or Missus Rost. Just Mercy is fine by her. That might tell you the type of grown-up she is.

This is a *good* place, let's get that straight. The Southern Ohio Children's Home is out of a fairy tale, dead mothers and all.

I was helping Mercy with our latest sad story. We waited on the front porch that Saturday morning for the nuns to arrive with the drug baby. Mercy was checking her phone for updates from Sister Hazel, and I was checking the gray sky for spring rain. I try to help Mercy every day, when I'm not causing trouble. I don't try to cause trouble, but somehow that's where I end up. Usually for daydreaming or forgetting what I'm supposed to be doing and instead doing something I'm *not* supposed to be doing. Mercy doesn't have harsh punishments. Not like the punishments I've heard about from other kids when they confess what their families from *before* did—like hit them or not feed them. It's nothing like that here.

When I do get in trouble, my punishment from Mercy is "the Look," then being sent to clean a bathroom or take out the nursery's diaper bin. I don't mind doing chores, but I do mind "the Look" because I do not want to disappoint Mercy for one second. "The Look" is a silence where she says to me, *What have you done now, Willa Johnson? You are eleven years old, and you know better.* Then she'll say aloud, "Go. Think about what you did. When you're ready to apologize, you may come back."

I'm always ready to apologize right away. Mercy wants me to think about it first though, so when I do say *I'm sorry,* it's coming from a place that makes my apology real, and I know what I'm saying is true. Sometimes, when the words come out right, with meaning inside them, Mercy gives me a rare hug. In those moments, I take a deep breath, I smell her lavender perfume, and I feel safe.

I came to the Southern Ohio Children's Home when I was seven, after my grandfather died. Pop-pop was another grown-up who loved me a lot. He used to sit in his recliner and watch the Cubs, even though Ohio is not near Chicago and we have our own baseball teams. His trailer was filled with candles and hearts because that's what Grammaw loved. Pop-pop kept every piece of her, to make himself feel like she was still there. Even the clothes in her closet. When Momma died, I tried to keep her with me too, but there hadn't been much left. After I moved in with him, Pop-pop had to quit fixing cars because his emphysema made it so he needed to take his oxygen tank everywhere.

I was happy living with Pop-pop, but the sad part was

that Momma was dead, and by then, Pop-pop was dying, too. Sad-happiness.

While Mercy and me waited for the drug baby, I thought about that baby's story. The happy part was that it was coming to meet Mercy. The sad part was that its mommy, daddy, or maybe both, were addicted to the same kind of drugs many grown-ups around here are addicted to. Mercy and my teacher, Miss Samantha, are always telling us that when someone's addiction is bad, they'll take anything, because they get sicker when they *don't* take drugs. It's kind of confusing. They teach us that the point is not to take them in the first place. Drug abuse and the problems that come with it is something we talk about every day, I swear, because nearly every kid at the Southern Ohio Children's Home has a story to tell that has to do with opioid drugs. Even Miss Samantha. Her baby sister died from opioids. Drugs are everywhere. You'd think they're growing on our trees.

Sister Hazel's rust-covered green van finally sputtered up the pebble drive from County Highway J, the words *Ministry of Hope* painted on each side. The van stopped. Or died. I couldn't tell.

"Ministry of Hopelessness, more like," I said. "Driving around in that van."

"If you can't say something nice, Willa—"

Mercy is trying to teach me not to say mean things.

"But it's true!" I lashed out in a tone. I can't help it sometimes.

Mercy glared at me. I knew better than to apologize before thinking about it, so I pursed my lips and didn't say anything more.

Normally when I talk in a tone, Mercy is patient with me.

Not today. Mercy was in a mood. I wanted to ask her what was wrong, but I knew she'd never tell me. *My troubles do not need to be anyone's troubles but my own*, is what she'd say.

Mercy puts herself together like a watercolor painting, with her long gray curls and loose, flowing clothes. Today her hair was pulled back in a headband she'd probably left on after washing her face. She hadn't even done her makeup, and she always does her makeup. She says it covers her brown age spots. She was still clutching her cloth napkin from breakfast, which I thought was strange.

I could tell there was something Mercy wasn't telling me. I watched her as she watched Sister Hazel and Sister Constance fuss with the van door and the drug baby's car seat.

There used to be things my momma wouldn't tell me, but I'd always find out.

I was going to find out with Mercy, too.

"Got a new one for you, Mercy," Sister Hazel said as she walked toward us. "Hardly used. Ha!"

Mercy closed her eyes and shook her head. She hates when Sister Hazel makes that joke. Probably because it isn't funny.

Mercy had been expecting the "hardly used" baby. She had *not* been expecting the police car that was coming up the drive. The car pulled behind the Ministry of Hopelessness van. A kid who looked every bit a criminal scowled at us from the back seat. The kid had a bruised face and purple mohawk and was wearing a ripped shirt.

We don't have many visitors at the Southern Ohio Children's Home. Today was busy.

"Willa, please tell Miss Lupe to get the last crib ready for the new baby." Mercy was staying focused on the drug baby, not the police car.

I didn't ask Mercy what would happen if another baby came after we used the last crib. The home has gotten more filled up since I arrived four years ago, and Mercy's always running out of money. She says it's because of the "crisis in our community." I know which crisis she means—the drug crisis—but it seems like there are a lot of other crises tied up with that one.

"You want me to go inside now?" I whined. "Things are just getting good."

"Now, Willa!" Mercy hardly ever raises her voice at me.

"But I don't even know that baby's name!" I raised my voice back.

"What would you like to call her, Willa?" Sister Hazel asked. She is a thousand years old. Her pale skin has wrinkles like mud cracks in a dry riverbed.

"What about Hope?" Sister Constance suggested.

"Not Hope!" I said. We already have three Hopes, thanks to Sister Constance, Our Lady of Perpetual Hopes.

Unlike Sister Hazel, Sister Constance is young. She's always trying to recruit me. She says how she'd wanted to be a nun ever since she was my age and that she'd never trust a man more than Jesus. *At least He keeps His promises, unlike what's running around our town*, Sister Constance says. *The promise of Eternal Life is a safer bet. I'm with the Lord.* Though I don't know how she knows the Lord keeps *His* promise of Eternal Life since she's not dead yet, is she?

Sister Hazel carried the baby in its car seat to Mercy, who cooed over the sweet thing while checking all its fingers and toes. Then she passed the baby off to me.

"Now, please go inside, Willa, and take the baby up to Miss Lupe," Mercy said calmly.

The baby was swaddled tight in her car seat. The skin on her face and hands was a splotchy mix of red, purple, brown, and yellow.

The policewoman slammed her car door shut and headed toward Mercy, taking off her hat and scratching her scalp with a long, glittery fingernail. Her black hair was braided into perfect, straight cornrows held together in a low ponytail.

"Willa, go!" Mercy said in a stern tone.

"Fine!" I huffed. "And by the way, I will call this baby Calamity. That's more like it." I took the baby in its carrier and stomped up the front porch stairs, making a show. "Miss Lupe!" I shouted. "Calamity's here!"

But instead of going inside and missing the excitement, I stopped and bent over one of the flower boxes lined up along the white porch. I learned long ago that if you're doing chores, you turn invisible. I rocked Calamity's carrier and weeded and turned invisible. Miss Lupe could wait, because I knew there was something Mercy wasn't telling me.

"Good morning, Mercy," the police officer said. She and Mercy nodded at each other like old friends. I watched as she turned and introduced herself to the nuns. "I'm Deputy Bell."

"What brings you by, Belinda?" Mercy asked.

"I got a domestic call this morning and was hoping you might be able to help."

"Oh, Lord, have mercy." Sister Hazel stood between Deputy Bell and Mercy, interrupting what wasn't her business. Sister Constance was hanging on every word from her seat in the van.

"Mr. and Mrs. Springdale have been having a hard time with their child, Kacey," Deputy Bell said. "We got a call from them this morning, so I responded with another visit to their home. Kacey was out on the lawn with a packed bag and a bloody lip."

"How old is Kacey?" Mercy asked.

"They're thirteen." The police officer looked back at her car. "You see, they—"

"'They,' meaning Kacey?" Mercy asked.

Deputy Bell nodded. "Kacey goes by they/them," she said.

"Why? Are there two of them?" Sister Hazel snorted, making another bad joke.

"Just Kacey," Deputy Bell said, annoyed. She did not bother spelling things out for Sister Hazel. She didn't need to explain it to Mercy. Or to me. Kacey would not be the first kid at the Southern Ohio Children's Home who went by they/them. I was not surprised that Sister Hazel didn't know about people having different pronouns, living in a convent with she/her nuns.

"Good thing there's only one of them, and good thing it's not a baby, because Mercy is out of cribs," Sister Hazel blabbed.

"And money," Mercy added.

"That's nothing new," Sister Hazel opened her big mouth again.

"I know everyone is always looking to you for help, Mercy," Deputy Bell said.

"Maybe it's time I sell that land," Mercy said. She pointed past the barren field and black oak tree, toward the crooked chain-link fence and *No Trespassing* signs.

"The old Midlands school property?" Sister Hazel couldn't stop butting in. She didn't even know what she was talking about because there wasn't a school there. I'd've known if there was.

"Yes. The abandoned reformatory school," Mercy said. "We don't use it. I'm already in touch with my cousin Meredith to see if she has legal advice to offer. The inheritance from her mom is gone—I stretched it as far as I could—and the state doesn't cover nearly enough per child."

I stopped rocking Calamity in her car seat and looked down the hill past the ravine where we were forbidden to ever go. All I could see were trees. There wasn't any sign of this reformatory school they were talking about.

One of our rules at the home is that we can explore anywhere in the fields on our "going out" adventures. The former farmland used to be inhabited by Indigenous people—the Shawnee Tribe. We sometimes find their arrowheads and mail them back to the Tribe's main office in Oklahoma. We can't go past the ravine, which is a far walk across the field. I never thought about it. I didn't know it was Mercy's property.

I was thinking about it now.

"Was there any mention of payment from Kacey's parents?" Mercy asked.

"I only spoke to their father," Deputy Bell said. "I was the one who suggested Kacey come here. I imagine Mr. Springdale can make a small donation. He didn't, ah …" She walked closer to Mercy so that Sisters Hazel and Constance would stop listening in on the conversation. They are so nosy.

"He didn't know what else to do," Deputy Bell said. "He doesn't feel right about any of this, but his wife is having a problem with Kacey. Like I said, this wasn't my first time visiting their house."

I quietly took a seat in a nearby porch chair and rocked the sleeping Calamity with my foot. My legs are long, which is something I got from my momma, along with the freckles covering my whole body, which I wish she'd kept for herself. I am happy she gave me her hazel eyes though.

"Do Kacey's parents understand that they are temporarily relinquishing their parental rights?" Mercy asked. "I'll need them to come sign some forms. Preferably with a lawyer."

Deputy Bell nodded again.

"Mrs. Springdale wants Kacey to go to a religious treatment facility," she said. "Mr. Springdale's not having it. He's got Kacey's back, as far as I can tell, but he feels they aren't safe around their mother. I have to agree. Maybe you could buy them some time to sort out their issues."

"I don't know how you do it, Mercy," Sister Hazel said. "All these years, and things are only getting worse. I do pray though. Lord, how I pray. Lord, have mercy."

Sister Hazel walked back to the Ministry of Hopelessness van. From inside, Sister Constance waved goodbye with a hopeless look on her face before sliding the door closed. I know we all prayed for that van to start, which it did on the third try. The nuns drove their sad van back to County Highway J.

"Here's Mr. Springdale's phone number." Deputy Bell pulled a piece of paper from her pocket and handed it to Mercy.

"We'll make sure Kacey is safe while their parents figure out the right thing to do," Mercy said.

"Honestly …" Deputy Bell said, looking like she was finally ready to say the thought that had been picking at her brain ever since she'd stepped out of her car. "Getting out of their house will be good for Kacey. They're a good kid."

"They all are," Mercy snapped.

Don't get Mercy started, I'm telling you. She loves all children and hates a lot of grown-ups. I could tell she already wanted to hate Kacey's mom, but she couldn't afford to hate their parents too much.

She needed their money.

Kacey is unique because they're what you call a "dumped" child. That means their parents are not dead. Most kids at the home have dead parents in the sky, from the crisis in our community.

My momma died when I was six, and I came here when I was seven. I'm eleven now, all grown up practically, even though I don't want to grow up. Ever. I remember how scared I was when I first got here. When Mercy bent down to shake my hand, I thought she was the tallest woman I'd ever seen. She is not mean like Miss Hannigan from Little Orphan Annie, and life here is not hard-knock like people might think.

But new kids usually don't arrive by police car.

"What'd you do?" I asked Kacey when they stormed up the porch with their backpack.

Kacey snarled at me like a rabid dog. "Exist," they said.

None of us kids ever ask questions about *before*. We know to avoid a sore subject, and *before* is a sore subject for all of us, no matter how long you've been at the home. *Before* is a scab that bleeds every day for the rest of your life, even if you think sometimes it's healed over.

"I hate my life," Kacey said.

Mercy always says that using the words "I understand" is magic, because you don't need to say any other words to help a person feel better. But, same as with saying apologies, you have to mean it from someplace deep inside or the magic won't work.

I could understand if Kacey hated the whole world when Deputy Bell dropped them off at the Southern Ohio Children's Home. I do not hate my life, but when I had first came to the home, I hated everything and everyone. I even hated Mercy.

"I understand," I told Kacey. And I meant it.

The Southern Ohio
Children's Home

My teacher Miss Samantha says that for someone who's eleven years old, I am "wise beyond my years." I am one of the oldest kids at the home, and there aren't many of us close to my age. That's why I was hoping right off that Kacey would see me as someone who could be their friend.

I took Kacey and Calamity up the princess staircase—the kind that winds in a curve and has a white banister—in the front hall. I gave the baby carrier to Miss Lupe in the toddler room, where she was finishing changing a diaper. She has a lot of helpers, but she's always the one changing a diaper. I help Miss Lupe with the little kids in small ways all the time, like wiping their noses or hugging them when they cry or sometimes changing a diaper myself.

"Hello, precious!" Miss Lupe said, smiling at the new baby.

"You can call her Calamity," I said, sticking with my name and not Sister Constance's.

Next I led Kacey down the hallway to my bedroom, which I

share with the other older kids. Sixty or so kids of all ages live in the home, give or take. I've gotten used to all the screaming little voices—they even make me happy sometimes—but I could tell they were already hitting Kacey's nerves.

"Where's the bathroom?" they asked.

I pointed at the door across from our bedroom. "Right here."

Kacey bolted and slammed the bathroom door behind them without saying a word.

I stared at the closed door. What if Kacey stayed in there all day? What if I had to pee?

"I'll be across the hall!" I shouted and hoped Kacey heard me.

We call our bedroom The Fortress. We pretend it's a magical place where everything we say inside can't escape. It's our hideout. Our safe, quiet place.

Honestly, if we didn't all live at the Southern Ohio Children's Home, I'm not sure that Justin, Roy, Elizabeth, and me would have chosen each other for friends. That is both a good thing and a bad thing. Good because I am with people who are different from myself, which Miss Samantha says is important in life. Bad because I could use a kindred spirit, like the kind Anne has in the book *Anne of Green Gables*. Someone you can tell your "inmost soul" to, as Anne says. Anne is also an orphan, but she is the kind who is looking to be adopted. I am not.

The main window in The Fortress is a circle above the home's front door. A rainbow rag rug covers the wood floor. There are beanbag chairs and three dressers, although we only use two because the drawers don't work on the third one and Roy has a fit when they don't push in. There's also a closet for shoes and hanging-up clothes, and a small desk and chair that we fight over because that's our throne.

Justin was sitting at the throne, reading the encyclopedia. He has a crown of black curls. His eyebrows are usually squeezed together from thinking so hard. Justin is twelve and is smarter than all of us combined. Probably because he's a big-time reader. He's already read through that encyclopedia set twice. I think he'd stop breathing if his face wasn't stuck in a book.

Roy was playing solitaire on his bed, cursing at the bad cards. His red hair was a mess of curls, like usual. He never remembers to brush it. Like me, Roy is eleven, but unlike me, he is not wise beyond his years. He swears *a lot*, especially when we're in The Fortress. Roy's white skin was turning red as the Queen of Hearts because he was losing.

"*Damn* it!" he said. Those words meant he might whip the deck across the room any second.

Roy likes to fight so much he even gets Justin going, and Justin is a pacifist. Justin's idol is Dr. Martin Luther King Jr. Justin always has a sad smile in his eyes, probably because he's so wise.

HATE CANNOT DRIVE OUT HATE, ONLY LOVE CAN DO THAT. That's what it says on the poster over Justin's bed.

One time, Roy kept pulling bookmarks out of Justin's books, which is real annoying even if you're not reading a hundred books at once. Justin finally lost it and punched Roy in the head. You better believe Roy punched Justin back, because Roy's family did it that way. Roy says his family is "white trash." Mercy tells Roy those words are not allowed.

Roy is scrawny and Justin is sturdy, but if I had to pick a winner, it would be Roy. We break up their fights as fast as we can because Roy is "troubled," and we don't want him to go somewhere for "troubled" boys, which would be nothing like life here. Roy is not *all* bad. Plus, he's learning to be better, thanks to help from Mercy and Miss Samantha.

In the corner of The Fortress, Elizabeth hugged her Lovey-Pup and looked out the window, probably dreaming about being adopted by a forever family. Unlike me, she wants to get adopted. She is ten and is the youngest of us older orphans. She is also the loneliest. We have to let each other be lonely—or mad or sad—because we don't know about each other's *befores*, except that some or all of it isn't good.

I've taken Elizabeth "under my wing." She likes me to put braids in her straight blonde hair so she can sleep in them to make her hair wavy. I also help take care of her stuffed dog because it pulls her mind back from the place it's always going. I pretend to give Lovey-Pup shots and fix his ear infections and treat him for heartworms and fleas.

The Fortress is the second-best room in the home. The circle window has a ledge where you can sit and read, or stare across the fields to County Highway J. Some nights when the moonlight shines bright, the whole moon practically fits in that circle. It's magic when that happens.

"Mercy said there's an abandoned reformatory school out past the ravine," I said. "And we have a new roommate. Kacey. They're hiding in the bathroom."

I sat down on the rag rug. Justin, Roy, and Elizabeth joined me in a circle, where we like to have our talks.

"*Great!* A new roommate!" Roy yelled and rolled his eyes so hard I thought they'd fall out the back of his head. Then he punched Justin on the arm for no good reason.

"Stop it, Roy." Justin brushed him off.

"What does *reformatory* mean?" Elizabeth asked. She looked scared, like always.

Kacey finally came out of the bathroom and entered The

Fortress. We got a good look at their swollen bloody lip and purple mohawk and couldn't help staring.

"Kacey, this is everyone," I said. "Everyone, meet Kacey."

Justin and Roy waved and said hello.

"I'm Elizabeth. I like your hair."

"Thanks." Kacey ran a hand through the purple stripe down the center of their head. It made their blue eyes look extra blue.

"You can have that bed." I pointed to the bunk above mine.

Kacey flopped their backpack onto the mattress then crossed their arms and stared out the window, pretending to ignore us.

"I know there is something else Mercy's not saying," I said to everyone on the rug.

"Like what?" Justin asked. "It sounds like she already said something if she told you about this abandoned school."

I shrugged. I didn't dare tell them my deepest fear—that Mercy was going to get rid of me because she needed the room for more drug babies. What if *that's* what she wasn't telling me?

"You haven't heard of the Midlands Christian Academy for Boys?" Kacey asked.

We stared at them, everyone hearing their tough voice for the first time. We all shook our heads *no*. I wondered if this was one of those things that regular kids know about. I have one regular friend: Finn. He works with me at All Creatures animal shelter. He tells me about regular life at Shawneeville Central High School.

"We never knew about it." I patted the rug next to me, hoping Kacey would sit with us.

"Everyone knows about the Midlands reform school," Kacey bragged. They walked to our circle but didn't sit. "It closed a long time ago. They abused the boys who went there."

Roy and Justin flinched at Kacey's words. "Why?" they both asked.

"Because they were bad kids," Kacey said. "Like me."

Elizabeth looked worried as she rubbed Lovey-Pup's threadbare ears.

"We aren't allowed to go past the ravine," I said. "I guess now we know why."

The fact that Mercy was keeping such a big secret was making me feel sad-sadness. I didn't feel any happiness even at the corners. There was no sad-happiness, or happy-sadness. Just sad-sadness. I pulled out the thoughts I keep stored for those sneaky moments when all at once everything is unknowable. I thought about my momma and the feel of her hug after she'd give me a chocolate chip cookie we'd just baked together.

"Are there any video games here?" Kacey asked, pulling me out of my thought.

"Yeah, right," Roy said.

"Mercy doesn't let us play video games," Justin said.

"Mercy doesn't let us do anything," I added.

"That's not true!" Elizabeth shouted.

Elizabeth was right, but I was mad at Mercy. There was something she was keeping from me—from us all. Midlands Academy felt like the beginning of the secret, not the end.

I wished for the ten millionth time that I had my momma back again, because then I wouldn't have my sad-sadness, everything-is-unknowable, Black-Hole feeling.

"We have regular games in the library," Justin said to Kacey. He was already back reading again.

Kacey looked like they'd rather be inside a video game where they could shoot lasers from their eyeballs and burn everything down.

"Come on, I'll show you," I said. I was worried Roy and Kacey might end up in a fight if we gave them half a chance, and I could tell Elizabeth needed her quiet time. Plus, I still wanted to try and be Kacey's friend.

"Whatever." Kacey shuffled out the door behind me.

I took them down the hidden back staircase that goes to the kitchen. I needed a cookie.

"There's lots of hidden stuff in this house," I said to Kacey.

"Hidden stuff?" they repeated.

I nodded. "This is an old mansion with secrets—secret staircases and laundry chutes, hidden closets under the stairs and passageways to the basement, a safe in the wall behind a painting. There's even a dumbwaiter."

I saw on Kacey's face that they'd never heard of a dumbwaiter before.

"It's a tiny elevator for food and drinks," I explained. "Mercy had it closed off because you can't have a tiny elevator in a house full of toddlers. Too tempting."

Kacey followed me down the back stairs with the worn carpet to the kitchen, where Charlie and his crew are always cooking or baking something that smells delicious. No one was in the kitchen now though because they were on a break between meals.

"I like to use these back stairs so I can steal cookies," I said. Kacey did not look impressed, but I was trying.

I promise you, Charlie doesn't mind if I help myself to some cookies. I knew he wouldn't mind if I gave one to Kacey. Charlie has a smile for everyone and teases you like you can't ever try any of his food. *Hands off!* he says, and then he looks at his right-hand woman, Emily, to make sure she passes you a still-hot blueberry muffin, which she does while putting a finger to her lips, like it's some big secret. Emily has Down syndrome and was raised by Mercy since she was two. She's grown up now, but Mercy arranged it so she'd never have to leave if she didn't want to.

I dream about doing the same thing as Emily—staying at the home my whole life.

I went to the secret place in the pantry where Emily keeps the cookie jar. I grabbed two and handed one to Kacey.

"No thanks," they said.

"You sure?"

Kacey nodded. They were not letting me in one inch.

I'd have to be patient for Kacey to stop growling at me. It's like when Finn and me bring a stray mutt into the shelter, and they are showing us their teeth and have their hackles up. As soon as they figure out we're going to spoil them with treats and pets, they turn soft and never want us to stop rubbing their belly.

I ate both cookies myself and led Kacey out the back kitchen door, past the little farm where we keep the chickens and grow flowers and herbs and vegetables.

"My favorite chicken is right there—Henrietta. Isn't she pretty?"

I could tell Kacey didn't want to notice anything, but I caught them sneaking a look at Henrietta anyway.

We went around to the front porch and crossed the threshold together again. Neither of us was stomping this time.

To the left of the front hall is the *best* room in the Southern Ohio Children's Home: the library. Everything about the library makes you look up. From the white arched doorway entrance, to the tall ceilings and windows, to the bookshelves that go all the way to the top. Even the white ladder that rolls along one wall so you can reach the books up high. There is also a quotation on the wall that Miss Katherine—Mercy's aunt—had painted when she first made the library:

—James Baldwin

It is a perfect quote for a library, especially a library in a residential children's home where there is plenty of pain and heartbreak. I didn't know who James Baldwin was until I found him on the Black Scholars shelf. Turns out, he was friends with Dr. King.

We used to try touching Mr. Baldwin's words by sneaking turns on the rolling ladder, even though it's only for teachers and helpers. Miss Samantha had to tie it off because one of the kindergartners got his finger smashed beneath a wheel. Now we can't sneak rides on it anymore.

I always get a feeling of pride when I walk into the library. Miss Samantha has taught us how to be library experts, both here and at the Shawneeville Public Library. I might have been bragging on the Southern Ohio Children's Home by bringing Kacey here, but I didn't want them to think they'd ended up someplace bad. Not like that secret school where boys were abused.

The library has a faded red couch, four study desks, two wing-back chairs with the buttons all torn off, and a giant wooden desk that had belonged to Miss Katherine when she lived here.

I sat at the desk and grabbed the display-stand book—Mercy switches them out twice a week, to always keep us reading new books—and pretended like I wasn't paying attention to Kacey, who was finally taking things in.

"Who are these people?" they asked.

I spun around to look at the pictures hanging on the wall behind me.

"That's everyone who's lived here," I said. "We take a group photo every year."

I looked at the photos with Kacey. Some faces, like Mercy's and Charlie's and Emily's, are in every photo going back to when Mercy had first started the home. Twenty-one framed pictures in all. Some faces only show up in one picture. Others, like me, are in more than a few. You can see me growing up from a scared seven-year-old to the most recent photo, taken right after I'd had a growth spurt.

"That's me last year." I pointed it out for Kacey. "I got lice after that and had to get my hair cut short. I'm growing it out. I can almost get it in a ponytail."

"I like your hair better now," Kacey said, comparing me to my photograph.

"You do?" I touched my hair and smiled, even though I wasn't sure I agreed with them.

Kacey nodded. "It's different from most girls' hair."

"Thank you," I said, taking it for a compliment, because I know it's good to be different.

Kacey looked at each photograph like they were looking for themself.

"Who's that?" They pointed to a small photo that was out of place among the bigger frames.

"That's Miss Katherine and her husband and daughter. They

were the family who lived in this house before they gave it to Mercy. This was Katherine's desk."

"Why'd they give the house to Mercy?" Kacey asked.

"Miss Katherine was Mercy's aunt. More like her mother. And Meredith—" I pointed to the little girl in the family photo, "she's Mercy's cousin. She's the only one besides Mercy who's still alive, but she doesn't live in Shawneeville anymore."

"Is Mercy nice?"

I nodded. "She loves us all like we're her own. Even though, you know … we're not."

Looking at Katherine's photo made me wonder if Mercy ever missed her aunt the same way I miss my momma. She had "took Mercy in," the way Mercy tells it. I didn't know anything about Mercy's real mom. Had Mercy been a dumped child, like Kacey?

I shook the thought away. I'd almost forgotten why I brought Kacey to the library in the first place.

"We should have some games around here somewhere," I said and checked the cupboards beneath the bookshelves. "I can't ever remember where they're at."

"Maybe they're hiding in the dumbwaiter," Kacey said.

I laughed because it was funny, but also because I was relieved to hear Kacey making a joke.

"What happened to your mom and dad?" Kacey sprung the question on me while they searched the shelves.

"My mom died from drugs, and I never had a dad."

It's not hard for me to say those words because they are simple facts of my life. Kacey looked surprised, probably because their parents were perfectly alive.

"I've lived at this home for longer than any other home in my life," I said. "My momma and me never stayed with my

Pop-pop and Grammaw when she was alive because Momma was always mad at them. We moved around a lot, like if she and some boyfriend were fighting, or if she needed money or drugs. Her 'medicine.' Now I know what her medicine really was, but I didn't know when I was five. I don't blame her for being hooked on drugs. I blame the drugs and the company making them. I wish every day that she didn't have to die."

I must have been wanting Kacey for a friend more than I knew, to come right out and tell them about my *before*.

"Sorry about your mom," Kacey said. "Sometimes I wish my mom was dead." They rubbed their sore lip.

"You can't know what it's like to have your mom be dead until it happens. Even if you hate her, you'd be sad."

"I doubt it," they said. "I'm not going to miss my parents while I'm here."

I couldn't tell if Kacey was lying or not, and I couldn't tell if they would be my friend or not. I might have wanted a kindred spirit, like Anne, but I got a feeling that Kacey didn't.

I went to the L. M. Montgomery books on the General Fiction shelf and picked out the first one in the *Anne of Green Gables* series.

"You ever read this?" I asked.

Kacey shook their head.

"You should read it," I said.

They tucked the book into the pocket of their cargo pants.

The *Anne* books are my favorites, and not because she's an orphan. I love them because they take me to a place other than where I'm from. I can dream of a different life, even though I know I am safe here. I sometimes do not feel safe, like when I'm afraid Mercy will get rid of me, or when I try to picture my future. That is my uncertainty. The Black Hole of My Future. I try not to think about my life when I'm a grown-up, because when I do, that Black Hole appears.

I wish I could be a kid and live at the Southern Ohio Children's Home forever.

"I do miss my cat," Kacey said quietly.

"You have a cat?" I caught Kacey secretly wiping a tear from their cheek.

"Her name's Domino," they said.

"I love cats! And dogs. All animals, really. I work at All Creatures animal shelter with my friend, Finn."

Kacey walked to a shelf on the other side of the library and hid their tears while pretending to look for the games we couldn't find. They'd accidentally showed me their soft side.

"Maybe Miss Samantha moved the games to our classroom," I said, thinking out loud.

"Hey, is this one of those secret hidden things you keep talking about?" Kacey asked.

I looked across at Kacey and rubbed my eyes, because I swear, I was seeing double. They were standing next to an extra shelf that I know for a fact wasn't there just a second ago.

"How'd you do that?" I asked.

A row of books at Kacey's shoulder stood open to reveal a secret bookshelf behind the regular one. Kacey pushed the front shelf closed, and I heard something catch.

"Up here." Kacey looked inside the shelf and pointed to a latch at the top corner. It was painted white to blend in with everything else. They pushed the latch, and the row of books opened.

"Don't tell me you never noticed," Kacey said.

I should not have been surprised, because the home is full of secrets. But still, I was.

"Kacey, you found a new secret about this house!"

"I did?" Along with being surprised, I could tell that Kacey was proud of themself.

"I wonder if Mercy knows. What's in there?" I shoved Kacey aside to see for myself.

I saw a dozen slim black books in a neat row, covered by a thick layer of dust.

"They all look the same," I said.

Kacey reached in and grabbed one, then opened it. "It's someone's diary," they said.

"Can I see?"

Kacey handed the book to me and grabbed another for themself.

When I touched the diary, I swear it talked to me.

READ US.

"Did you hear that?" I asked, looking around.

"Hear what?"

"We have to read them," I said.

"Whose are they?" Kacey asked.

I flipped to the front page and looked inside the cover.

"Katherine Ann Rost," I read.

"The person who used to live in this house?" Kacey asked.

I nodded. "Mercy's aunt!"

"Does this house have ghosts?" Kacey asked.

"Elizabeth swears she hears ghosts all the time," I said.

"I just got the biggest chill up my spine." Kacey shivered.

"Me too!" I agreed.

"Willa!" Mercy's voice suddenly shouted from the hallway.

Kacey and me both screamed as if we'd heard a ghost.

"What do we do?" Kacey whispered.

"Hide it!"

I grabbed the diary from Kacey, and they pushed the bookshelf closed. I shoved both diaries up the back of my T-shirt and faced the doorway, where Mercy was entering the library.

"Yes, ma'am?" I said, red-faced, my freckles hot.

Mercy stood beneath the arched doorway, looking regal. She had "put her face on."

"I've been searching all over for you two. Are you settling in, Kacey? I called your dad. I know you left in a rush today, so he's going to drop off more clothes. And a hug."

"Fine," Kacey huffed. They had the world's biggest chip on their shoulder. Rightfully so, I thought.

"I'm sorry for everything you've been through," Mercy said, ignoring Kacey's chip. "Why don't you and I have a chat in the kitchen? Willa, you can head back upstairs."

"I know," I said, with a tone.

"Excuse me?" Mercy said.

"I was going to go anyway!" I yelled at Mercy. I was mad because I didn't want to leave Kacey yet.

"What's gotten into you, Willa?" Mercy asked.

"Nothing!" I yelled again.

Mercy looked like I was embarrassing her. I suddenly felt scared that she'd get rid of me right then and there. I turned and ran out of the library so fast, hiding the diaries so Mercy couldn't see.

At least now I had a secret I could keep from her.

Forgetting What Came Before

As soon as everyone was asleep in The Fortress, I dug out a plastic bag of oatmeal cookies Finn had given me at All Creatures the day before. I asked Kacey if I could climb up to their bunk.

"Yeah, sure," they said, like they didn't care, but I know the first night is the hardest, no matter how tough you're trying to be.

We'd taken the first two diaries we saw, which happened to be from 1957 and 1958. The first two that Katherine had written. The hard-covered black journals had metal plates with the years etched on and locks that didn't work, lucky for us. We'd found Miss Katherine's secrets, and we knew without needing to say it out loud that we had to keep her diaries to ourselves. Was her spirit watching over us right now?

We read together using a flashlight Kacey had thrown into their backpack that morning.

"It's good you brought a flashlight," I whispered.

"I packed it just in case. You never know," Kacey said.

"You never know what?" I asked.

"If you're going to need to run away," Kacey said, which scared me.

I bet Kacey never would've thought they'd be using their escape flashlight to read secret diaries with a new friend.

"I'm glad you're here, Kacey," I said. "You won't want to run away."

I showed them the bag of oatmeal cookies, as if cookies could make everything better.

August 27, 1957

Mother and Father gave me a diary for my birthday. This is my first time having one, and I'm not sure what to say. It has a lock, so I know I can say secrets.

Kacey and me felt bad about the secrets part, but secrets that old must have grown out of the diaries that keep them. We made our choice and kept reading.

Prescott Jr. and Eleanor got married a month ago, and now they're back from their honeymoon. They went to Japan. I wish I could've gone, but who'd want a tag-along 12-year-old on their honeymoon? Now Press has moved into his new house with his new wife.

Their wedding was in the yard. Father rented big tents, and everyone danced late into the night. Some of the boys from Midlands Christian Academy helped with serving drinks and picking up and things. I don't see boys from there much, even though it's just on the other side of the ravine. I couldn't help it, I stared at them—probably because Mother told me not to. She wasn't talking about just staring, though. I know Mother, and she was talking about making eye contact. The only way she looks at boys from the reformatory school is down her nose. But I am not rude like that.

I was making eye contact with the boy who kept coming over and filling up my water. He wasn't that much older than me. I liked his smile, so I smiled back and said thank you every time he came by. He might have been teasing me, giving me all that water, but I don't care. We were having fun. I wanted Mother to see me having fun with him.

I was too shy to dance, but I watched the grown-ups. The band played "Loving You" by Elvis for Press and Eleanor's first dance as Man and Wife. One of Mother's lunch friends said Father's house is even bigger than Elvis's house. Here is a secret: I am in love with Elvis.

Press is working full-time with Father now. I'll never work with Father. I'll just get married someday.

Katherine Ann Rost

Katherine had given us information about Midlands reform school in her very first entry.

"We have to read all her diaries, even if it takes all summer. Will you be here all summer?" I asked.

Kacey shrugged. "I have no idea."

I heard Mercy's footsteps coming up the hall and scurried down to my bunk. She always pokes her head into our room before her bedtime, and I didn't need to be in more trouble.

"Pretend you're sleeping," I whispered to Kacey, who turned their flashlight off just in time.

I heard them secret-crying in their bunk later, when I couldn't fall asleep. We all cry, especially at first. But the diaries would give Kacey something to think about other than being mad at their mom, and me something to think about other than being mad at Mercy.

I'd thought I was an expert on the Southern Ohio Children's Home, but there was a lot I didn't know. As I tried to fall asleep, I thought about the land on the other side of the ravine, including the fact that it is Mercy's land. I also thought about the school on that land—a ghost school haunting Shawneeville.

We'd never gone past the ravine or the chain-link fence and the *No Trespassing* signs. I'd never even wanted to before, but now I needed to see that school with my own eyes. This is how I get in trouble. My mind gets set on doing something and I can't unset it until I've done the thing it's set on.

I pictured the great black oak tree that stands smack in the middle of the field between the house and the ravine. It gives us shade on hot summer days and leaves to jump into on cool autumn days. If we don't want anyone to find us, we hide on the other side of its fat trunk. I imagine that tree has been here since the Shawnee were living on their land, that's how big it is.

We have secret Forgetting Ceremonies by that tree. Those were my idea. I got it from a book where people burned the thoughts they wanted to let go of forever by writing them onto a piece of paper and setting it on fire. Many of us living at the home would like to forget our *befores*. We can't set anything on fire though—Mercy doesn't let us anywhere near matches. So instead, we write down our *befores* and put them in a shoe box, then bury it beneath the black oak tree. Justin always starts off our ceremonies with a land acknowledgment for the First Nations we've forgotten, even though they still exist. One of Justin's favorite topics besides Dr. King is Indigenous histories. He knows the people who were here first, before being forced off their land—the Shawnee, Miami, and Osage, to name a few. But mainly Shawnee.

We don't ever ask what's in each other's Forgetting Letters.

Now that Kacey was here, it was time for another Forgetting Ceremony, and I was going to convince everyone to have it in an even more secret place.

"Miss Samantha, can we have a going out today?" I asked when we were together in our classroom later that week. "We need to show Kacey around."

"We want to take her to the black oak tree," Roy said.

"Take *them*," Miss Samantha corrected Roy. She didn't even look up from the math lesson she was giving to one of the six year olds.

"I keep doing that!" Roy bounced on his toes and punched the air, his skin turning red.

He was messing up using "they" and "them" for Kacey's pronouns, but he would apologize and try again until he'd get it right. Mercy gave us a big lecture about respecting people's identities, even though she didn't have to. I knew it was especially important for us to respect who Kacey is because their parents were not.

Kacey was locking themself in our bathroom less and less, and I hoped that meant they were feeling better about being at the Southern Ohio Children's Home.

"Apologize and try again, Roy," Miss Samantha said.

Roy didn't hesitate, even though he hates apologizing more than anything. "Sorry, Kacey. 'We want to take *them* to the black oak tree' is what I meant to say."

Kacey nodded but didn't say anything. I could tell they appreciated it, though.

Miss Samantha is a champion multitasker. Our classroom is filled with students as young as six. We help teach them when we're not doing our own work and when Miss Samantha has her hands full, which is every day. I love teaching math because I'm good at it. Plus, it's fun to see the little kids get so happy to come up with the answers, even if they're not right, which is fine, because what's more important is that they love doing math.

I was hoping Miss Samantha wouldn't mind my not helping today. She gets anxious toward the end of the school year and worries she hasn't taught us enough.

"Would it be okay?" I asked again.

"Yes, Willa. Fewer bodies in this classroom would actually be helpful right now. Go now, so you all can be back in time for lunch. And don't forget to sign out."

Miss Samantha has long hair, big eyes, and red nails. Today, she was wearing a necklace of colorful beads. I especially love her buttery voice. Her words come out soft but not quiet. You never have any trouble hearing her, but everything she says sounds like it's wearing a blanket that someone's granny knit for them. I imagine Miss Samantha's voice is how my momma's favorite country music singer would sound if she was talking instead of singing. I remember all Momma's favorite Alison Krauss songs because we listened to them a billion times.

I rounded everyone up, including Kacey.

"Where are we going?" Kacey asked.

"You'll see." I didn't want to tell them about the Forgetting Ceremony in front of Miss Samantha.

We signed out on the whiteboard near the classroom door and left.

"We're going to the black oak tree," Justin said, pointing it out for Kacey. Now that we were outside, we could see it across the field.

"What's at the tree?" Kacey asked.

"Nothing," I said. "We just need to make some plans for our Forgetting Ceremony."

Kacey looked at us with question marks in their eyes.

"The Forgetting Ceremony is where we write down what we want to forget and put it in a shoe box to bury it," Elizabeth explained.

"Do other people come to the Forgetting Ceremony? Like a graduation?" Kacey asked.

"No way," Roy said. "This is secret."

"No one knows about it but us," Elizabeth added. Having this secret between us made Elizabeth happy, because this was not a scary kind of secret.

"Should we have the ceremony someplace new this time?" I asked. "Because Kacey is with us now, and we could celebrate new beginnings and put the box in a different special place?"

I wasn't sure if anyone would agree with me, but I had to try.

"Like where?" Roy asked.

"I was thinking we should have a chance to see that land before Mercy sells it," I said.

"You mean go past the ravine?" Elizabeth grabbed Lovey-Pup. She acts young for her age and still brings that stuffed animal everywhere. I felt bad about asking her to break the rules, but maybe it would help her see that she didn't need to be afraid of everything all the time.

"We have time to go pick a new spot and still be back for lunch," I said. "No one will even know. They can't see us once we're past the tree."

"I don't want to get in trouble," Justin said.

"Don't worry, we'll go fast," I said.

"I want to go!" Roy jumped up and down.

"We should find that school," Kacey chimed in, giving me a secret look. We'd read about the reform school together in Katherine's diary, and this felt like something kindred spirits would do.

"It's been sitting there this whole time, and we never knew anything about it," I said.

"I found a couple old newspaper stories about it online," Justin said. He always knows about everything before anybody else.

We were nearing the black oak tree now and could see the dip in the land before the ravine. It was just ahead, but still farther away than I'd imagined. The field can play tricks on your eyes like that. It can look bigger close up and smaller from far away, like from our bedroom window.

"What did you learn about the reform school?" I asked Justin while we walked.

"I only had time to read one article about when it closed in 1998." Justin has a photographic memory for dates and numbers. He knows the birth years of all the kids at the Southern Ohio Children's Home, which is unbelievable because there are so many of us. "And, fun fact, 1998 is the same year the Southern Ohio Children's Home opened," he added.

We all thought on that coincidence as we passed the tree and got closer to the ravine.

"My momma always said there's no such thing as a coincidence," I said.

"What does that mean?" Elizabeth asked.

"I have no idea." And I didn't. But I did like talking about my momma.

My gym shoes were wet from walking through the long field of grass still damp with sunrise dew. Our spring rains were often more like flash-flood downpours, and when it rains a lot, the ravine floods. The ravine wasn't flooded today, but it wasn't low, either. The sound of water reached my ears as the *No Trespassing* sign came into view. The stream bubbled over rocks and branches.

"I'm scared," Elizabeth said.

"It will be okay, I promise," I said. "We're all together, aren't we?" I held Elizabeth's hand and glanced back at the old mansion, which looked small from far away. Like a dollhouse.

Roy crossed the slippery path of fat stones that dotted the stream, followed by Kacey and Justin. Elizabeth and me went last. Water flowed across our shoes and socks, getting us wet as we jumped from one muddy bank to the other. It wasn't more than twelve feet wide.

On the other side, we had to slow down because there were branches to climb through. We didn't know which way to go until we saw a spot where the chain-link fence had been pulled down. We climbed over it and crossed the threshold into forbidden territory.

The woods were thick and closed in over us.

"Wow," Elizabeth gasped. Her hand loosened its grip on mine.

The morning was sunny with a few clouds, but once we entered the trees, a peaceful green shade covered us.

The beautiful woods were also full of mosquitos, which we had to keep swatting away from our ears and legs and everywhere because no one had brought any bug spray.

"This way," Kacey said, pointing out a path. "I bet deer probably use this."

"The Shawnee probably used it when they lived here, too," Justin said.

We walked in single file. All we could hear was the crunch of the dried leaves that carpeted the forest. All I could smell was damp dirt.

Soon, we came to a clearing, and there it was—the Midlands Christian Academy for Boys. The building was covered in moss, vines, fallen dead branches, and buckthorn. It looked at us like it'd been waiting for a visit this whole time. Well, since 1998, I guess. Last century.

"It's spooky," Elizabeth said. She looked up into the sky, probably looking for ghosts.

"It sure does look like a ghost school," I said.

"It didn't look like that in the picture I saw online," Justin said.

"But that's definitely it," Kacey confirmed.

There wasn't a sign or anything saying this was a school, but there it stood, just like Mercy had said. On our land … Mercy's land.

The main building was two stories tall and white, only it didn't look white anymore, with its paint peeling and black mold and green vines growing everywhere. It was like the forest was giving the reform school a hug. With so many vines squeezing it tight, it didn't look like you could open any doors or windows. Two long cement-block wings stuck out on either side, making a V. That was probably where the classrooms were. I counted five more smaller buildings, all spread out into the woods—each one identical to the next from what I could see. Maybe those were the dorms where the boys had slept at night.

We looked around, amazed that this all had been here and that none of us had ever known our closest neighbor was an abandoned school. I didn't know if it was actually haunted, but one look made you feel like it was, like this building was full of ghost boys who went to school every day, the same way we went to Miss Samantha's classroom every day.

"Can we leave?" Elizabeth asked. "It's giving me the creeps."

"It's just because there are so many overgrown things here," I said. I didn't want to tell Elizabeth that I thought it was creepy, too.

"Did the newspaper say why it closed?" Kacey asked.

"All it said was that the students were failing," Justin said.

"That's not the whole story," Kacey said.

"What happened here?" I wondered aloud, but nobody knew.

A picture of the Southern Ohio Children's Home flashed through my mind, abandoned and covered in vines, just like these buildings. Could the same thing happen to our home someday?

"What if it really is haunted?" Roy snuck up behind Justin and grabbed his shoulders. "Boo!"

"Cut it out, Roy," we all said together because we are so used to telling Roy to cut it out.

Kacey was picking up sticks and putting them in a pile. I noticed logs in a circle.

"Is this a fire pit?" I asked, bending down to help Kacey clear more sticks and wipe off the logs. "It looks just like ours."

When we have bonfires in the fire pit by our garden, Charlie helps everyone roast marshmallows, and Emily makes sure no one gets more than anybody else.

"This is the perfect place for our Forgetting Ceremony," I said.

"No, it's not," Elizabeth said. "I'm never coming back here. Can we please go now?" She started walking backwards in the direction we had come. "Please?"

She looked like she'd already seen a ghost, but her imagination is always showing her scary things. She must have seen scary things before she came to the Southern Ohio Children's Home. She'd been full of bumps and bruises and a broken arm when she showed up. Mercy couldn't start taking care of her fast enough.

"We'll go in a minute, I promise," I told her.

Justin and Roy were walking in the opposite direction of Elizabeth, exploring around the dorm cabins.

"Look over here!" Roy waved us over. "Look what we found!"

Kacey and me ran to see, and Elizabeth did too, even though she wanted to leave.

Justin and Roy pointed up to the trees, and we all saw it: a sanctuary in the forest. Somehow, the trees were growing in two straight rows with an aisle down the middle. The sun shone through the branches, blessing us all.

"Someone has already been here," Justin said. "It looks like we're in a church."

"That's what I was thinking!" I said.

Justin stood in the middle of two dozen or so aspen trees that were set apart from the rest of the forest. Their silver, narrow trunks stretched to the sky with branches spreading into a ceiling of swaying green stained glass. Everything else about Midlands Academy was gloomy, disorganized, and forgotten, but these aspen trees were on purpose, growing in a way no other trees were. The bright bark and new leaves made me feel hopeful in an unhopeful place.

"Someone planted these trees a long time ago," Kacey said. "They're so tall. And trees don't grow in straight lines like this."

"It's pretty," Elizabeth said.

"We should go back now," Justin said. "We found what we were looking for."

I shook my head. "I want to let go of my past here, in these trees," I said. I couldn't stop looking up at the branches hanging over my head in neat rows.

We heard a creaking sound coming from somewhere in the woods.

"I want to go now!" Elizabeth was ready to run back to the ravine. Everyone turned to leave when we heard another creak and some rustling.

"What was that?" Justin asked.

It was too loud for a squirrel or chipmunk. And it couldn't have been the trees blowing and creaking like they do in the wind, because there wasn't any breeze.

I followed the sound with my eyes and saw a cabin just past the tree sanctuary. It was really more like a shed, since it was smaller than the dorms and made from dark wood instead of concrete block. The mossy brown building looked even more ancient than the rest of the buildings and would probably fall down if a big bad wolf huffed and puffed at it.

I was about to turn back with the others when the door of

the shed opened, and a man stepped out. Elizabeth let out a startled scream before we all froze, scared stiff.

The man was carrying a flowerpot in one hand. He was dressed like a teacher on a TV show with plain khaki pants and a plain collared shirt. A gray pit bull full of muscles stood close to his side. They both approached us through the leaves, staring at all of us, but mostly at me because I was closest.

I backed away slowly, not taking my eyes off the man. His gray-blonde hair was stringy and straight and looked like it needed a trim. A scream got stuck in my throat.

Justin, Kacey, Roy, and Elizabeth were behind me. We all took slow steps backwards. I still couldn't look away from the stranger, his dog, or the old shed.

"Run!" Roy hollered all of a sudden.

As soon as he screamed, the giant dog barked, and everyone else started crashing back through the sticks and leaves. My feet wanted to sprint with them, but instead, I felt glued to the forest floor. If I ran, would the dog chase us?

"What are you doing here?" the stranger asked me in a whisper. He seemed startled, not angry. He gave a hand command for his dog to sit, which it did right away. The man dug a treat out from his pocket and rewarded the dog, his eyes staying fixed on me.

"Why are you here?" he asked again. We were both confused.

"Just … just looking around," I stammered.

The stranger glanced up at the aspen trees, as if he was listening for something. Then he looked back down at me. I wondered in that moment if he was the one who'd planted them.

"What's your name?" I asked. I was betting that someone who'd made something so beautiful and who had such a well-cared-for dog couldn't be mean.

"Never mind my name," he said. "Just go. It's not safe for children here."

"Why not?" I asked, knowing I was pushing my luck.

"You need to go," he said again, more firmly this time.

With that, his dog growled, and I ran all the way back to the Southern Ohio Children's Home.

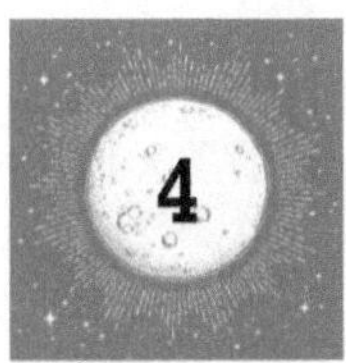

The Midlands Christian Academy for (Bad) Boys

Kacey discovered how delicious the food is at the Southern Ohio Children's Home, especially the dinners. I didn't always get dinner when I lived with Momma. Sometimes I'd only eat candy or SweeTARTS, which might sound good, but it will make you sick and you'll still be hungry.

Charlie says his secret ingredient is love. He loves food, and he loves us kids. I never met anybody more full of love than Charlie, and you can taste that in what he cooks for us. My favorite is his lasagna, but he only makes that once or twice a year because it takes all day. My other favorites are macaroni and cheese and fish sticks (two favorites in one meal), and hot dogs on the grill.

For dessert, Emily usually makes homemade cookies or chocolate cake or fruit popsicles. Finn's mom, Mrs. Harbour, used to bring us cookies once a week, but she doesn't bake as much ever since she got Parkinson's. She has it "early-onset" because she's too young to have that disease but she got it anyway. Now she mostly bakes only for Finn and Mr. Harbour.

One night after dinner was over, when everyone was getting ready for bed, I finally got Kacey to sneak some cookies from the kitchen with me. We ate them later as we read Katherine's diaries after lights out.

"Don't you think we would have been friends with Katherine?" I asked them.

"Maybe," Kacey shrugged. "It's kind of weird, reading all her thoughts. She sounds *so proper*." Kacey whispered in a British accent, which made me laugh.

"That's how they talked back then," I whispered in my own fancy accent.

Some diary entries were more interesting than others, and we read plenty of boring pages in between the good stuff. But there was a lot of good stuff. We'd started keeping a notebook where we copied down entries that had information about the reform school. We were learning so much about Midlands all of a sudden, including the fact that Katherine was as curious about it as we were.

September 10, 1957

Mother took me to get new saddle shoes and bobby socks for school. I love when school begins. My favorite class in sixth grade is Social Studies with Miss Brewer. She always gets a tear in her eye because we are focusing on Civil Rights this year. Landmark legislation was passed in Congress, despite a filibuster (there's a word I'd never heard). Miss Brewer says she feels history while we're living it. That's what makes her a good teacher.

We're going to debate the Civil Rights Act and create a mock Civil Rights Commission to discuss voting rights and integrating schools. I wish someone could desegregate Shawneeville. All the white kids either go to Shawneeville Central (except for two colored girls in the senior class, who are twins) or to Immaculate Conception. Midlands Christian Academy has some Negro students, but none of the boys' families even live here.

Mother has a rule that I'm never to cross the ravine by Midlands Academy because the kids there are juvenile delinquents, and I must "<u>stay away</u>." She doesn't even know any of them, so why should I believe her? Even if it is a school for reforming bad behavior ... I don't want to know what Mother thinks about the Civil Rights Act, although I could guess. Mother and Father say things by not saying them, such as their disapproval of anything that's not how it's "supposed" to be ... including people. And manners. If I forget to put my hands in my lap at dinner, I'll get a stern look. I think that saying things without saying them is worse than if you just say them out loud. But Mother and Father would never say their feelings out loud.

Katherine

"Katherine's mom was so *mean*," I whispered, huddling close with Kacey's flashlight.

Kacey pointed to the part about things being how they're "supposed" to be.

"That's like me and my mom," they said. "Me not being how I'm 'supposed' to be."

"But you're yourself. Everyone is just their *self*." I felt *my* self getting angry, but I didn't want to raise my voice and wake up Elizabeth, Roy, or Justin.

"I know," Kacey said, shrugging, like they were used to their mom being this way and there was nothing they could do. It must have hurt inside more than they were showing.

March 29, 1958

Mother and Father have been fighting about an incident that happened at the reformatory school. Mother is upset. So am I. This is the only time in my life I can remember feeling the same way as Mother about anything. But, of course, she won't talk to me about it.

A boy was killed there. Well, we don't know if he was killed or if he died of natural causes. But it doesn't really make a difference. He's dead, and no one is investigating or trying to figure out what happened. I check the paper every morning, but there hasn't been another story printed since the first one when the police were called. The boy was at Midlands because he was an orphan. He wasn't even a juvenile delinquent. He just didn't have a family.

It's not fair. It sounds like they weren't doing a good job taking care of him. He was sick, and then he got in trouble for something. The newspaper didn't say for what. They punished him and left him outside in a shed. It was freezing that night, and he died. That's all anyone will say.

Mother keeps telling Father that he's responsible for that boy's death. Not responsible, but "complicit." What does "complicit" mean, and why would Father be responsible in any way? He never even sets foot on the Midlands property (neither does Mother). He's always either at work or driving to Cincinnati in his new Cadillac.

Father is on the board for the academy. Does that make him complicit? It's not like Mother to care about anyone who goes there. She's too preoccupied by appearances and being a socialite. Maybe she's embarrassed by Father being associated with Midlands?

Every time I see them fight, they tell me to go up to my room. All I can do is stare at that field and wonder what is going on across the black ravine. Do boys always go to that shed when they get in trouble? Do the teachers know? Is anyone looking out for them? They might need reforming, but they're still just kids.

It makes me feel silly for the things I worry about ... things like if I'll get an A in Social Studies, or if I'll get my favorite sandwich (bologna) for lunch, or if I'll finish sewing my skirt in time for the spring dance. I also worry about if Elvis will have to fight in the war now that he's in the Army. These are silly things to worry about. Except for Elvis. But what if I had to spend the night alone in a dark shed? I would die, and not just from the cold.

When I grow up, I will not be old-fashioned like Mother and Father. I will not care about appearances. And I will never drive a Cadillac.

Katherine

It was hard not to have nightmares after reading about that boy dying at the reformatory school. There probably *were* ghosts haunting it after all.

"We can't ever tell the others," I whispered. Kacey agreed.

I could tell Justin had been upset by our trip to the abandoned school, but he was keeping it in tight. I cannot be inside his head, but I believe it would be even more troubling to learn that a boy died over there if you are also a boy without a family to come get you if you're in trouble or being treated unfairly.

After finishing the diaries from 1957 and 1958, we swapped them out for two new ones. We made the switch when the library was empty during quiet time before dinner. Just like before, we hid the books under Kacey's covers.

While I'd been looking forward to getting the new diaries to read, I was dreading dinner for practically the first time ever. Not because of the food, but because Mercy was wanting to have "a talk" with us. I knew exactly what the talk was going to be about, too.

I had found out that Miss Samantha had told Mercy about our sneaking over to Midlands. She hadn't caught us right away, but she'd noticed Elizabeth being sadder than usual, saying very few words and never letting go of Lovey-Pup.

"Elizabeth," she had finally asked, getting down on

Elizabeth's level and talking to her with her sweet-as-honey voice and understanding eyes. "Is there something you're holding on to inside?"

I knew I was in trouble when Elizabeth's chin quivered.

"I'm here, sweetheart," Miss Samantha said, rubbing Elizabeth's back.

That's a trick she and Mercy and Miss Lupe have for talking to kids. They never say *It's okay* when you'd think that would be a comforting thing to say, because they understand better than anyone that for us, usually it is *not* "okay" and to say so would erase our feelings. Instead, they say *I'm here*, or *Take your time*, or they say nothing at all and just rub your back and wait. It works, I swear, it really does.

Finally, Elizabeth pointed at me, then put her head on the table and started to cry. It made things look worse, like I'd done something *really* bad. It was fair for her to blame me, since it was my idea for everyone to go past the ravine and find the abandoned reformatory school. She had started off scared anyway, and then we saw the tree sanctuary, which probably has ghosts. And then that stranger came out of the shed and made Roy scream. It was all too much and had sent Elizabeth over the edge.

"Willa, you and I need to have a chat," Miss Samantha had said before using her magic to pull the whole story out of me. I tried not to be mad at Elizabeth.

I didn't mind that I would get in trouble for what I did. I did mind, however, that it would make it a lot harder to go back to the reform school again. I needed to talk to that stranger. I knew he wasn't mean and wouldn't kidnap me. When you're around enough grown-ups who are not kind, you can spot the ones who *are* pretty quick. That stranger was kind. So was his pit bull, who was only protecting him when he growled. Did he know any of the boys who had gone to Midlands? Did he know what had happened there? If Mercy is going to sell the land, shouldn't someone give him a warning?

Kacey was my kindred spirit in wanting to go back. They needed to get all our questions answered, too.

Miss Samantha joined us when we sat down at our usual table in the gigantic dining room. It used to be a ballroom, for back when people danced at balls. That's how old the mansion is.

I know that Mercy gives Miss Samantha free meals as part of her job. I also know that Miss Samantha doesn't make a lot of money. I didn't mean to overhear their conversation when Miss Samantha was asking for a raise, but my ears are expert at hearing things they're not supposed to. My momma used to say a lot of words not meant for children, but I heard them anyway. Usually because I was strapped into my booster seat in the car or trying to fall asleep in the back of some boyfriend's trailer. I didn't understand the words half the time because I was so little, but when you're overhearing voices, it's impossible *not* to listen. That's how I heard Miss Samantha tell Mercy she needed more money. Mercy can't afford to pay her any more than she already does, but she offered her meals to "offset the cost of food," which is a pretty good deal because Miss Samantha loves Charlie's and Emily's food, too. She'd be crazy not to.

"What were you thinking, Willa?" Miss Samantha was asking. "Breaking Mercy's rule like that? You know you're not supposed to go down past the ravine, and especially not with Elizabeth. You're responsible for the younger ones when you're going out. I'm surprised by you, making such a poor choice."

There was a lot I could have said to Miss Samantha about

our discovering Midlands Academy, but I was trying to keep my mouth shut to prevent myself from getting into more trouble, since I was planning on being a troublemaker again soon with Kacey.

"I'm sorry," was all I said.

I wished I could make Elizabeth feel better, but she looked like she might start crying again just from thinking about it all. She sat slouched in her chair and didn't touch her food. Roy stole a piece of garlic bread from her plate when she wasn't looking, even though there was a basket full of garlic bread right in front of him.

"Hey, give that back," Kacey said, and Roy did, only because he was surprised someone caught him. Kacey pointed to the basket and he took a piece from there instead.

Miss Samantha was preparing me for the getting-in-trouble conversation I was about to have with Mercy. I was thinking of what chores I could do to turn invisible.

"Did you know that the Midlands Christian Academy for Boys was right there?" I asked Miss Samantha, trying to change the subject so we could stop talking about me and my poor choices.

"I'm curious about it, too," Justin chimed in. "I've tried looking it up, but I can never find much information before hitting a dead end." I was grateful to Justin for helping me change the subject, even though he didn't know that's what he was doing.

"Oh boy," Miss Samantha sighed and ate more garlic bread. It was a spaghetti and meatballs night, which is almost as good as lasagna. We also got a big bowl of salad with any kind of dressing we want: French, Italian, or ranch, which is my favorite.

"Well," Miss Samantha said when she finished chewing, "I knew about Midlands Academy, but it closed when I was a little girl. There have been some articles about it in the paper over the years, Justin, but honestly, I'd never given it much thought. I'm too busy at *our* school."

"Articles about what, exactly?" Kacey asked.

"Mostly about the buildings, I guess. Because they're abandoned." Miss Samantha kept putting food in her mouth so she wouldn't have to talk. That only made me want to talk about it more.

"What happened to the students who went there?" I asked.

Miss Samantha shrugged.

"I'd like to do more research on Midlands Academy, as part of my *History of the Land* project," Justin said. "Would that be okay?"

Each of us always has a research project we're working on, and it can be about any topic we choose. Justin would start a new research project every day if he could. Right now, mine is about the homeless pet crisis. Miss Samantha started Kacey off on a research project about gender expression in cultures around the world. That was part of why Kacey was loving school for the first time. They hadn't been allowed to study or even talk about gender expression at their old school.

"I would like to tell you yes, Justin," Miss Samantha said, "but first I need to do some research myself. I'm not sure what all you'll dig up, so let me get back to you on that. For now, keep going with Ohio's Indigenous people. You're about ready to present that to the class, I think."

"Okay," Justin said. I could tell he was disappointed. He gives a presentation practically every week and sometimes even teaches the class if Miss Samantha is too busy or has to have a meeting with Mercy. I'm telling you, Justin is really smart, and not just for his age. When he grows up, he will invent something new or be President or a Supreme Court justice. Or maybe he'll be in charge of his own school.

I noticed Mercy walking across the dining room toward our table, stopping and greeting the other tables on her way. When she reached us, she pulled up a chair right next to me.

"Mercy, isn't it time to have another one of our fundraisers?" I said, still trying to talk about a different subject other than me getting in trouble.

It didn't work. I was in trouble off the bat.

"Willa," Mercy said, "all of your going-out privileges, except for volunteering at All Creatures, are suspended for two weeks."

"That's not fair!" I said. Now I had something new to be mad at Mercy about, even though I was sorry and it was my fault.

"The rest of you are not in trouble," Mercy continued, "but if anybody visits the reformatory school again, you *will* be in trouble. Especially now that you know it's there, and now that you know you're *not* to go."

We all quietly looked at our plates. Roy's neck and cheeks turned bright red.

"But how come you never told us about it before?" I asked. It would have been better if I'd kept my mouth shut, since I was the one who was in trouble. But I didn't.

"Midlands Academy isn't any concern to us, other than it being vacant and unsafe," Mercy said.

"What I don't understand," Justin said, "is why they didn't just tear it down?"

I was grateful again for him taking the attention off me. Justin can be as stubborn as I am when it comes to finding out about things. The difference is, he wants to find out about things to make himself smarter, while I usually want to find out about things because I am curious. *Curiosity killed the cat*, is what my momma used to tell me.

"That's a good question, Justin," Mercy said. She took a bite of spaghetti and looked like she wanted to think about his good question for a minute before she told us her thoughts. Mercy never speaks with food in her mouth. Sometimes, you can eat an entire meal with her, and she won't say a single word. She just points to her cheek full of food to show us that she can't speak because there is something other than words in her mouth.

"There is a history with the reformatory school that has made it difficult for anyone to know what to do about it," she finally said.

Kacey and me gave each other a big secret look across the table.

"Rather than do anything," Mercy continued, "everyone has done nothing, which has left the property abandoned and dangerous. Unfortunately, sometimes we deal with problems by not dealing with them at all. We pretend a problem doesn't exist, or even worse, that the problem is somebody else's."

"That's why we've been pretending like Midlands isn't there," Roy suggested. "It's like a ghost!"

"No such thing as ghosts," Elizabeth said, even though she was the one always hearing them.

"What is its history?" Kacey asked, like a reporter digging for more information.

Mercy looked at me sideways before answering, maybe because *I* was in trouble and didn't deserve additional information. She probably wanted me to cover my ears, which I would never do.

"When Midlands Christian Academy was open"— Mercy began anyway and we all leaned forward, even Miss

Samantha—"it was ostensibly for 'troubled' youth. Juvenile delinquents." Mercy uses words like "ostensibly" all the time because she wants us to have big vocabularies. She doesn't ever talk to us like we're dumb kids. I did not know what "ostensibly" meant, but I would look it up in the dictionary later.

"The young boys who went to Midlands might have made a bad choice, or they might not have had a family," Mercy went on. "When the school was finally shut down, it had become evident that those students had not been receiving a proper education."

"What do you mean?" Justin asked. "Why didn't they get a proper education?" He looked angry, which was surprising because he is always so calm, even when Roy antagonizes him.

"I mean …" Mercy took another bite of food to stall. I was starting to wish we could clear all the food from the table already. "The teachers and administrators at that school were more 'troubled' than their students."

"I knew it!" I blurted out. "Why do kids always get blamed when it's the adults messing everything up?"

I looked over at Kacey, thinking this was the same kind of situation they had with their mom and dad, who thought Kacey was "troubled" even though they weren't at all. It was Kacey's parents who were troubled. They're the ones who gave Kacey a bloody lip and made them move to the Southern Ohio Children's Home. Not that it was all sad-sadness with their story, because now I got to have Kacey be my friend.

"Sounds like they didn't know the golden rule," Kacey said. "How 'Christian.'"

"That's all I'm going to say about its past," Mercy said. "More importantly now is its future. Something has to be done with the Midlands property, and it's fallen on me to sort it out.

Legally. The time has come to deal with it, whether I'd like to or not."

"Seems like you'd rather not," I said.

"That's not for you to worry about, Willa," Mercy said.

I gave Mercy a giant eye roll for treating me like a dumb kid.

"Is there any way I can help, Mercy?" Miss Samantha asked.

Mercy's shoulders relaxed. "Thank you, Samantha. I'm sure I could use your help. My cousin Meredith is coming with a copy of her mother's will. Meredith is a lawyer."

I raised my eyebrows and looked across the table at Kacey again. This was new information. I practically forgot that Meredith would be all grown up by now. I'd still been imagining her as the little girl with pigtails from the picture in the library.

"What would truly help is if everyone"—Mercy said *everyone,* but looked at me—"stayed away from the Midlands property."

I held my lips between my teeth, thinking about all the trouble Kacey and me were going to be in for when we didn't stay away from the Midlands property.

"What about the stranger?" Elizabeth asked.

I shook my head at her, but it was too late. That secret was out.

"The stranger?" Mercy repeated.

I wanted to kick Elizabeth under the table. Kacey, Roy, Justin, and me had guilt written all across our faces. Elizabeth kept staring at Mercy with a scaredy-cat look in her eyes.

"Willa," Mercy said my name but didn't ask the question. I knew what it was anyway. *What have you gone and done now, and who is this stranger that's terrified Elizabeth?*

I had no choice but to tell her.

"We saw a man in the woods with his dog. He isn't bad,

though. I *know* he isn't bad. He even made a cathedral of trees at the reform school, and he told us we should leave because it wasn't safe for children."

I tried saying the fewest words possible, but they all came out too fast and it was way more words than I should have said. I was panicking from being guilty.

Miss Samantha looked down like *she* was the one in trouble, and soon, so did everybody else. It was their way of showing they knew how much trouble *I* was going to be in. None of us could look Mercy in the eye.

Mercy kept her words to herself for two or three long minutes. Maybe it was a full hour, I don't know. I pictured myself running into the woods and back into the tree sanctuary to hide, so I wouldn't be in trouble anymore.

"I'll call Deputy Bell," Mercy finally said. "There shouldn't be anybody on that property without my knowledge. Willa, your punishment has now been raised to three weeks, because you put everyone in harm's way."

"What?!" I shouted. "That's not fair! We were *not* in harm's way. I told you, that stranger was nice!"

"His dog growled at us," Elizabeth tattled.

"Elizabeth!" I sprang from my chair, pushing it back so it scraped the floor.

Everyone in the whole dining room looked at me. One of the toddlers started wailing.

"Willa, that's enough," Mercy said. "Go upstairs. Now."

"Fine!" I stormed off before anyone could see the tears stinging my eyes. I didn't care about missing Emily's dessert.

Some days, I don't know why Mercy doesn't just get rid of me.

Helpless Creatures

I AM ALWAYS BEGGING MERCY for a kitten or a puppy, but she can't let us have pets at the Southern Ohio Children's Home. Imagine taking care of stray dogs and stray cats on top of taking care of stray kids. Feeding creatures costs money, as Charlie and Mercy say. (Moe, my manager at All Creatures, says that, too.)

We do have chickens, but they're cheap because they eat our food scraps. Chickens will eat anything, even chicken nuggets. It's disgusting. They are not smart birds.

The chickens are not considered pets because no one needs to look after them or take them for walks. Also, they give us eggs. We have twelve chickens, give or take, depending on if a fox or hawk gets one. It's sad when that happens, but it's a happy day for the fox or the hawk. Happy-sadness.

We can get pullets, which is what baby chickens are called, or we can get stray chickens from the shelter to re-establish our flock. They lay 2,000 eggs a year. I know because we do math problems about chickens and eggs. The kindergartners love it, I swear. Charlie is always making scrambled eggs and egg casseroles, and Emily bakes a lot of cakes. Chickens are a "win-win."

Even though they're not technically pets, I still take care of them that way and spend a lot of time in the coop. Especially with Henrietta. She is a buff-colored Orpington who likes to sit in my lap. Miss Samantha is the one who suggested I do an internship at All Creatures because she saw how much I love the chickens.

"Animal shelters always need help cleaning cages and walking dogs," she'd said.

The first time I went to All Creatures, I rode my bike there with Justin. We met Moe, and he had me and Justin helping five seconds after we walked through the front door. I loved it right away, but Justin never went back because he said it smells worse than a porta-potty.

Riding my bike to All Creatures is the only going-out I do by myself because it's real close and because I text Miss Samantha from Moe's phone when I get there. It's in Courthouse Square, just up County Highway J, past Finn's house. It's only a ten-minute ride from the Southern Ohio Children's Home. Shawneeville is a small town like that. There are mostly farms, then a couple neighborhoods with tiny houses or trailers. Then there's Courthouse Square, where there are restaurants and a coffee shop and the animal shelter and a bike shop and a store with everything under five dollars. There is also one ice cream shop and one frozen yogurt shop.

Taking my own self somewhere on my bike is freedom. I go to All Creatures at least once a week. I'm usually relieved to have a break from my life, either because I'm in trouble or because I need time to myself. Miss Samantha tells us it's important for us to have time to ourselves. She worries we don't get enough, so she is happy for me and my internship.

I was especially glad for it now that I was grounded for three weeks.

Reading Katherine's diaries was also helping time pass while I was in trouble. Kacey and me had already made our way through 1959 and 1960 and had added a handful of entries to our diary notebook. We kept noticing more and more injustices every time Katherine wrote about Midlands Christian Academy for Boys.

<u>May 1, 1959</u>

The seventh graders participated in a mock trial today for Law Day, something created by President Eisenhower. We're supposed to celebrate equality and justice under law, but it's hard to celebrate equality and justice when <u>in</u>equality and <u>in</u>justice are part of Shawneeville. Just look at Midlands Academy and how unfairly they treat the boys who go there.

I got in trouble for calling Tommy Billhart a member of the Ku Klux Klan. Tommy isn't actually one, but his father is, and that is close enough. I spoke the truth, but I'm the one who got in trouble. Here we are arguing over equality, but no one can say anything about someone being racist without paying a price.

I was only supposed to be playing a witness in the trial, but instead I got sent to the principal's office.

Katherine

Both Kacey and me could relate to being in trouble.

"I've been sent to the principal's office a bunch of times," Kacey whispered.

"Really? Mercy would've sent me to the principal's office a million times by now if we had one," I said. We laughed. When you get in trouble enough, you get used to it.

We'd also copied a diary entry from February 4, 1960, because it was the first time Katherine had mentioned Mercy. Not by name, because she wasn't named yet, but Katherine's brother and his wife were having a baby. Since Katherine was Mercy's aunt, we knew her brother and his wife had to be Mercy's parents. Kacey and me were pleased when we puzzled it all out.

<u>February 4, 1960</u>

There have been more stories about the shed at Midlands Academy. Whispers and words-of-mouth. We hear about it at Shawneeville Central. Mother and Father know about the abuse, but they are not doing anything about it except saying things like, "Let the new director handle it."

They hired a man at Midlands named Mr. Winter. He is small and still has pimples. The boys at Midlands could beat him up if it weren't for his security guards.

Mother took over a casserole to welcome Mr. Winter. I begged to go so I could get a look at the reformatory school with my own eyes. She finally agreed. It felt like a different world, being there. Midlands was nothing how I imagined. For one, we didn't see a single student while we were there. Not one. Isn't that strange? Where were they? Hiding?

Mr. Winter gave me the creeps. I hid behind Mother like I was a little kid again. I saw the shed outside his office window. It made me sad to look at. I was thinking about boys my same age having to spend the night out there, cold and alone.

Mother and Father are more worried about the communists than what's happening in our own backyard. They're also busy fawning over Press and Eleanor because they're "finally" (as Mother would say) having a baby. Everyone wants them to have a boy, which I find insulting.

Father took Press with him to play golf with President Eisenhower. The President was in Ohio meeting with business leaders, and now Father thinks they're best friends. He even got their photo taken with his golf group. He had it framed and put it in our front hall, so it's the first thing anyone sees when they walk into our house. I know it's exciting that he played golf with the President, but I don't want my friends coming over and seeing that picture. It makes Mother mad, the way I won't bring anyone over. She wants to show off.

She'll never understand.

Katherine

"Mercy's grandfather played golf with a president? Wow," I said, even though Katherine would not have wanted me to be impressed.

"Do you think the shed is the same one where we saw the stranger?" Kacey asked.

I nodded. "It has to be."

Kacey and me were still hatching our plan to visit the stranger again, as soon as I got back my going-out privileges. Sometimes I do not "learn my lesson," Mercy says. But reading Katherine's words only made everything more urgent. We felt connected to Katherine's ghost. We were a trio of kindred spirits, with Katherine actually being a spirit.

<u>August 30, 1960</u>

We're moving to a new house. Press is officially taking over Rost Pharmaceuticals, and Eleanor is going to have her baby any day now. Mother and Father want Press and Eleanor to move into the family house—our house—but they never will, because Eleanor only likes new things. This house is old and full of family secrets. I'm used to the howling and creaking sounds it makes. Eleanor hates it though. When she comes for supper, she says, "Does it smell musty in here?" Mother pretends not to hear.

I'll miss the view from my window, especially at night when there's a full moon. The moon was bright last week when one of the boys from Midlands sprinted across our field in his pajamas. It wasn't the first time. I think that's the real reason Eleanor won't live in this house. It's too close to a reformatory school. I also think it's the real reason Mother wants to leave. At first, she tried to ignore it. Then she tried to "get involved," but Mr. Winter won't return her calls. When we move to the new, modern house that Mother wanted, near Courthouse Square, she won't have to think about Midlands, or Father's complicity, because it won't be in her backyard.

Father will continue to own our old house along with the school's land. I found out that he gets special breaks on his tax bill because the school is on his property. The last time he was away on a business trip, I was curious, so I looked through the papers he keeps on his desk and discovered that he gets money from the state of Ohio for the school's land lease. I believe that this is his "complicity." He profits while boys are being abused.

The moon was shining so brightly I could see the boy's eyes. He didn't seem afraid. He actually looked happy to be running away. Wild. For the first time, I tried to help. I ran downstairs and out the front door. When he saw me, he smiled but kept running. He disappeared into the trees.

I can't tell Mother and Father. They'd say, "Those boys are at a reformatory school for a reason. Mind your own business."

Katherine

"My mom's a nightmare, but Katherine's parents sound worse," Kacey said.

I felt so sad whenever Kacey talked about their mom. I know my momma loved me just the way I am, even if she was terrible at being a mom.

I stared out the window to think, the same as Katherine had done when she'd lived in this house.

"The moon is shining bright, like when that boy ran away," I said.

Kacey stared, too. "I know why he was smiling," they said, wiping a tear from their cheek.

"Try and have sweet dreams," I whispered, then crawled down to my bunk, where the moon glowed in a white circle across my bedspread.

"Willa-gorilla! It's kitten season," Moe said when I arrived at the shelter. He has pet names for everyone, even if you're not a pet. "I need the empty kennels disinfected and prepared for the onslaught. There are ten that need scrubbing, and then you can walk the dogs."

"Got it," I said.

Moe is about the same age as Miss Samantha—an adult, but not an old adult. He might be homeless, or maybe he just always stays at All Creatures for the animals. He loves them and takes good care of them, but he does not take good care of himself. He only eats McDonald's and Taco Bell. I'm not even sure he showers. He definitely never gets his hair cut or shaves his beard. He told me he wanted to be a veterinarian back in the day, but he couldn't get into vet school. He said it was probably for the best because he couldn't have paid for it, anyway.

I was cleaning the kennels when Finn showed up. Finn loves animals, same as me. He's fifteen and is almost done with tenth grade at Shawneeville Central, where his dad teaches English. He's named after *Huckleberry Finn*, which is his dad's favorite story from when he was a boy.

"Hey there, Willa." Finn picked up a rag and bleach spray to help with the kennels.

"Hi, Finn." I always feel shy around Finn when I first see him because there are usually a lot of days between our shifts. And he's cute. Anyone would think he was cute—I swear I don't have a crush on him. He has brown hair that flops in his eyes, and he's good with the animals. He's especially good at walking the big dogs, who can tug real hard on their leashes. I've seen Finn pick those big dogs up and put them on the exam table for Moe to check their paws and teeth. I'm strong, but I can't pick up a pit bull and put it on the table.

"Mercy is going to sell some property that has a secret abandoned boys' school on it," I told him.

"For real?" Finn handed me fresh newspapers to put in the clean kennels.

"Yes," I said. "The school closed a long time ago, but she needs to sell it now."

"I bet the property is really valuable," Finn said. "Maybe she needs the money."

"Mercy always needs money. Do you know about that school? It was for 'juvenile delinquents.'" I used air quotes to talk about juvenile delinquents. I couldn't picture kids being criminals.

"Do you mean Midlands Christian Academy?" Finn asked.

"I knew you'd know about it!" I said. "Everyone does but us."

"My dad worked there," Finn said.

"Your dad *worked* there?" I repeated.

Finn nodded. "For a little while," he said. "Before he started at Shawneeville Central."

"Can I come over for dinner again soon?" I asked, feeling excited about this new information.

Finn laughed. I know I shouldn't invite myself, but I also know Mrs. Harbour loves having me because she said she'd always wanted a daughter and I was the closest thing she got. Mrs. Harbour and Mercy are old friends, which is why Mercy lets me go over to their house for dinner.

"I'll ask my mom," Finn said. "I'm sure it'd be fine."

I knew it'd be fine. I'd just have to find a way to get Mr. Harbour to talk about when he worked at Midlands. Did he know the whole story of why it closed and why everyone abandoned it? And what did he know about the "juvenile delinquents" who went there?

"Want to walk the dogs now?" Finn asked.

There were seven dogs in all. Finn took four, and I took three.

The dogs get real happy when we leash them. They wag their tails and tug like they'd walk themselves if we let them. We filled our pockets with treats and headed out for our usual route around Courthouse Square, toward the park overlooking the creek that flows out to the Ohio River.

The courthouse is the pride of Scioto County. I've never been inside, but I've walked in circles around it a thousand times with the dogs. The building is a perfect square made of red brick, and it has giant columns and a clock tower. It's from the old days, when Shawneeville was full of jobs and prosperity thanks to the tire factory and the shoelace factory. That was before the factories closed and the drugs started. The courthouse still looks stately and proud, like it remembers what Shawneeville used to be.

Finn walked the largest dog, a Newfoundland-Bernese mix. I know a lot about dog breeds, the same way I know a lot about chicken breeds. The small dogs on my leashes were yipping their heads off. Our walks are never quiet or peaceful, but that's okay because the dogs are so happy to be outside. That makes Finn and me happy.

I love animals so much because they are reliant on the kindness of others to survive. They are trusting, and no matter how many mistakes you make, they love you back.

"Do you think these dogs love it at All Creatures so much they want to stay?" I asked.

The dogs pulled on their leashes when we stopped at the traffic light to wait for the green.

"They probably like it well enough to stay until they get adopted into a real home," Finn said.

"Maybe they consider themselves to be living in a 'real' home already, Finn," I said. I couldn't help having a tone in my voice.

I get frustrated with Finn sometimes because he will never understand what my life feels like. He has his "real" parents and his "real" home. How could he possibly understand that as far as I'm concerned, I *also* live in a "real" home.

"I'm sorry, Willa," Finn said "That was a stupid thing for me to say to you."

"All these dogs care about is that they're being fed and watered and petted," I said. "They care about feeling loved. Moe takes good care of them, even if he smells."

"You're right about that." Finn laughed as we all crossed the street together.

Finn and me have a lot in common, but we are also very different. He's so regular that sometimes around him I feel embarrassed about things like my momma. I never bring her up around him. Finn's parents are the kind of people who help the people who are in trouble, like Momma was. I'm not "trouble" like her, but I am a troublemaker, even if I don't want to be. Maybe it's inherited. Sometimes I notice mine and Finn's differences like they're shouting at me. Those are times when I want to get away and go ride my bike as fast as I can.

That's how I was feeling for the rest of our walk.

When we got back to the shelter, I was fixing to leave without saying goodbye.

"Is everything okay, Willa Wonka?" Moe asked.

"I'm fine," I lied. The easiest white lie there ever was. "I'll see you soon, Moe."

"I'll ask my mom to call Mercy about dinner!" Finn shouted after me.

We were in the sweetness of late spring, but you could feel summer rearing up with blazing hot days to come. I always wish spring could last longer.

I turned my bike's flashing lights on so the cars could see me. Thankfully, there weren't many. I would make it home in time for dinner if I pedaled hard enough. Even if I didn't, Charlie always has leftovers in case anyone misses a meal because they're sick or sad or have lice or whatever. I knew it was a hamburger and hot dog night, and I was already hungry enough for seconds.

My tires crunched the pebbles along County Highway J.

Spring peepers made frog sounds in the ditch. Soon I heard a different sound.

I pulled my bike off to the side so I could have some silence and listen harder. Something was singing with the peepers. The sound was unmistakable—*mew, mew.* Hadn't I just come from the shelter where we'd been getting ready for kitten season? And here was a kitten. I saw it now, all by itself in the ditch on the side of the road. I'm drawn to stray animals like a magnet. Like there is a compass inside of me pointing toward helpless creatures.

"What are you doing out here all by yourself?" I asked the kitten.

I looked around in the grass, but there was no momma and no other tiny kittens. Only this one, all orange and fuzzy and soaking wet. I put my bike down to pick the creature up. She might not have liked it, but there was nothing she could do about it.

"You should be happy I found you," I said. I lifted the poor baby from the grass to make sure it wasn't injured. "Aren't you a lucky thing?"

Maybe a hawk had dropped her there in the ditch. Or maybe a human had dumped an entire litter of kittens on the side of the road and a predator had already got the rest of them. Not everybody in Shawneeville has enough money to take care of pets. I didn't have any other explanation for why a kitten would be out in the middle of nowhere all by itself.

"Come on. I'm taking you home," I said.

I put the kitten inside my shirt and rode one-handed the rest of the way to the Southern Ohio Children's Home. (I can also do no-handed, but that wouldn't be safe for a kitten.) I named the kitten Clover, after a four-leafed clover, because she was lucky and because her fur reminded me of the nutty brown of a clove, like Henrietta's buff-colored feathers.

"You have to help me keep you a secret. That's our deal, Clover."

Normally, I would not sneak in a pet. Normally, I would not do something to get myself in deeper trouble than I was already in. But things were not normal lately. Not with Mercy, or the abandoned school, or the stranger. Secrets were floating all around like ghosts.

I figured I could use a creature to take care of, to help me with my worries creeping in. Another secret for my own while I was trying to figure out everybody else's. I could let Kacey in on this secret, too. Kacey was still missing their cat more than they were missing their mom and dad. At least I'd be doing something kind, even if I was breaking Mercy's "No Pets" rule.

I leaned my bike against the garden shed and snuck inside with Clover. We went up the princess staircase while everyone was at dinner. I made her a home in my closet. I knew the most important thing for her would be a warm, dry, and safe bed. She'd be fine with milk and water overnight, then I'd pedal back and get kitten food from Moe in the morning.

I just had to pray that Clover, my newest secret, would stop meowing.

Secrets and Ghosts

JUSTIN HAS READ PRACTICALLY EVERY book in the Southern Ohio Children's Home library. He goes there every day, no matter what, to read more. While Kacey was spending their days tucked away in Miss Samantha's classroom and working on their gender research, I was going to the library. I wanted to keep an eye on Justin and the secret bookshelf to make sure no one else accidentally found it. Kacey and me especially didn't want *him* finding the bookshelf.

Justin wants to know everything, even the things he doesn't know he wants to know. All he wanted to know about lately was Midlands Academy, same as me.

I found him reading three books he'd pulled from the library shelves. He'd curled himself into the red couch in a blanket that Mrs. Harbour had knit. I swear, there are at least a hundred Mrs. Harbour blankets scattered all over the Southern Ohio Children's Home. I sat at Miss Katherine's desk and flipped through the latest book on the stand: *A Wrinkle in Time*. The dad in that book is stuck on some other planet, and his kids are trying to get him back. I've never tried to get my dad back, because he is dead. Plus, all I know about him is that Momma hated his guts because he's the one who started her on drugs.

"If we broke *our* rule and crossed the ravine, so could the ghosts," Justin said, taking a pause from reading books to look up at me. It seemed that ghost boys were haunting him, and he only knew half of what Kacey and me knew from Katherine's diaries. I couldn't let him figure out more.

"They cannot," I reassured him. "Ghosts have to stay where they're assigned."

Justin clutched his book and flipped through the pages. He likes books in his hands better than books online. One time, he tried reading the newest version of the encyclopedia on the internet, and it made him so mad. He just kept pressing links to whatever sounded interesting.

"How do I know what I haven't read yet? What if I miss something?" he'd said.

I understood how that would be frustrating to a person like Justin who likes to finish their books. How could he finish the internet?

"Willa, I need your help, please." Mercy appeared in the library doorway like a ghost herself.

I nearly fell off my chair. "Coming."

I put Mrs. Whatsit back on the bookstand and ran to be in Mercy's good graces.

"Good morning, Justin. Visiting with a friend?" Mercy asked, pointing to his book. Justin is better friends with books than he is with people.

"Yes, ma'am," Justin said.

Mercy smiled proudly, and Justin blushed. Getting a proud feeling for yourself is special, even when Mercy and Miss Samantha show us practically every day they're proud of us.

"Let's go, Willa."

Justin sank deeper into his blanket and his book while I followed Mercy into the hall. She opened the front door, letting in a fresh gust of spring air. I was grateful for cool mornings and open windows. Mercy had got central air conditioning last year because summers are getting hotter, and window units are running up her bill. I hate the heat, but I would not use AC all summer if it meant saving Mercy money.

We walked through the front door together and stared at the driveway.

"Is another kid coming?" I asked, knowing Mercy couldn't take any more.

"No," she said. "My cousin, Meredith, is coming."

I nodded, but I had questions, like why did Mercy look nervous? And what would the little girl with pigtails look like now?

"Where does she live?" I asked Mercy something easy.

"New York City," she said.

"New York City is a long way from Shawneeville," I said.

"It sure is. She's not staying long, even though we have a lot of work to do. I'd like you to help take her bags up to my bedroom."

"Got it," I said.

Mercy's bedroom is another forbidden place, but Meredith was a special exception. I still had more questions wanting to spill out, like when was the last time Mercy saw Meredith? And what did she know about Midlands Christian Academy for Boys? But I kept my mouth shut to avoid irritating Mercy, who was clearly "stressed out." I could see it in the deep furrow between her brows.

Just when I thought I couldn't keep quiet any longer, a black SUV with dark windows pulled up the drive.

"Here she is now." Mercy sucked in a breath. She looked at me and smiled. I hadn't ever seen her this nervous before, and I didn't know what to do. So I gave her a thumbs up, like I give Elizabeth or Roy when they need encouragement on something hard, like Spanish lessons.

The SUV stopped, and a man in a dark suit got out and opened the back door for Mercy's cousin-lawyer. Meredith stepped onto the pebble drive in the highest high heels I have ever seen. They were black, just like the rest of her outfit, including her sunglasses and gigantic leather purse. This was not a Shawneeville lawyer, I could tell that right away. Meredith was too fancy and too rich. She flung off her sunglasses and stuck them on top of her head to hold back her long, dark brown hair.

"I like what you've done with the place," Meredith said to Mercy while the driver got her enormous suitcase. It looked like Meredith had packed for six months. Now I realized why Mercy asked me to help—she was still punishing me.

"That's a big suitcase for someone not staying long," I whispered to Mercy, who stepped down from the front porch and ignored me.

"Thank you for coming, Meredith. It's good to see you," Mercy said.

"I've been avoiding coming back as long as I could, but here I am," Meredith said with a sigh.

They gave each other a not-so-huggy hug.

"I'll take that!" I said and grabbed Meredith's suitcase.

Mercy quickly introduced us. "Meredith, this is Willa. Willa, meet my cousin Meredith."

"Hi," I said, struggling to pick up the suitcase. It had to weigh more than me.

"It's nice to meet you, Willa," Meredith said. "I'm taking that."

Meredith grabbed her suitcase out of my hands and lugged it to the front door in her high, high heels.

"I can do it!" I said.

"Absolutely not," Meredith said.

"Really, Meredith, Willa knows where to take it ..." Mercy said.

"So do I!" Meredith was inside the Southern Ohio Children's Home and halfway up the princess staircase before I could even try and help.

"She's strong," I said.

Mercy nodded and gave me one of her looks, like she agreed with me but she also knew a lot more about the situation. We weren't supposed to have visitors running around the Southern Ohio Children's Home, but anyone could see that Meredith was special. How could she not be?

She'd had Miss Katherine for a mom.

"Turns out Mom changed her will right before she died. Look ..." Meredith handed Mercy a small envelope.

Meredith had got herself settled and peed (her words, not mine). Now, she and Mercy were walking in the garden.

"What's this?" Mercy opened the envelope and unfolded a yellowed slip of paper.

I had followed Mercy and Meredith out the back door with two glasses of Emily's delicious sweet tea, still trying to be helpful. Emily has a sweet tooth, so she always makes her tea extra sweet, as she likes it.

Meredith inspected every plant we'd planted so far, which were mostly herbs and peppers and tomatoes. We also had kale and lettuce that were growing like crazy. That's bad for Roy because he hates salad. I could eat salad with ranch dressing every day. We had also planted marigolds to keep the deer away. Our garden makes a lot of food. We'll have more than a thousand tomatoes before summer's over, I swear. And Charlie will make a hundred jars of tomato sauce.

"Your mom never told me anything about changing her will," Mercy said.

"Me neither," Meredith said. "I found it at Dad's house."

I put their tea on a milk crate and picked up a basket so I could pull weeds and be invisible. My ears were on high alert.

"When I was in high school, Mom and I had this system," Meredith said. "I never wanted to be interrupted while I was studying, so if she had something to tell me—like what was for dinner, or if some boy had called, or if she wanted company watching *Murder, She Wrote* or *The Golden Girls,* she'd write it in a note. Then, she'd put that note in an envelope in Grand-daddy's cigar box, which I kept on my desk for pens and pencils. That way, I'd find her note when I was ready."

Meredith paused, as if she got distracted in her memories.

"I hadn't been to Dad's house since he died, you know," she sighed. "I only stopped by for a few minutes before coming here, to see if I might be able to stay there. But I can't. Not without Dad there. Thanks for letting me stay here with you."

Mercy nodded, and Meredith started back in on her story.

"Anyway," she said. "Out of habit, I sat down at my old desk, and there was the cigar box, right where it always was—on top and to the left. I opened it. It still smells like sweet tobacco and pencil shavings. Wouldn't you know, I found this envelope. It's just like Mom, to leave me a message but keep it a secret and have me find it only when I'm ready."

I was starting to think I could spend my whole life discovering Katherine's secrets.

Mercy read the cigar box note over and over. I put down my basket of weeds and checked the chickens. Meredith sauntered past the coop in her high heels. Chickens don't need you to do much for them besides clean their poop and give them food and water, but I pretended like each chicken needed petting and examining right then and there. It's a good thing Henrietta and me are such great pals, because she sat in my lap and let me pet her and pet her. Anyone from New York City might think this is something you have to do with your chickens.

"She wrote you a letter about changing her will over twenty years ago?" Mercy asked. "And never told you?"

"Apparently," Meredith said. "She must have placed it in the cigar box before she died. When she was still sick. When Dad moved out of this house, he must have brought the box with him without ever touching the note."

Meredith put her giant sunglasses back on, even though a cotton-ball cloud had floated in front of the sun.

"I'm sorry I've been so absent, Mercy," she said. "All I ever wanted was to get out of Shawneeville. It was hard enough to come back after Mom died, with memories everywhere. When Dad died, it seemed impossible. I can't believe he's been gone two years already. I miss them both so much."

Mercy dropped the letter and walked over to give Meredith a real hug. Mercy is full of love, but she is not a hugger. She doesn't even hug us kids all that often, unless someone gets a scrape or has a nightmare. I imagine if she actually was a hugger, she wouldn't be doing anything but hugging kids all day long.

So it surprised me when she hugged Meredith that way. A huggy-hug, like she meant it. The kind of hug I didn't know Mercy knew how to give. It was like how she makes us wait to apologize, to make sure we mean it in our heart when we say an apology. Or how she teaches us that when you say "I understand," you have to feel it deep inside and really understand. It looked like Mercy had that same philosophy when it came to hugs. It seemed like she felt that hug deep inside.

"You're here now," Mercy said.

I don't know why, but watching Mercy hug Meredith, with Henrietta sitting on my lap, made me want to cry. Maybe it was Miss Katherine's spirit watching over us, feeling that hug, too. Maybe Meredith was crying, but there was no way to tell with those giant sunglasses on.

"Hopefully, the addendum to her will is still hidden somewhere, too," Mercy said. "A lot of things could have happened to it in the twenty years since your mom wrote it. Especially since there are a lot of children in the house now, with little fingers finding things. And breaking things. And tearing things up."

I was going to have to look up the word "addendum" in the dictionary.

"Mom would have been purposeful about this," Meredith said. "I trust she put it someplace safe. She'd have wanted it to survive beyond—"

"Beyond another generation." Mercy cut Meredith off, like she knew what Meredith wanted to say before she said it. Both of them knew exactly what kind of woman Katherine was.

"That's right," Meredith said. She picked up the letter from the ground. "She *had* to put her hope in future generations. So she would have wanted the addendum to be found *now*. Not then."

"Your mother has a way of staying with us, doesn't she?" Mercy smiled.

This time, I knew Meredith was crying even though she was smiling, because a fat tear escaped from underneath her sunglasses.

After meeting Meredith, I was almost starting to feel like part of a regular family. She didn't know how close Kacey and me had gotten to her mother. We had a regular routine of sneaking diaries from the hidden shelf, sharing flashlights, reading every night, and writing down the words we wanted to keep. Like when Katherine wrote about getting married.

June 21, 1967

I am back at this house full of secrets and ghosts, but on my own terms. I'm ready to make changes. I'm writing in my diary from the same window where I used to write as a young girl. Now here I am, a married woman who is turning 22 in a couple of months. Yes, married!

Mother is mad at me for eloping and refuses to set foot in this house—my house—which is just as well. The last thing I wanted was some big wedding where Father could show off the way he did when Press and Eleanor got married ten years ago. Mother might be mad at me forever, for denying <u>her</u> my wedding celebration. But it was worth it since Edward and I went to France and Italy for a month after convincing

Soon after I found Clover, I started bringing her up to Kacey's bunk to read alongside us. My new kitten had spent her first couple nights sleeping under my covers. She loved snuggling and slept quietly. Probably because she was so tired from living in a ditch for who knows how long.

"A kitten!" Kacey whisper-screamed when they met Clover. I was worried the others would wake up, especially when Clover meowed. But kitten meows aren't loud, thank goodness.

"How'd you get a kitten? What's its name?" Kacey asked.

"Clover," I whispered. "She found me when I was riding my bike."

Kacey petted Clover and nearly cried tears of joy, while Clover purred and purred. Breaking Mercy's "No Pets" rule was definitely worth it to see the smile on Kacey's face.

I was going to All Creatures more than usual since I was grounded from everything else. That made it easier to sneak back supplies, like food and litter. Moe is angry that I won't bring Clover to the shelter to live and be adopted. Plus, he knows I am breaking Mercy's rule. But I can't take her. I love Clover. She's the only pet I've ever had who is truly my own. We've already adopted each other.

Momma and me had a cat once who traveled around with us when "home" wasn't a thing that existed. I was only five years old, and that cat—named Midnight, because it was black—was kind of mean, but I loved it anyway. Momma took it from a friend who couldn't feed it anymore, thinking she'd be able to feed and take care of it better. But after a couple weeks, Momma hated Midnight, and I was the only one caring for him, which was hard because I was five. I couldn't exactly walk to the store and buy cat food, even though I tried. Momma left Midnight behind at one of the houses we'd stayed at. I don't even know whose house it was. I never got to say goodbye to Midnight, because Momma never told me she was ditching the poor thing. Ever since Midnight, I have always wanted my own cat.

I am going to bring Clover to Moe for spaying though. He'll see how much we're family, but I know he's still going to be so mad. More than anyone, Moe knows the danger of falling in love with a stray animal. It's happened to him eight-hundred times, and now he's living in an animal shelter.

"Clover makes me miss Domino," Kacey said.

"You'll see her again," I said, not really knowing if Kacey

would see their cat again or not, but it hurt my heart to think they wouldn't be reunited someday.

"We have to keep Clover a secret," I whispered.

Kacey crossed their heart. They knew just how to pet Clover behind her ears and under her chin. I was grateful to have a partner in crime, because taking care of a kitten is a lot of work, believe me. Especially if you're also trying to keep that kitten a secret. We figured how to sneak Clover into the bathroom, where we lock the door and wear her out playing with kitten toys before putting her back in the closet for another nap.

Clover does wake me up in the middle of the night sometimes, and going back to sleep is hard when you're a mom. I remember Momma used to complain about that.

One night, while I was lying in bed awake with Clover, I ended up reading ahead in Katherine's diary.

"Look!" I showed Kacey. They were already half asleep, but I couldn't keep my discovery for myself. "Katherine says how she got the quote for the library wall!"

I had almost screamed when I'd read about Katherine's library—*our* library.

October 7, 1967

I've been canning tomatoes and making jam for a week straight. Edward and I could become self-sufficient in this giant house and not have to rely on my family for anything ever again. We are real hippies. Mother abhors our lifestyle, so I must be doing something right.

Edward has been especially inspired by his work lately. Thurgood Marshall was sworn in as the first African American Supreme Court justice. It's got Edward thinking about putting his name in for the open judgeship in Scioto County. He hadn't given it much thought before now, because starting a law practice was hard enough. But he is inspired.

Other men Edward's age are being drafted to go fight in Vietnam. I'm grateful he's practicing law, so he won't have to go. Still, he's troubled by the inequity of a deferment process that gives advantages to men with education and financial privilege. We both know that the students at Midlands Academy graduate straight into battle. Many are happy to.

I want to lend books from our house to Midlands. I'm changing Father's office into a library, and I've been cleaning everything out. I found a stack of his LIFE magazines. There was a profile of James Baldwin in an old issue called "Telling Talk From a Negro Writer." Inside, I found a perfect quote to inscribe on the library wall:

YOU THINK YOUR PAIN AND YOUR HEARTBREAK ARE UNPRECEDENTED IN THE HISTORY OF THE WORLD, BUT THEN YOU READ.

I wonder if Father read that article. Do he and Mother even understand pain and heartache? They "help" those less fortunate, with her luncheons and his land donation for Midlands. Being privileged is their goal; they'll never see it as a problem.

Katherine

"What does she mean about privilege being a problem?" I asked Kacey.

"Maybe it means they're giant snobs?" Kacey said. They yawned and reached out their arms for Clover.

"Katherine's own daughter is the most privileged person I ever saw in my life," I said, giving Clover to Kacey.

Kacey was worn out from our late nights, which was fine by Clover, who snuggled up to their chin and made biscuits with her paws on their shoulder.

"Sweet dreams," I whispered to Kacey and Clover. Then I kept reading.

Sanctuary in the Woods

WHEN ROY HAD FIRST CAME to the Southern Ohio Children's Home, he would use swears a lot and call us bad names—especially Justin, because Justin is smart, and Roy is jealous. Roy had grown up with his family swearing all the time, so Mercy had to have a special lesson with him about why he had to stop cussing us out.

"When you call people bad names," she'd said, "it hurts their feelings." She'd talked to him like he was a three-year-old who needed this obvious fact pointed out to him. But that was the weird thing about Roy's family's cussing—they'd done it so much, Roy had stopped noticing. Mercy needed to unlearn him. "If you continue using words that are hurtful, you cannot live at the Southern Ohio Children's Home. Do you understand, Roy?"

Mercy scared him so bad when she said that. The thought of one of us getting kicked out scared us all. She'd given the lesson to everyone, making sure we all heard her words. And Roy *did* learn his lesson. At least we thought he did, until he and Justin got into a fight over the right way to do long division. Roy finally gave up and called Justin a whole string of bad names, including *jack-cuss* and *stupid frigging swear-word-hole* (but with the real swears). Then he called Justin the F-slur—one of the worst bad words there is. This time, Roy knew how bad it was and that he was hurting Justin's feelings. (I told Roy that if he wants to be smart, he should be nice to Justin, so Justin would help with his homework instead of fighting him over it.)

We punished Roy by ignoring him for a full week. Then, we made him write an apology letter to Justin, explaining why what he had said was wrong. Justin kept that letter. Roy had better thank his lucky stars that Justin is a pacifist. We promised Roy we wouldn't tell Mercy, because she said she'd kick him out. *There are lines that cannot be crossed, such as disrespecting others,* she'd said.

Having this information on Roy comes in handy sometimes. Like when he found out about Clover.

She was meowing one night after lights out, and Elizabeth was scared there was a monster in the closet.

"It's not a monster, Elizabeth. I promise you," I said. It almost made me laugh, thinking about a little kitten being a monster. But Elizabeth is what you'd call a scaredy-cat.

"I can hear it," she said.

Justin and Roy couldn't hear Clover as good because their bunk is on the other side of The Fortress. Plus, Justin reads in bed with headphones squeezing his ears. He doesn't wear them to play music, they just make the world quiet for him.

"I'll get the monster for you, Elizabeth." Roy jumped off his top bunk. He wanted to smash Elizabeth's monster.

"No!" I said.

"Leave it alone!" said Kacey.

But it was too late. Roy was already opening the closet door, ready to punch something.

I hopped out of my bed to save Clover from Roy.

"See? It's not a monster, Elizabeth," I said, pulling Clover out of the closet to show Elizabeth, while trying to shield my cat from Roy.

Elizabeth smiled and pet Clover.

"You are in so much trouble!" Roy said.

"If you tell Mercy, I'll tell her what you called Justin!" I said.

Roy looked at the ground, ashamed. I knew he wouldn't snitch on me. He glanced at Justin out of the corner of his eye. Justin didn't hear us. Either that, or he was pretending. He looked over, saw Clover, and then kept on reading his book, like everything was normal in The Fortress and having a kitten was fine by him. Justin prefers to mind his own business if he can. He is wise in more ways than one.

I probably shouldn't talk too much about Roy not learning his lesson though, because I have a hard time learning my lesson, too.

That night, with Clover safely out of hiding and in the bed with us, I helped Kacey write a letter to their dad to ask about their cat, Domino. We also kept reading Katherine's diaries as fast as we could. I was worried Roy or Elizabeth or Justin would find our notebook the same way they'd found Clover.

<u>July 10, 1969</u>

I'm now the librarian (volunteer, part-time) at Midlands. It was not easy getting a foothold inside those closed doors. Mr. Winter is still as frosty as his name suggests. I have yet to see the shed outside his window being used, but my imagination gets the better of me. I fear I might not be dreaming up the worst of it.

I took a box of Father's books that had been collecting dust. If I can see one young man smile at the small kindness of receiving a book, I will feel better, if only for a moment. Edward says I'm collecting happy moments to replace the bad moments that have come to pass.

I've been distraught by the war and Nixon's failed promises to withdraw troops. Surprisingly, being at Midlands has been a bright spot. Mother and Father have no idea about my involvement. Mother had always told me to stay away, but now she can't keep me away. Father still sits on the board and collects on the land-lease. Does he still get tax breaks? I wonder if there is a way for me to change his agreements. Probably not. At least, not until I am the owner of this land. We don't discuss it, but I know that when Mother and Father pass, this property will be mine.

Katherine

"So the property was hers, and then she gave it to Mercy," Kacey whispered, reviewing the facts.

"That must be right," I said. "But before Mercy can sell it, she has to check Katherine's will."

"Is that why Meredith came?" Kacey asked.

I nodded. "Meredith told Mercy that Katherine had changed her will at the last minute and that she hid some secret part of it here. In this house."

Roy tossed and turned in his bed, saying, "Stop it." Sometimes he talks in his sleep. Kacey and me stopped talking just to be safe.

We eventually got to the part of Katherine's story where Meredith was born and Katherine became a mom.

<u>**February 9, 1973**</u>

Edward and I are so in love with our baby. Meredith was born a week ago, 7 pounds, 9 ounces. We are barely getting any sleep, but we don't care. Even though she's completely reliant on us, she is so CAPABLE. I don't know how to explain it, except that I feel I know her already.

But what will I do now? Stay home and play house? There are women at this very moment who'd love nothing more. Women who are campaigning <u>against</u> the Equal Rights Amendment and against men and women being treated equally. Sometimes I wonder if equality will ever be possible. People must believe in our laws if they are to be effective. Congress passed the Civil Rights Act almost ten years ago to outlaw discrimination, but don't tell me discrimination doesn't still exist. Some days I am plain angry. People around here aren't angry about anything, which doesn't feel right. To them, life is good in our "picture-perfect" town!

I find thresholds unsettling. Birthdays, and the New Year, and now motherhood. Still, I am grateful for the promise of change. For a new generation. When we can't accomplish our dreams, we must look to the next generation to save us. Progress comes so much slower than I'd like.

Mother, Father, Press, and Eleanor came over to meet Meredith. Eleanor brought her own daughter for once, and how Mercy has grown. Everyone was as overjoyed as we are. For a moment, I felt like my family was honest and real. I think Mother dreamed of having a dozen grandchildren running all around, but she only has two. And two girls at that. Even though life is different from what she'd imagined, she seems content. I wonder if she might be softening around the edges. I do catch Mother looking askance at her daughter-in-law, even though Eleanor is every bit the socialite as Mother. A mirror of privilege. Mother sees herself in Eleanor, but because it is not her own reflection, she can be honest about what she is looking at.

Katherine

There were so many things in Katherine's diaries I knew I'd have to ask Miss Samantha about, like Civil Rights and Equal Rights and a lot of other kinds of rights. I had so many ideas for more research projects, I was starting to feel like Justin.

When my three-week going-out grounding was finally done,

Kacey and me didn't waste any time sneaking out to Midlands all over again.

It was easy enough for me to pretend I was going to All Creatures.

"Moe must be overjoyed with all the help he's been getting, Willa," Miss Samantha said.

"He sure is," I white-lied.

I felt bad lying to Miss Samantha, but I prayed she wouldn't notice when she didn't get a text from Moe's cell phone. She was playing phonogram bingo with the six- and seven-year-olds, using puzzle words like "laugh" and "tough" and "mother" and "father." I used to think "mother" and "father" were special puzzle words for orphans, because it might be puzzling why we do not have mothers or fathers. I couldn't read when I came to the Southern Ohio Children's Home, even though I was seven years old. I hadn't ever gone to school enough. Miss Samantha had me reading words within one week, I swear. Sometimes she doesn't notice other things when she's teaching real hard, like whether or not Moe texts her when I get to All Creatures.

Kacey signed the whiteboard for a going-out along with Justin and Roy. Then, Kacey told Justin and Roy they'd have to do their own going out, just the two of them. They might have known what Kacey and me were up to, because they might have heard us planning in The Fortress. They might also have known it'd be better if they *didn't* know, so they shrugged and ran off in the opposite direction of the black oak tree, toward a stick house they were building. Elizabeth stayed in the classroom where she could announce the phonograms for the bingo game.

Luckily, the day had not started off rainy and was only a little hot. We'd had a couple hot days already, but you could still feel a coolness in the morning breeze. I rode my bike toward

County Highway J but veered off the driveway and walked back to the black oak tree. I hid my bike on the other side so no one could see it if they were looking from the home.

Kacey was already there waiting for me.

"Did you bring the cookies?" they asked.

I pulled the Ziploc bag from my backpack, along with two bottles of water. We wanted to have something to give to the stranger, so maybe he'd let us stay for a minute and talk. That is, if he was there, since Mercy had called Deputy Bell on him.

It's not safe for children here, is what he'd told me. I was grateful for Kacey's company. I needed them, but I knew they needed me, too. It felt like we'd been friends from before we knew each other. I wanted to ask Kacey more about their family or any friends who might know they were at the Southern Ohio Children's Home, but I also didn't want to bring up a sore subject. Their *before*.

We walked to the ravine, long grass swishing under our feet. Even though it was getting hotter outside, Kacey wore baggy pants and a long-sleeved shirt, like they did every day.

"Mercy can get you some summer clothes," I said. "She gets them donated from the Methodist church or the Ministry of Hopelessness."

"I like wearing my own clothes," Kacey said.

"At least your pants will keep the bugs off," I said, remembering our last visit to the school. "Dang-it, I forgot bug spray." I was wearing shorts and a T-shirt and was about to get eaten alive by mosquitos.

"Here," Kacey pulled a white sheet from their pocket, the kind you put in the dryer to make it so your clothes don't stick. "Rub it on your skin. It keeps the bugs away. I already put some on my neck."

Sure enough, as soon as we crossed the ravine, climbed over

the bent chain-link fence, and entered the thick woods, bugs flew all around but didn't bite me.

"That dryer-sheet trick works good," I said. Kacey smiled.

We walked toward Midlands Christian Academy as quietly as we could. Past the fire pit and to the tree sanctuary, tiptoeing even though the sticks and dried leaves and pine needles on the forest floor gave us away. It smelled like campfires and Christmas.

"Are you scared?" I whispered.

My own heart thumped in my chest from sneaking out, and from sneaking up on the stranger.

"Nah," Kacey said. "I don't care if anything bad happens to me."

I suddenly felt like I didn't know Kacey at all. I hoped they were only being a show-off.

"I care if anything bad happens to you," I whispered. "But nothing bad will happen. This is a nice stranger. I can tell. I really can."

I got the cookies out of the backpack and gave one to Kacey.

"Here, eat this." Cookies always make me feel better, and we had plenty.

Kacey took the cookie and ate it, and that made *me* feel better. Emily and Charlie were rubbing off on me.

I crossed the threshold into the aspen tree sanctuary and stood beneath the towering branches that swayed in the light breeze. Their green leaves danced high in sunshine that turned to shade before it reached me. The sanctuary was even more peaceful now with some grown-up leaves on the trees.

I heard the same slow creaking sound I'd heard when we'd first found Midlands. I looked toward the dark wooden shed just in time to see its door open with a groan.

As if he'd been waiting for a visit, the stranger stepped out of the shed with his dog. He grabbed a walking stick that was leaning against the wall. This time, his dog wasn't growling.

"Hello?" I said, trying to sound friendly. I didn't want the ghosts to tell us we had to leave.

The stranger spied me in the tree church. Kacey stepped up to my side. I felt braver with them next to me.

The stranger walked toward us, keeping his dog content with regular treats from his pocket. He was wearing blue jeans and a button-down shirt. He smelled like bug spray.

"Who are you?" the stranger asked. "What are you doing here? I thought I told you to leave." He sounded worried.

"We brought you some cookies." I pulled the cookies and water bottles from my backpack and laid them on the ground beside the aspen trees.

"What's your name?" I asked.

"My name's Jack," he said after a pause, like he wasn't sure if he wanted to tell us his name or not. "Jack Thompson."

"I'm Willa, and this is my friend Kacey."

"Nice to meet you," Jack said.

I pointed to the gray-haired pit bull mix. "Who's that?"

"This is Benji. Benji, sit. Paw. Speak." Jack went through the series of commands and Benji did exactly as he was told, right on cue.

Kacey and me clapped our hands after Benji's tricks, like we were his audience.

Jack picked up the cookies. "How did you know I have a sweet tooth?"

"Just lucky, I guess." I didn't mention that it'd be weird if he *didn't* like cookies. "Can I pet your dog?"

"Sure," he said. "Benji won't bite. He looks tough, but he's a softy."

I reached out and let Benji sniff my hand. Then Benji gave me his paw, as if to say, "Pleased to meet you." That made Kacey and me laugh. A second later, he was rolling on his back so I could rub his belly.

"See what I mean?" Jack said. "A big softy. Now, tell me, Willa and Kacey, why do you keep visiting a place where you shouldn't be?"

I could have asked Jack the same thing, since Mercy said he was trespassing. I was starting to wonder if he lived in that shed. He ate a cookie while he waited for me to answer.

"We need information," I said. "We weren't sure you'd be here though. Someone might have called the police about you." I didn't want to rat Mercy out, and I didn't want to tell Jack too many things about us—like that we live in a residential home for kids just across the field.

"Deputy Bell?" Jack guessed.

"How'd you know?" Kacey asked.

"She visits me from time to time, but I haven't seen her in a while," he said. "When I first started fixing things up back here, she followed me down the driveway to see what I was up to. She lets me do my thing. She has her hands full around here."

"That's true," I said. "There is a crisis in our community, after all."

"Ha!" Jack laughed and smiled so big when I mentioned the crisis in our community, like it was the funniest thing he ever heard. I don't think it's funny, but at least I was breaking the ice. "A 'crisis in the community' is one way of putting it," Jack said.

"Did you plant these trees?" Kacey asked, pointing at the cathedral.

"I sure did. I started moving them a long time ago," Jack said. "Aspens don't like the shade, so I moved them over to this spot. It used to be a clearing. They share a strong root system by now. I've always dreamed of making a community garden here, but I can't do it by myself. Still, these trees were my first attempt. They give me a place to pray."

"I pray a little," I said. "Not for anything much ..." *Like to talk to my momma again*, is what I didn't say. I pretend I still talk to Momma, and I write her letters that will never get read. I don't pray too hard though, because I do not think my prayers will be heard or answered.

"What do you pray for?" Kacey asked Jack.

"I pray for the boys who went to this school," Jack said. "Sometimes I feel like they're talking back, telling me to remember."

Kacey and me looked at each other and then looked around at the forest and the abandoned buildings. There was no one there but us.

"It's their spirits," Jack said. "Right there, in these trees." He looked up at the aspens as if he could see boys climbing them.

"What do they want you to remember?" I asked.

"Who they were," Jack said. "They came to this school but never left. All scared. Same as I was."

Jack kicked over a log with his foot. He leaned on his walking stick and sat down. Benji found a stick to chew on and laid down at Jack's feet. Kacey and me each pulled up our own log stool. We sat inside the sanctuary, with Jack on the outside. Drops of rain tipped the leaves above our heads. The pitter-patter made me feel sleepy.

"When it rains, it reminds me of them crying," Jack said.

"Crying over what?" I asked.

"You don't want to know," Jack said.

"Was it because they were bad and got in trouble?" I tried again.

"That's what everyone believed … that juvenile delinquents deserve to be treated poorly," Jack said.

"But wasn't it a Christian school?" I asked. Kacey rolled their eyes.

"There wasn't anything 'Christian' about this school," Jack said.

"Why do still you come here?" Kacey asked.

"I visit Shawneeville every summer. I'm a music teacher. A choir director back in Virginia, where I live. It's hard for me to describe why I come here. I never imagined I'd ever run into anyone at Midlands, except maybe Deputy Bell. This is a forgotten place."

"We never even knew it was here until a few weeks ago," I said. "And I've lived in Shawneeville all my life." I could see from Jack's face that my saying this made him sad.

"One summer," Jack said, "a while back, when Benji was just a puppy, we passed through town. I ended up taking a part-time job at the library and got a rental for a couple months. One day, Benji and I came back here for a walk. I was scared at first. Scared of what I'd find. Turns out I didn't find much, but what I felt was something sacred. Peaceful. I felt the boys' memories. Who's going to remember them if I don't? That's why I still come here. It's for them. And that's why I'd like to plant a garden here. You could call it my memorial to them."

I wondered where Jack would put these memories if Mercy sold the property.

"You went to school at Midlands?" I finally asked.

Jack looked me in the eye and nodded. He still had a sad look on his face.

"You don't seem so bad," Kacey said.

Jack laughed. "Thank you," he said.

"Did you have a teacher named Henry Harbour?" I asked, thinking it'd be a long shot.

Jack raised his eyebrows at me. "He made us read *Huckleberry Finn*."

"He has a son named Finn!" I said. "I never read that book yet. I know Mr. Harbour, too." I had a butterfly-like feeling inside when Jack said he knew Finn's dad.

"The teachers here were mostly bad," Jack said, "but Mr. Harbour was good, even if none of us appreciated Mark Twain the way he wanted us to." Jack looked like he wanted to laugh again. He kept laughing at things I didn't understand. "The good teachers never stayed, though," he added.

"We heard that's why the school closed," Kacey said. "Because the teachers were bad."

Jack grabbed one of the water bottles we'd brought and took a sip.

"We weren't learning much here," he said. "Except how to grit your teeth when a belt came out."

I saw Kacey flinch from the corner of my eye.

"My daddy laid his hand on me once before he died," Jack said. "For talking back to my mom. But it wasn't anything like what they did here. My daddy loved me. There was no love at this school. None."

I thought about how much Miss Samantha loves me.

"Do you mind if I ask why you went here?" Kacey said.

"My parents were killed in a car crash," Jack said. "My dad was about to start a job at the shoelace factory. We were driving from Virginia to Ohio, to our new home, when a truck came out of nowhere and nearly swiped off the front of our car. I have a bad leg to show for it, but my mom and dad died pretty quick."

"I'm sorry," I said. "My momma died, too. So did my dad, but I never knew him."

"You don't ever get over it, losing your parents so young," Jack said. "I'm sorry to hear about your mom and dad."

Jack was having a lot of emotions, talking about his parents. Who knows when was the last time he'd talked about them.

"My parents didn't have any money," he went on. "We were dirt poor, with no family around. And what family was left in Virginia didn't have enough to feed another mouth. I didn't have any other options. That's how I ended up at Midlands."

"Life is so unfair," I said.

Kacey looked at the school, then back down at their feet again, like they were looking inside themself. The pitter-patter of the rain grew louder. The woods smelled like wet earth.

"Why has Midlands Academy been sitting here abandoned all these years?" I asked. "Like it's invisible and no one can see it?" I had really been needing to know the answer to this question.

"Nobody wants to touch this place," Jack said. "The town abandoned it when they shut it down. The same way they abandoned the students who went here. There is a *responsibility* that has been abandoned as well."

All of a sudden, Jack seemed mad. Not mean, but mad.

"This school is a ghost because no one, not one living soul, will take responsibility for what happened here," Jack said.

"What happened here?" I asked, like a whisper. Like when you want to find out about a secret you're scared to know.

Jack shook his head. "You probably shouldn't come here

anymore," he said. "Benji and I won't stay much longer anyway. We're heading back to Virginia soon."

Fat raindrops hit our bodies. Jack shook his head again as rain fell on his face.

"We should go," Kacey whispered. They bent over and dug a hole in the dirt.

"What are you doing?" I asked.

"I'm forgetting," Kacey said. "I'm leaving this behind." They pulled a piece of paper from their pocket and put it in the hole, burying it. I knew it must have been their Forgetting Letter.

I had a thousand more questions, like what was it like to have Mr. Harbour as a teacher, and if anything bad had ever happened to Jack at Midlands. We knew some of what had happened, but only as much as Katherine had known, which definitely wasn't all of it.

But I knew we had to leave.

"Thank you, Jack! We're going to visit you again!" I called out as we ran, trying to beat the rain.

I don't know if Jack heard me. Maybe he was praying or somewhere else far off, feeling raindrop tears and sad-sadness.

The ravine was filling up with a flash flood, drowning everything in the blink of an eye. Our shoes got soaked and soon, so did the rest of us.

We grabbed my bike from behind the black oak tree and kept running in a straight line, straight across the field toward the Southern Ohio Children's Home in "Noah's Ark Rain," as Miss Samantha calls it. Kacey and me might as well have jumped into a swimming pool. The sky turned dark as midnight right as it started thundering and lightning. It was like we had made the ghost boys—the ones who knew about the parts Jack wouldn't tell us—angry and sad. Maybe they knew Mercy was wanting to sell the land, which would keep Jack from ever making them a memorial garden.

We came in through the side door, into Miss Samantha's classroom. Rivers of water were streaming down our legs. Miss Samantha was waiting inside with Roy and Justin, who had come in as soon as the rain started. They'd had to tell the truth about why Kacey was not with them.

Miss Samantha silently gave each of us a towel to dry off. I knew I was in big trouble because Miss Samantha has a "Look" too, like Mercy's. She just doesn't use it as much because of the soft spot she has inside for all the mistakes we make.

I prayed hard, like Jack. I prayed that Miss Samantha wouldn't tell Mercy.

As usual, my prayers were not heard or answered. Miss Samantha told Mercy right away.

To the Letter

MERCY STARTED OFF MY GETTING-IN-TROUBLE talk by saying I was making more "poor choices" and she might not trust me to leave the Southern Ohio Children's Home ever again. That punishment will backfire though, because it is one of my life goals to never leave Mercy.

The last time an older orphan left the home to go live with a foster family it was a 14-year-old girl named Brandi. A family from two towns over said they could take her in after their own teenage daughter died of a drug overdose. That family wanted a foster child to help heal from losing their girl and maybe also to help solve the crisis in our community. Brandi said she was fine, but she cried and cried when that family took her away.

I never want to go live with a foster family or get adopted or anything.

Never.

I had my family, and they died. Everyone at the Southern Ohio Children's Home is my family now, even though Mercy is not my mom. I don't know what that means for me when I grow up. Will Mercy not have room for me anymore? Will she have to say goodbye to me someday and send me away so she can take in more kids? The Black Hole of My Future opened wide.

"I told you never to go across that ravine," Mercy said while I was still dripping wet. "Now you've gone and done it two times, and you dragged Kacey with you." Mercy acted like Kacey was some innocent bystander, but they'd wanted to go just as much as I did. Maybe Mercy was feeling sorry for Kacey because they'd been asking every day if there was a letter from their dad in the mail, but he hadn't written back yet.

"I'm sorry." I apologized to Mercy right away, even though I wasn't feeling it in my heart yet.

I knew Jack had something to tell us, and that he'd created something beautiful in the woods. I also knew that Mercy would like his tree sanctuary. She would probably even want to help him plant his garden, because even though he might be as old as Mercy, Jack is an orphan—same as me and the other kids.

"What am I going to do with you, Willa?" Mercy said, which scared me.

She was pacing back and forth in The Fortress after kicking everyone out and closing the door. My soaking wet T-shirt and shorts and socks were dripping all over the carpet. Kacey had got to take a hot shower and put on dry clothes, but not me, because I was the "ringleader."

It was a fish sticks and macaroni and cheese night, and I didn't want to miss dinner. I also wanted my getting-in-trouble to be over as fast as possible because Clover was in the closet, and when she knows I'm in The Fortress, she meows and expects me to open the door and give her food. I prayed that Clover would somehow stay asleep until Mercy was gone, which didn't seem possible. Except maybe it was, because cats sleep twenty hours a day, and Clover is no exception.

Mercy finally stopped pacing and stared at me like something had shifted in her brain, as if she wasn't mad anymore, but curious.

"Why do you insist on going there, Willa?" she asked, doing her magic. She does it with her eyes, where you feel like she is with you and not against you. Like she is on your side. Her eyes see inside you, and you can see yourself in them, and you see that she loves you. It makes you relieved but tearful, because having someone love and understand you is rare.

"What is at that abandoned school that is of so much interest to you?" Mercy asked again, looking at me on my level.

I didn't want to lie about Jack, but if I *didn't* lie about seeing him, I was afraid I'd get in worse trouble.

"I don't know," I lied.

So many people were lying and keeping secrets about Midlands Christian Academy for Boys. Now I could count myself among them. At least I had company.

"You don't know?" Mercy asked. She didn't believe me.

I shrugged my shoulders and tried not to look guilty.

"Hopefully the police got rid of the trespasser," she said. She sounded annoyed.

"He's the *least* of their problems," I said. "Because of the crisis in our community," I added, though I didn't need to explain it to Mercy. She has five dozen orphans to show for it.

Mercy let out a big sigh from down deep and sat on my bunk. She put her head in her hands, like she was going to cry.

I sat down next to Mercy in my wet clothes and rubbed her back, like she'd done for me one thousand times, whenever I was sad.

"Sometimes it's hard to know what to do, Willa," she said.

"Maybe you could call Deputy Bell and talk to her about it?" I suggested. "Or Meredith?"

Mercy took another deep breath. She sat up tall and pulled herself together, like she'd made a decision.

"That's it," she said. "Meredith is going to have to stay longer and help me. I can't navigate this situation with the Midlands property without legal expertise. We'll find Katherine's letter, and then I'll know what to do. Aunt Katherine always knew what to do."

I agreed wholeheartedly with Mercy and almost said so, but I didn't want to give away that I'd been reading all of Katherine's diaries.

Once she'd made up her mind, Mercy finally left, which was good because my bedspread was wet and Clover was starting to meow.

I could hardly believe it, but I'd escaped being in trouble again.

Even though we keep doing school all summer at the Southern Ohio Children's Home, we celebrate a "last day" of school. Mercy gives a presentation acknowledging that we're graduating into the next grade level (sixth grade for me). The very next day, we go back to Miss Samantha's classroom, like nothing had even changed.

For summer school, Miss Samantha lets us do fun stuff, like read a book all day or make cookies with Emily or build a stick house or sit with the chickens. I was planning on sneaking to The Fortress to read a diary if no one else was there. Or petting Clover. Or staring out the window and thinking. It's good to think when you have a cat purring on you.

We didn't have much homework lately because Miss Samantha had been wrapping things up for our last day of school, so I'd been working on my Forgetting Letter. Kacey had inspired me after burying theirs in the tree sanctuary. The things I want to forget don't change from year to year, but I keep not forgetting them anyway. If I put them in our Forgetting Ceremony, I hope I will truly forget them eventually. Maybe when I'm Miss Samantha's age. I hope I will become a different person by then. Someone who is not the person you might have thought I would have become, based on how I started out, because my starting out was not pretty. Miss Samantha reminds me that it's not like I could have done it any different. I was only a kid.

The thing I wish I could forget the most is when I thought I was watching Momma die right in front of my face from her using drugs. I wish I could set fire to those memories inside my head.

I gave up on my Forgetting Letter and wrote a letter to Momma instead.

Dear Momma,

Are you the Momma you always wanted to be? Watching over me? Loving me? Wishing you could still make cookies with me?

The problem is, I'm here and you're not. I cry every day from missing you, and it's hard to find secret places where I can cry. I need you, Momma. I need to feel you loving me. I pretend I'm okay, but I'm not.

Even though you left me, I love you forever. I will always be
Your daughter,

Willa

I added my note to the shoebox full of unsent letters to Momma that I keep under my bed and flopped back on my pillow. I'd had The Fortress to myself a lot since I escaped being in trouble, because Mercy had told the others I needed "space." I wished I could tell Mercy that I have good intentions, but she knows as well as I do that the road to hell is paved with those.

Soon, we found out that our last day of school was going to be different from usual. Instead of having a graduation presentation, we were going to have a scavenger hunt for a secret letter.

Mercy and Meredith gathered us in Miss Samantha's classroom.

"There is a secret letter written by my mom hidden somewhere inside the Southern Ohio Children's Home," Meredith said. She acted like she was telling us about a big prize.

"And we get to find it?" Elizabeth asked, excited as she gets for Easter morning egg hunts.

"You sure do." Meredith was wearing high heels, of course, and blue jeans so tight it looked like someone had painted them on her body. She kept running her fingers through her long hair, like she was raking out itches. Sometimes, I got the impression that Meredith couldn't hold her own body still, like a three-year-old who can't keep her energy inside.

Mercy stood next to Meredith, looking glad but also nervous.

"Don't break anything," Mercy said. "And please don't make a mess."

"What kind of letter?" Justin asked.

"We won't know what kind of letter it is until we find it," Meredith said. "But I will tell you that my mom most likely put it inside an envelope."

"Can we read the letter?" Roy asked.

"No," Mercy said, fast and hard.

"Please?" we all said together, except for Kacey, who is too old to beg like a puppy.

"Let's make a deal," Meredith said, like a lawyer. "Mercy and I will read it first, and if it is appropriate for your young ears, we will read it to you."

This made everyone happy enough to help find the secret hidden letter.

Roy ran off to the kitchen, Elizabeth stayed in Miss Samantha's classroom, and Kacey and me headed to the library.

"She already hid all her diaries there," Kacey said.

"Maybe her secret letter is in the library, too," I agreed with Kacey's thinking.

Justin beat us to it. He was already taking books off the shelf one at a time, flipping through each page.

"Are you going to check every page of every book?" I asked him.

"That would be impossible," Justin said. "Maybe there's a specific book that would have the letter?" The wheels inside his brain were turning and turning. "But what book? If we don't know what the letter is about, we don't have any clues."

Kacey and me needed to check the secret library shelf, but we couldn't do it with Justin there.

"We know she loved James Baldwin," I said, and pointed to the quote on the wall:

You think your pain and your heartbreak are unprecedented in the history of the world, but then you read.

Justin raced to the Black Scholars section.

I wanted to find that letter so bad. I'd known about it since hearing Mercy and Meredith talk in the garden. Maybe I wanted to be the one who found it because I knew about it first. I wanted to give Mercy reasons to keep forgetting that she hadn't punished me yet for going back to Midlands to see Jack. What if she was still considering making it so I couldn't leave the Southern Ohio Children's Home ever, even for All Creatures? That really wouldn't be the worst thing in my world, but I would miss seeing Finn. Plus, I still needed to get Clover spayed.

Maybe I felt like it was my letter to find because I knew Katherine best, along with Kacey.

We searched for days. By day three of hunting the whole house, the only things anyone had found were some missing toys and books, one of Mercy's hoop earrings, a couple of Charlie's recipe cards that had slipped behind his cookbook cabinet, and a shoebox full of photos from before I was at the Southern Ohio Children's Home, with Mercy looking a lot younger.

Otherwise, no one had found a thing.

"How can we find something when we don't know what it is?" Roy kept asking over and over.

Sometimes, when I'm frustrated or sad or need to make myself feel better, I read the toddlers their bedtime book while Miss Lupe sits in her rocking chair, drinking cucumber water. She has a melatonin tablet and closes her eyes. After the scavenger hunt turned out to be so unsatisfying, I decided to do the toddler read-aloud.

I brushed my teeth, put on my PJs, then read the toddlers a silly book. I'm good at doing voices to make them laugh. I read

Interrupting Chicken and got them so riled up that Miss Lupe might have been mad if it weren't for her melatonin. When I finished reading, I took the kids to bed, along with Miss Lupe. I gave them each their stuffed animal and tucked them in tight, most of them still giggling at me. I truly hoped they'd have sweet dreams.

As I walked from the toddler room back to The Fortress, I passed the children's playroom. I never go in there unless I need to help disinfect all the toys, which is just about the worst job there is, but we have to do it regularly, especially during flu season.

For some reason the playroom dollhouse caught my eye. It's a copy of the Southern Ohio Children's Home—an antique that sits high up on a display shelf and out of reach of the little kids because it's fragile. It looked like a light was on inside the dollhouse, like some tiny person was in there reading a book or making cookies or singing lullabies. That light drew me in.

I looked real close at the dollhouse for the first time ever. There were columns across the front porch, a black front door and shutters, and even The Fortress's circle window. Exactly like real life. I turned the dollhouse around carefully, hoping I wouldn't break it. I wanted to see the inside better. I pretended that a small Willa doll lived inside and slept in the tiny bedroom, with a doll cat hiding in her closet.

I guessed that the inside was decorated to look the way the real house used to, when Katherine's family had lived here. Probably all the way back to when Katherine was a little girl. Way before it got turned into a residential childcare facility. The dollhouse Southern Ohio Children's Home was fancier than the real-life Southern Ohio Children's Home. It had glass chandeliers and flower wallpaper and a dining room table set as if a dollhouse-sized president was coming over for dinner. In The Fortress, instead of three sets of bunkbeds, there was a single giant canopy bed. I couldn't imagine ever sleeping in a bed like that, with velvet curtains hanging down. Clover would tear those up—her claws are sharp even though I trim them.

There were also a lot more fireplaces in the dollhouse Southern Ohio Children's Home. Mercy must have had the real versions closed off for safety. In the dollhouse, each fireplace had a little fake fire blazing, one in the kitchen, the dining room, the library and study, and even the bedrooms. The princess staircase in the front hall looked the same as it does now, except the real staircase doesn't look as grand anymore with its worn carpet and nicks in the wall.

The real difference was a tiny grandfather clock standing in the front hall.

"That clock is nowhere I've seen in the Southern Ohio Children's Home." I must've been talking to dollhouse Willa. "Where is that grandfather clock now?"

I carefully picked up the miniature clock to get a closer look. Its face had a sun and a moon, and beneath the face was a cabinet door. I tried to open it, sliding my fingernail underneath. The door gave, and I gently pulled it open.

A key fell out and landed on my foot.

"How did that get in there?"

I picked up the key. I could see right away it wasn't a dollhouse-sized key but a regular-sized one that would fit inside a regular-sized lock. It was shiny and gold and looked like no one had touched it in a long time.

"A clue!" I said.

The key felt like magic, and I wondered if Katherine was there guiding me.

"Thank you, Miss Katherine," I said, just in case.

I kissed the key and put it in my pajama pocket, then went straight to tell Mercy.

"Where did you find this?" she asked. Mercy and Meredith were drinking chamomile tea in the kitchen. Mercy inspected the key as though it was a rare artifact.

"In the dollhouse in the playroom," I said. "Inside the little grandfather clock."

"The grandfather clock?" Meredith took the key from Mercy to get a look for herself.

"But we don't have a grandfather clock," I said.

"We do," Mercy said, smiling like a Cheshire cat. "Come on, Willa. Get the others. We're going to my bedroom."

"Your bedroom?" I said.

Mercy's bedroom is the one room where only Mercy can go. That's why I've never seen the grandfather clock before. Mercy calls her bedroom her peaceful sanctuary, so I'd pictured it looking like a church with stained-glass windows, like the little Methodist church where Pop-pop used to take me before he couldn't breathe anymore because of his emphysema. That cement block church was painted mint green inside and smelled like crayons, maybe because of the candles at the end of each pew. I imagined Mercy's room smelling like crayons, too.

After three long days of searching, we stood outside Mercy's bedroom in our pajamas—Kacey, Justin, Roy, Elizabeth, and me—trying to be first inside when Mercy opened her door.

"I found the key. I should go first," I said.

Roy shoved me aside. I was too tired to fight, but I was

determined to get credit for finding the key and 'hopefully' the letter, too.

"The grandfather clock has been passed down to the oldest male child in my family for generations," Mercy said. "At least until my mother decided it didn't match the décor in her new home." Mercy looked at Meredith when she said *my mother*.

"It was still here when my mom and dad moved in, even though it was supposed to have belonged to Uncle Press," Meredith added.

"But here it has remained," Mercy continued.

"Why the oldest male child?" Elizabeth asked. "Why not a female child?" She was nervous about entering Mercy's room, even though Mercy was right there and had said it was okay.

"That is a good question, Elizabeth," Mercy said. "I don't have a good answer, other than the fact that we live in a patriarchal society."

Elizabeth furrowed her eyebrows and looked at Justin.

"The patriarchy is an ideology upheld by men and women alike that instills male dominance in our social and political systems," Justin rattled off. He is as good at defining things as if he is reading straight from the dictionary, even though sometimes it doesn't make sense to the rest of us.

"Impressive," Meredith said.

I could see on Elizabeth's face that she still didn't know what the patriarchy was.

"The patriarchy is stupid," Kacey said. Elizabeth seemed more satisfied by that explanation and nodded like she understood now.

"Can we go in?" Roy pleaded, hopping back and forth on his toes like he had to pee. That's what he does when he gets excited and anxious at the same time. You have to watch out for him then, because he might punch you from not being able to hold his body together.

Mercy opened her bedroom door, and we stepped inside her sanctuary. It did not smell like crayons, but it did not smell like Mercy either. The room was as big as our bedroom where all five of us sleep. Papers and stacks of mail and old newspapers and cardboard boxes and school supplies covered everything, which felt strange since the rest of the home is clean and organized. Mercy must put all the things she doesn't know what to do with in her bedroom.

"We should have been searching in *here* for the letter. Look at all this stuff!" Roy said. I was glad he said it and not me, because I was thinking the same thing, and Mercy is always telling me to think before I speak, even though it is a hard thing to do.

"Yes," Mercy said. "I can't seem to find a place for everything. I've been trying for years." She seemed embarrassed about how messy her bedroom was, and I guessed that was the real reason why we weren't ever allowed in here. If our bedroom looked like hers, we'd be in so much trouble.

We followed Mercy and Meredith through the mess, winding single file on a narrow path through the piles. A mattress with blankets was shoved into one corner. Meredith's bed, I thought.

"This bedroom has never *not* been a mess, Mercy," Meredith said. "Do you think any of these boxes are my mom's?"

"Maybe?" Mercy said. "I've honestly lost track."

"See? I told you we should've been looking *here*!" Roy shouted.

"You are so right, Roy," Meredith said.

"Well, we're here now," Mercy said as she approached the

grandfather clock in the corner. The top of it nearly touched the ceiling.

"Does it work?" Justin asked.

"Goodness, no. This clock is from a different time," Mercy said. "I could never wind it because I didn't have the key. Willa?" Mercy held out her hand, and I pulled the gold key from my pocket.

It looked even shinier next to the dusty old clock, which was plain and dark brown. The clock had a long cupboard in front, just like the one in the dollhouse. The clock face also showed a sun on the bottom right corner and a full moon on the bottom left corner.

"Can I open it?" I was afraid to ask, but I really wanted to find that letter.

"You can try." Mercy stepped aside.

I walked to the grandfather clock and put the key into the keyhole. I turned it to the right and the left, but it didn't catch on anything. I wiggled it around and tried again until finally it grabbed on the lock. I slowly turned the key to the right. When it stopped turning, I pulled. The door creaked open.

"Yes!" I said quietly. I have always had a way with opening doors.

"You did it," Elizabeth whispered.

"What's inside? What's inside?" Roy asked, hopping on his toes again.

Everyone stepped closer, crowding me. Inside the clock, we all saw a weighted chain and pendulum, bright and shiny as the key. A piece of paper was taped inside the door.

"The letter!" Justin said.

But it wasn't the letter. It was just a list of names.

"Silas Rost, 1820," I said. "That's what it says at the top. There are all these names on here too, ending with Prescott Rost, 1944, and Prescott Rost Jr., 1981."

"My father," Mercy said.

Everyone looked at Mercy with surprise, because she has never once talked about her own father. In many ways we considered her to be an orphan like us.

"The patriarchy," Meredith said.

"Is there anything else in there?" Kacey asked.

I stuck my head inside the clock and sneezed. "There's a lot of dust."

"There's got to be something!" Roy shouted. "I want to see! Can I see?" He was hopping more and more to try and see, until he somehow hopped right on top of me and pushed me inside the clock.

"Ow!" My head hit the pendulum, which clanked against the weighted chains. I had to punch my hand down into the bottom of the cupboard to try and catch myself, and when it punched down on the right side, the other side tipped up, like a seesaw.

"Roy, get off me!"

I swear, Roy always is trying to fight you, even when he isn't.

Mercy and Kacey pulled Roy off so I could get myself out of the clock, but my hand sure hurt. So did my ears from all the clanging.

"Look, there's something in there," Justin said. He put his hand in the same spot where mine had been and lifted up the bottom panel. Sure enough, there was an envelope taped underneath.

"I'm going to call this a grand*mother* clock," Elizabeth said.

"I like that, Elizabeth," Mercy said as she reached past Justin and untaped the envelope.

"*I* found it," I said, rubbing my hand, even though I knew Justin had found it. But if it wasn't for me, *no* one would have found it. Not that Mercy was going to give me a prize. Except for maybe letting me be in less trouble.

"Get ice for Willa's hand." Mercy left her room, letter in hand. "And then go to bed!" She called behind her.

"But … aren't you going to read it to us?" Roy ran ahead of everyone, turning bright red.

"It's late," Meredith said. "Maybe tomorrow. We'll have to wait and see."

Kacey rolled their eyes and sighed in frustration.

"It's not fair!" Elizabeth whined.

We shuffled out of Mercy's bedroom. I would've made a bigger stink if my hand wasn't starting to throb. I also felt a headache coming on.

I wasn't surprised that Mercy didn't read us the letter. It was going to be another secret no one would talk about.

9

The Ties of Kinship

Finn's house is the kind of house a kindergartner draws, with a big rectangle, triangle on top, square windows, rectangle door, and a circle doorknob. It has a porch with a swing, and a lamp in the front window that is always on. It smells like apples, inside and out. No one ever fights or raises their voice.

You could never imagine fighting with Mrs. Harbour. When you're with her, you want to be good, because she's good to everyone. She makes you feel like you could never do anything wrong, anyway. And if you did do something wrong, she'd be patient and understanding and let you have your mistake and never be cross. Momma would have liked her if they'd known each other when she was alive, even though Momma was a fighter. Momma was always arguing with Grammaw about everything no matter what. Sometimes kinship does not come from blood.

One time, Finn got in a car accident. He was driving to the CVS to get his mom some Tylenol and chocolate. (She'd needed Tylenol, but Finn had added the chocolate because he's good that way.) Mr. and Mrs. Harbour hadn't known he'd gone to the CVS. He only had his learner's permit, and he was supposed to be driving with an adult in the car. But sometimes in Shawneeville, you feel like no one's around, so no one will notice. Plus, there are people overdosing on drugs in the bathroom at the CVS, and that is a problem that *does* need noticing. Who cares if Finn takes a quick drive with his learner's permit to do something nice for his mom?

He missed a stop sign, and someone ran into the side of their old Chevrolet. The car used to be Mr. Harbour's, but Finn got it after Mr. Harbour had bought a new Ford with Bluetooth. Finn was okay after the accident, but the car was not. Finn got a ticket, and the police officer escorted him home with blue and red police lights on. Then he stood there while Finn told his parents what happened.

Most parents would yell at their kid for smashing up their car, but not Mrs. Harbour. She gave Finn a hug, and he didn't get in trouble at all. Mrs. Harbour knows what is most important at all times, and Finn being okay was more important than the car being okay. Finn was embarrassed and started crying. He'd been trying to do something good, and instead he did something stupid. Which is something I know all about.

"We all do stupid things," I'd told him. "Some things are worse than others. What you did wasn't so bad."

Finn will never repeat that mistake, and that is part of learning and growing up: being given the opportunity to make mistakes. That's what Mercy and Miss Samantha say when we make our mistakes, which is a lot. I was making more than my share lately, and Mercy didn't even know about Clover yet.

Mr. and Mrs. Harbour had got the car fixed, because they're not the kind of people who'd drive around in a smashed car. That's how their house is too, with everything as it should be. Finn finally got his license for real, and now he stops so hard at every stop sign and looks both ways five times, I swear.

Sometimes after All Creatures, he drives me back to the Southern Ohio Children's Home, like if it's raining or if I took a digger on my bike and I have a bloody knee.

I'd been anxious to have dinner at their house, so I could talk to Mr. Harbour about Jack and the boys' reformatory school. I knew there were things no one was telling me, and there must have been a reason why. Maybe it was something hard to talk about, which made everyone shut up. Like when Pop-pop stopped talking about Momma. After she died for real, I tried talking about Momma every day. I needed to keep her alive because I couldn't believe she was dead. But when I talked about her, Pop-pop acted like he couldn't hear me. Eventually, I stopped saying anything about Momma. Instead, I just scrolled through the pictures on her phone over and over and over again and listened to her voicemail message a thousand times so I could hear her voice. That was all I had left.

"How's your cat?" Finn asked when he let me in the front door to their house.

I'd parked my bike on the front porch by the swing. It hadn't cooled off even though it was dinner time, and I was sweating from the short ride over. Summer was here.

"Shh! I don't want your parents to know about Clover," I whispered. "What if they tell Mercy? But she's fine. I need to take her to Moe and get her spayed."

Moe had said he'd arrange to have Clover spayed for $25, and I already had almost enough money saved up to pay for it. He loves kittens but is serious about spaying and neutering because he hates kitten season.

"I can drive you there when it's time, if you want," Finn said. "It can't be easy riding your bike with a kitten."

Finn smiled at me like he does, and I knew I was blushing.

He is easy to be around. He is not all proud and argumentative, like most of the boyfriends my momma ever had. Finn listens when we talk. However it is that Finn is, I like it.

It was getting harder and harder not to notice Finn being cute. I worried that if I kept noticing, I might not be able to be a friend to him the way I'm used to, so I tried not to notice. Instead, I looked down at my own feet and followed him into the kitchen.

"Willa!" Mrs. Harbour is always so happy to see me. She pretends like she doesn't have early Parkinson's, even though she's wobbly and her voice shakes. I gave her a big hug.

"How's life at the Big House?" Mr. Harbour asked.

It was our joke, calling the Southern Ohio Children's Home the Big House, because that's another thing people call jail. But the Southern Ohio Children's Home really is a BIG house—a mansion—so that's why it's funny. Especially because it's the opposite of jail, although some kids at the home have a mom or a dad in jail, so that isn't funny. I know Mr. Harbour doesn't mean anything by it. When he talks, he's usually trying to make a joke. It's why his students love him so much and come back to visit him even after they've graduated college. Some of his "students" are old now, but they'll always be his students.

He was folding his newspaper at the kitchen table. Mr. Harbour always has a newspaper, like they print one every hour just for him. When he sits at their antique table, he takes up the whole thing with his large body and his newspapers. We have to pull the table out from the corner so four people can fit when I come over. That table is heavy and make of thick wood, and it's a big production to make room for me. Mrs. Harbour tells me *It's not a problem*, and *Don't think anything of it*, and *We love having you here, Willa*.

It's like she knows I feel like I don't belong with their family, but at the same time, I do.

"Life at the Big House is fine," I said. "Mercy has her cousin staying with us right now. Meredith. She's from New York City and only ever wears high heels."

"Meredith?" Mrs. Harbour exclaimed. "I haven't seen her in years! Please tell her Mrs. Harbour says hello."

I wasn't surprised that Mrs. Harbour knows Meredith. Shawneeville only has 20,251 residents. At least that's what the sign on the highway says as you enter town. Who knows if it's right because it's been there forever and a lot of people have died because of the crisis in our community. But a lot of babies are still being born and coming to the Southern Ohio Children's Home, so maybe the number is still perfectly fine because of the dying and being born cancelling each other out.

A lot of people know each other in Shawneeville, especially the Harbours. Mr. Harbour had even taught my momma in his English class, but it was by the time she'd started using drugs and was no longer the straight-A student she'd been her whole life leading up to that point.

"Was Meredith in your class?" I asked.

"She was. Honors English, senior year," Mr. Harbour said. "That would have been, what, '91? Start of the Gulf War. We spent more time talking about Iraq than Macbeth. Meredith had strong feelings about that war."

"She takes after her mother," Mrs. Harbour added. "Very civic-minded."

"Yes, she does," I said, but then bit my tongue. Mrs. Harbour wouldn't know that I know how much Meredith takes after her mother, because Mrs. Harbour didn't know that I was secretly reading Katherine's diaries.

"And her father, too," Mrs. Harbour went on. "He was very justice-minded. Meredith left Shawneeville in a hurry to go to law school."

Finn and me set the table and poured lemonade, and Mrs. Harbour put pork roast and potatoes on a serving plate that I carried to the table, while she brought over a basket of rolls. Finn put cooked broccoli in a bowl, and just like that we had a feast. I am surprised Finn is so skinny with all the food his mom makes. But he's getting taller and taller. He is at least a foot taller than me, and I am growing, too, so he must *really* be growing.

"Finn told me you taught at Midlands Christian Academy," I said to Mr. Harbour. I was scared to bring it up but did it anyway. I had to find out why no one ever talked about it.

I put butter on my roll and waited. Mr. and Mrs. Harbour looked at each other and then looked at Finn, like he'd told me something he wasn't supposed to.

"What?" Finn said. "You *did*. Right, Dad?"

I charged in with the details.

"Mercy is planning on selling the property where Midlands has been sitting abandoned all these years. That's why Meredith is here. To help. Before Mercy can sell it, she has to check Katherine's will, but Katherine added a secret part to it right before she died. I don't know what it says because Mercy won't read it to us. I didn't even know a school was there until recently, but everyone else knows about it. Isn't that strange?"

Mr. and Mrs. Harbour were frozen, like we were playing a game of freeze tag and they'd lost. I hoped spilling my guts would help them spill theirs.

"Oh my. Oh—" Mrs. Harbour suddenly started shaking more than usual.

"Are you okay?" I asked. I hoped I didn't make her Parkinson's worse.

"Is Mercy running out of money?" Mrs. Harbour asked.

"Mercy's *always* running out of money," I said. "That's the way it goes, running a home for kids during an opioid crisis."

Mrs. Harbour's eyes got big and then they got wet. Seeing Mrs. Harbour's worry made me worry more.

"I worked at Midlands my first year after I graduated." Mr. Harbour finally unfroze and jumped into the middle of our worry. "Right out of college. Don't remember too much, though. Except for being able to get a job at Shawneeville Central after, because I'd gotten some teaching experience. It would be good for Mercy to sell that property. Nothing but an eyesore."

Mr. Harbour didn't know what he was talking about. He hadn't seen Jack's tree sanctuary.

"Do you remember a student named Jack Thompson?" I asked, then held my breath.

Mr. Harbour stopped eating, which he never does.

"Oh my—" Mrs. Harbour said again.

We all sat there looking at each other like I'd said the biggest swear you ever heard. Finn finally shrugged at me. I had the feeling I was never going to know the truth.

I'd thought Midlands Academy was the secret. I was starting to think there were a whole lot more.

"I typically remember all my students," Mr. Harbour said. "But I don't remember one named Jack."

Was Mr. Harbour lying? He remembers all his students—he'd said so himself. He picked up his fork and started eating again.

I didn't know what to believe. He is not the kind of person who would ever lie. Ever.

Kacey and me had to rely on a dead woman to find out the secrets everyone was keeping.

"Katherine is the only person who's going to tell us any-thing," I said to Kacey while we were exchanging diaries from the secret bookshelf the next day.

The hardest part of our routine was waiting for Justin to take a bathroom break. He's in the library all the time during sum-mer school. Thankfully, Kacey is good at making a fast switch.

We'd made it through half the diaries, most recently read-ing Katherine's words from 1974 and 1975, without discovering any new information.

"Where is 1976?" Kacey asked, peering into the cubbyhole after Justin left.

"What do you mean?" I said.

"It's missing." Kacey stepped aside so I could peer into the shelf.

"Just what we need," I said when I saw the gap in years. "Another mystery."

We grabbed the next four diaries and went back inside the fort we'd made with library chairs and Mrs. Harbour blankets so we could secretly read during the daytime. I kept falling asleep reading at night, and so did Kacey, especially now that Clover loved snuggling their neck.

<u>November 7, 1978</u>

It tears me apart how parents, teachers, churches—and so many other institutions—fail us. We've failed Mercy. I'm grateful she can live here, but I must do more. I must work harder to right the wrongs we all accept.

When I was young and saw the world not living up to itself, I got angry. Mercy _is_ angry. She made her choice for a reason. However, she's also withdrawn. She's 18 years old, on the cusp of adulthood. But because of everything she's been through, she's more like a child—vulnerable and scared. Her mother thinks she's willful and disobedient. I will never forgive Eleanor and Press. We're no longer on speaking terms.

I will get Mercy's fire going again and help her release her joyful spirit. I'm thinking about Thanksgiving and what we can do to make this a special time. Hopefully, with Mercy at our house—along with Edward and silly, giggly Meredith—she can truly start to heal. We all can heal. Together.

I haven't told Mercy that I've tried to find Jack Thompson. Unsuccessfully, so far.

"Katherine and Mercy knew Jack!" I practically screamed from under our fort, forgetting our walls were made of yarn.

"He's not a stranger at all!" Kacey said. But I don't get it— _how_ did they know each other? What else does it say?"

Kacey and me huddled in close to read the rest of Katherine's words.

I came across Jack's letter in Mercy's bedside table. I gave it to her after I found it inside the library books he returned before he left. What

"She doesn't say anything about how they knew Jack," Kacey said.

"It must be from Katherine being the librarian," I said.

"Who's Jack?" Justin made Kacey and me jump out of our skin.

We'd been discovered, and I was panicking. Justin had been so quiet coming back from his bathroom break that we forgot he was using the library, too. I poked my head out of the fort.

"Hi, Justin," I said, and then hid inside the fort again.

Next thing you know, Justin crawled right inside with us.

"Who's Jack?" he asked again. He saw the diaries and our notebook spread out on the ground. "What are you reading?"

Kacey and me silently considered our options. We made a decision together without talking about it, the way you can with a kindred spirit. Kacey heard my inmost soul: Including Justin might help us out.

"Justin, can you keep a secret?" they said.

"I can keep a secret better than anyone," Justin said.

"It's true. He can," I confirmed. "Look." I spread the diaries out for him to see. "Want to help?"

"Help with what?" he asked.

"These are Miss Katherine's diaries," Kacey said. "We found them on a secret shelf here in the library."

"A secret shelf?" Justin asked.

"We'll show you," I said. "We're saving all her information about Midlands Christian Academy in this notebook." I handed our notebook to Justin, and he flipped through it.

"Jack is the stranger we saw in the woods," Kacey said.

"He's really nice," I said. "So's his dog. And he went to Midlands."

"I knew it!" Justin said. "I *knew* he must have gone there."

"Not only did he go to Midlands Academy—" Kacey started.

"He knew Mercy!" I interrupted, nearly screaming again.

"How?" Justin asked.

"We don't know," Kacey said. "Yet," they added.

"No one will tell us anything about Midlands," I said. "If you want to help us read, we'll find out information a lot faster."

"Tell me what to read," Justin said. He seemed as eager as we were, probably because his own research on the abandoned reformatory school was coming up short. He'd told Miss Samantha that it was as if the school had never existed. There wasn't anything more than a few old newspaper stories online.

We squeezed in to make the fort big enough for the three of us. Kacey gave Justin a fresh diary, and I took the notebook from him to copy down the entry about Jack.

"I wonder what Mercy did," I said, getting back to our work. "Her mother thought she was 'willful and disobedient.'"

"That doesn't sound like Mercy," Justin said.

"I can't picture her being disobedient, but I've seen her be willful," I said, thinking of the times Mercy had "imposed her will" on me when I was getting in trouble.

"Why did Jack leave?" Kacey asked.

"And why did he come back?" Justin added, looking through the diary.

A big piece was missing from this story.

"I wonder where his letter is now," Kacey said, reading my mind.

"Here's something else about Jack." Justin sat up and pointed to a page for us. He is such a fast reader. I had no regrets about letting him in on our secret.

<u>March 15, 1980</u>

I watch Meredith growing up in this old house. Some days it feels like everything has changed, while other days, it feels like nothing is different. The occupants are different, of course. The house is no longer formal. And Father's old study is loaded with books collected from flea markets and estate sales, and volumes the county library is taking out of circulation. It doesn't matter to me if nobody else wants the books. I want them. I even found a secret shelf where I can keep more books! Grandfather must have had the cubbyhole built to hide booze during Prohibition. There was still a bottle of gin in it, alongside the cobwebs.

"Katherine hadn't known about the secret shelf either!" I said. "Why did her grandfather hide gin?"

"We can research the Prohibition later," Justin said.

"Yeah, let's keep reading," Kacey said.

Midlands still has no library space of its own. I can't imagine a school without a library, but if I had to, it'd be Midlands Christian Academy for Boys. So I continue taking books over from our library. Mercy is helping me organize a card catalogue. She's been taking courses at the community college, working on her teaching degree. I couldn't be more proud of her. But when I look at how her life is turning out, I also think about how Jack's life is turning out. Where is he? I'm convinced both their lives are different from what they would have been, all because of one night that should have been magical. I imagine what would happen if he came back some day. But it wouldn't be safe. Not yet. Not now.

Mercy still won't speak to her mother and father. Press calls to ask after her, but Eleanor has not tried to reach out. Not once. Press must keep his calls secret from Eleanor. He's chosen his side, to Mercy's detriment. I cannot imagine the damage it does to a child to lose her mother, but in Mercy's case—and I hate to say this—she might be better off. We all want our mothers to be perfect for us, but motherhood doesn't work that way. Mothers are flawed humans, like every other human on Earth. I try to be perfect for Meredith, but I fail every day. Then, I wake up and try again. I don't know what else I can do.

Katherine

"If it's not safe for Jack to come back to Shawneeville, then why is he here?" Justin asked.

"He said he wanted to plant a garden—a memorial to remember the boys who went to Midlands," Kacey said.

"I wonder what happened the night that changed Mercy's life," I said.

"And Jack's," Kacey added.

"It must have been in 1976," Justin said.

"The year of the missing diary," I realized.

"Where could it be?" Kacey asked. We didn't have a clue. "Her diary only mentions one secret Prohibition shelf."

"Should we ask Meredith?" I suggested.

"We have to tell Mercy about Jack," Justin said. "Especially if she already knows him."

"No!" I yelled. "Mercy can't find out we talked to him again."

"What if he needs help?" Justin asked. "What if it's still not safe for him to be there?"

"He and Deputy Bell are friends," Kacey said.

"I would have gone to Midlands, like Jack," Justin said. "I'm not a 'juvenile delinquent,' but I don't have family. Same as him." Justin was taking it hard about Midlands and the ghost boys and Jack. I hadn't ever seen him cry all that much, but the thought of going to a reformatory school was too real for him. Tears rolled down his cheeks.

Kacey and me each gave Justin a hug, not knowing what to say to make him feel better.

If it wasn't for Mercy, Justin could have ended up in a bad place.

Secrets to the Grave

CERTAIN DAYS, I AM OVERCOME with sadness from missing my momma and anger that she had to die. During those moments, I go to the garden shed to dry herbs. No one can find me there.

Herbs were the one thing my momma could take care of. She grew them in empty beer cans with the tops cut off, and she kept them in a shoebox. Her shoebox beer can herb garden traveled easy, and she always remembered to water it even when she forgot to feed me. She grew basil and parsley and mint and rosemary. It smelled so good. *Eat your veggies,* she'd say, and I'd nibble on Momma's herbs to see how long I could keep the green bits stuck in my teeth.

I was trying to get some alone time in the shed, but Meredith found me after she turned on the garden hose to get some water. She wasn't like any other grown woman I'd ever met. Probably because she was rich. Even someone like me who's never been around a rich person in her life could tell how rich she was. She came from a rich family to start, but she'd made herself more rich in New York City.

I'd recently added a diary entry to our notebook about Meredith moving away:

<u>August 27, 1994</u>

Progress is hard to measure, but when I look at my life compared to Meredith's ... compared to Mercy's ... compared to my mother's, I see it plainly. I don't want Meredith to go to New York, but that is what it means to be a parent—a series of small releases until you let go of your child completely.

At least I'll still have Mercy by my side. She's made the best of a difficult situation and is satisfied but worn down. There are never enough resources. She's helping the nuns at the Ministry of Hope with a new foster program. Apparently, Eleanor stopped donating to the mission and had given Sister Hazel an earful after she discovered Mercy's involvement. Sister Hazel is old-fashioned at times, but now that she's no longer indebted to Eleanor, she sees Mercy for the smart, kind-hearted person she is.

Katherine

Meredith peeked inside the shed where I was hanging tied lavender stems on pegs. My fingers smelled like perfume. I rubbed lavender on my wrists and neck, and then I smelled like Mercy's hair, because Mercy washes her hair with the lavender soap we make.

"This was where my mom kept her gardening tools," Meredith told me. "But mostly she'd come out here to read. It was one of her favorite spots. Probably because it made her feel like she lived somewhere other than here." Meredith pointed in the direction of what used to be her family's mansion.

She was wearing a maroon visor, and her face was bright red from all the running she'd been doing. Meredith runs for miles and miles every day. If she isn't wearing high heels, she's wearing running shoes. I'd passed her on County Highway J while I was riding my bike. She has purple running shoes that I swear you can see a mile away, and she puts her hair up in a ponytail that swishes back and forth, thick as a horse's tail.

"Why didn't she want to live here?" I asked, because if I'd lived here with my own, alive mother, I'd be inside a fairy tale. I knew from Katherine's diaries, though, that her own, alive mother was unkind and snooty.

I followed Meredith out of the shed, where she turned on the spigot and drank from the hose. Mercy always tells us not to do that, but since Meredith did it, I figured it'd be okay for me to take a sip. It was one of those summer days that I knew was going to be hot until sunrise the next day, when it would be cool for one breath before getting hot again. I would need to give the chickens extra water.

"Living in this house meant a lot of things," Meredith said. "It was more than just a house. Do you know anything about my family?"

I knew way more about Meredith's family than Meredith knew I knew. I might even have known more about her family than she knew, because she'd never read her mother's hidden diaries. But I had to keep on keeping secrets because I didn't want to get in trouble for our "invasion of privacy." I shrugged and kept my mouth shut.

Meredith turned over a milk crate and sat on it. We always have a stack of them after our weekly milk deliveries.

"I bet Mercy hasn't told you anything," she said.

"About what?" I acted like I didn't know anything at all, so Meredith would be more likely to tell me *something*.

"About where she comes from. About this house. About why my mother would have written a secret addendum to her will on purpose, so that nobody would read it until now."

I pulled up my own milk crate to show Meredith I was interested in knowing everything she wanted to tell me. I kept tying lavender in my lap though, so it wouldn't look like I wanted to know *that* bad. Sometimes, when Mercy or Miss Samantha realize I am being nosy, that is their clue they *shouldn't* talk in front of me. I didn't want Meredith to feel like I was paying too much attention, which was hard because she was opening up about subjects no one was talking about, no matter how much I'd asked.

"My mom had a complicated relationship with this house and this land," she said. "Even though it was her family's, she never wanted it. But she was the only one left to give it to, because her brother built a compound—bigger and better, he'd say—up in Cincinnati. Hyde Park. Very fancy. Nothing but the best for Uncle Press and Aunt Eleanor. What a pair. Uncle Press died a few years before my dad died. Have you ever heard of Rost Pharmaceuticals?"

"I have," I said. I wanted to impress Meredith with my knowing about things. "That's the company that makes the drug that all the doctors prescribe. The one that everyone starts taking, and pretty soon they need more and then they start using drugs from the street and become addicts. That's why we have a crisis in our community."

Meredith looked surprised, but she didn't know how much we talk about the crisis in our community in class. Mercy believes we should not be "shielded," so the problem will not "perpetuate," which is a word I keep meaning to look up and keep forgetting to.

"I'm so sorry," Meredith said.

"For what?" I hate people feeling sorry for me. There might be a crisis in our community, but I am not a crisis. I am a force to be reckoned with. That's what Miss Samantha says. "There's nothing that's your fault that you need to apologize for," I said.

"I suppose you're right, Willa, because I can't say exactly what it is I'm sorry for." Meredith sighed. "This whole town, maybe. And me leaving it." She took off her shoes and socks and let the cold water from the hose run down her feet. "That's the short of it when it comes to my family."

"What's the long of it?" I asked, keeping my head down and tying lavender.

Meredith's toenails were painted light pink and matched her fingernails. There wasn't one part of her body that wasn't kept up. Even in her running clothes, she was perfect. My momma used to always say, *We can't have nice things*, and sometimes at the home, it feels like we can't have nice things. Everything's a raggedy hand-me-down. We hardly ever get haircuts, and when we do, Miss Lupe's cousin does them. Everyone has to wait their turn in line. Miss Lupe's cousin has to check for lice, too, and she always finds lice on someone's head (like mine, last year). Then she starts cutting everyone's hair real short after that.

We don't have nice haircuts or nice clothes, and I've never had my nails done. But everything about Meredith was so *nice* and *cared for*. I tried fixing my hair nicer while we were talking, but there was nothing I could do except put it in my too-short ponytail again.

"The long of it is … very long," Meredith said. "The long of it is why I left Shawneeville twenty-five years ago."

"Twenty-five years ago … you were so young."

Meredith looked like she was only twenty-five and a half. My momma was thirty when she died, and she had looked older than Meredith. But my momma was not *cared for*. She could not take care of herself or a cat or me. She could take care of a shoebox beer can herb garden, but now that I think of it, her herb garden wasn't good for anything because she never cooked unless it was something you could put in a microwave. So why did she even grow those herbs?

"I was twenty-one years old," Meredith said. "I got my college degree close by and wanted to go to law school. I wanted to go to the *best* law school, but I didn't want to leave my mom and dad. My mom and I especially were really close."

I chucked some scraps from the herb pile into the compost bin and waited a minute for what I knew Meredith was about to say again—

"I'm sorry!"

"I'm fine," I lied for the umpteenth time.

I sometimes run into these conversations where someone is talking about how great their mom is, and then they remember my mom is dead. It's happened enough so my gut tells me when someone realizes it after it's too late. Words come out of my mouth that I wish I could suck back in, so I get it. But I still hate these conversations because, like I said, I do not want anyone feeling sorry for me. It makes me mad. People should know how much I do have. Number one is Mercy. And my friends.

And All Creatures. And Finn. And Miss Samantha. I don't have my momma, but I don't have nothing.

On certain days, though, I might need to convince myself.

"Tell me about your mom," I said, keeping the conversation going.

"My mom was like no other," Meredith said. "Maybe everyone feels that way. Do you?"

"I never knew anyone who had a mom like mine," I said. "She wasn't like other moms. For bad reasons, though. Mainly because she couldn't be a mom, even though she tried and even though she wanted to and even though I know she loved me. I do know that for a fact."

"Of course she loved you," Meredith said.

"I just wish I could still feel it." Sadness swelled up inside of me.

I was sure Meredith's mom wasn't like other moms for good reasons. Katherine loved Meredith so much, she devoted her entire life to taking care of her, and that's probably why Meredith is still so good at taking care of herself.

"I wish I could still feel my mom's love, too," Meredith said. "But you know what? I feel it when I remember that she made me who I am. It's true what they say, that when a parent dies, they'll always be with you. Your mom is part of who you are, and that will never change."

"I know," I said, "but it's not the same."

"Do you still talk to her?" Meredith asked. "I talk to my mom all the time."

"I try to," I said. "I write her letters. I pretend like she's going to write me back, and like I know what she'd say. Sometimes, I can hear her voice in my ear."

"I won't pretend you didn't get a raw deal, Willa."

I wanted to tell Meredith thank you, but instead I sat quietly with her words.

"Lately, I've been thinking about my mom and how she taught me to be an activist," Meredith said. "From an early age, she'd talk to me about her passions, along with a lot of things other moms probably weren't telling their kids."

"That sounds like Mercy and Miss Samantha," I said. "They're always talking to us about stuff that maybe you'd think you shouldn't talk to kids about or that kids wouldn't understand, like drugs or gender expression or racism or the human body and what it means to give consent. I'm glad they do, though, because kids are smart. And we need to know about that stuff."

"Exactly. You do," Meredith said. "Kids are *so* smart. When I was growing up, people thought children should be protected from the bad stuff, so they pretended the bad stuff didn't happen. Or, like you said, that kids couldn't understand 'adult' subjects, like drugs and sex and politics. I'm not surprised Mercy has the same philosophy as my mom. She was always fighting for something. Civil rights. Women's rights. It's why I wanted to become a lawyer. My mom didn't have a career, but if she had, she would've been a senator or the governor of Ohio or ..."

"Or President," I said.

"Or President! Yes!" Meredith laughed.

She put her socks and shoes back on, and we walked over to the chicken coop. I picked up Henrietta. She's heavier than you'd think. At least fifteen pounds—big as a cat. A large cat. Probably because we have so many food scraps from the toddlers, who can be picky eaters.

"Could you please give them more water?" I showed Meredith the three chicken waterers.

She dumped them out in the marigolds and filled them with

fresh water from the hose. The chickens were drinking a lot every day. I know what chickens need to make them happy.

"So why didn't your mom like this house?" I asked.

"My mom didn't like what this house represented. She didn't like how ostentatious it is."

"What is ostentatious?" I asked.

"Show-offy," Meredith said.

"That makes sense. No one likes a show-off." I pictured one family living in the home, with maids and stuff. That definitely would have been a show-off kind of house.

"Although, when I was growing up here, it felt more like a hippie commune," Meredith said. "My mom tried hard to un-fancy everything. I had more fun in this house than she did, that's for sure. But after I went to law school and before she got sick, I already had my mind made up that I was staying in New York. That's why she gave this house to Mercy—so it could be used for something good. And now, it turns out, she wants the same thing to happen for Midlands Academy."

"What?" My ears perked right up when Meredith mentioned Midlands. "She wants something good to happen to that reformatory school?"

"She does. She always has," Meredith said.

"Is it because something bad happened there?" I tried pulling more out of Meredith.

"A lot of bad happened there," she said.

"Can you please tell me what happened there?" I asked. Maybe this was my chance to finally learn about the secrets everyone was keeping.

"Mercy really hasn't told you anything?" Meredith asked me.

I shook my head. "Not about Midlands. I never even knew it existed. All I know is Mercy wants to sell the property."

"Well, she can't sell it," Meredith said.

"What do you mean she can't sell it?" I asked.

"It's complicated, Willa. That school—" Meredith pointed in the direction of Midlands and Jack's tree sanctuary, over the ravine. She knew exactly where it was.

I knew then that she knew everything about it. My gut said Meredith knew things. The same way Mercy knew things. The same way Mr. Harbour knew things.

"That school is a subject nobody knows *how* to talk about, Willa. That's why I'm here, though. I'm going to help Mercy figure it out."

Then Meredith walked away, just like that. *Right* when we were finally getting somewhere, after she had just said all this stuff about how kids should know things, and how adults shouldn't keep things from kids. This was *my* future that Meredith wasn't telling me about, and that made me mad.

"What happened at Midlands Academy?" I shouted after her. "I'm not some dumb kid!"

Either she didn't hear me, or she didn't want to, because Meredith started running again. Running away.

Justin, Kacey, and me finished the rest of the diaries together, searching for answers about why Mercy couldn't sell the Midlands property. I'd told them what Meredith had said. With each passing day, we were feeling more anxious.

"Why would Katherine care so much about what Mercy does after she's already been dead and gone for so long?" I asked.

"It doesn't make sense," Kacey said.

We were in the library, each of us hiding a diary inside a

bigger book so we could close them up quick in case Mercy or Meredith came in.

"Maybe she's ensuring her family keeps its wealth," Justin said. "They've been rich for generations. I bet Katherine doesn't want anyone else to get their hands on their money."

"That sounds like something a selfish person would do. Katherine wasn't selfish," I said.

"And she hated most of her family," Kacey added.

Justin shrugged. "I don't understand rich people."

"Me neither," I said, turning a page.

We made a couple final notebook entries, with more clues leading nowhere.

<u>December 5, 1997</u>

My doctor hasn't given me much time. He did give me new pain meds, manufactured by Rost Pharmaceuticals, of course. Press can get pills for me, so I don't have to keep going back to my doctor. My brother has one sympathetic bone left in his body. But still, with his generosity he flaunts his privilege, like he and Eleanor always do.

Meredith will be home for Christmas. I'll tell her the news in person.

I have one dying wish: to close Midlands Christian Academy for Boys.

Katherine

I did not like reading about Katherine using pain medications made by Rost Pharmaceuticals, but she was using them because she was having a lot of pain. She wasn't an addict; she was dying. She couldn't have known that her family's company was about to cause a crisis in our community.

When we came to the last diary, we all felt sad about Katherine dying, even though she's actually been dead for a long time. It was different reading about it in her own words.

<u>**September 14, 1998**</u>

I'm finalizing my plans, which cannot happen now—not while Press and Eleanor might have a say. I don't have much energy, but what I must do has become so clear. Dying helps you see what matters in life.

These diaries will be stored in hiding. I'm going to leave a note for Meredith where I know she'll find it someday. It will tell her that I've hidden a letter, the addendum to my will. I'm not telling her where, but it will be inside the Rost family grandfather clock, a symbol of patriarchal power and a family fortune made through slick maneuvers, tax kickbacks, and overpriced drugs.

Maybe there will be a time after I'm dead when the world will be ready to move forward. Much of what I am asking hinges on Mercy, and she has already sacrificed more than anyone.

Now that Midlands is closed, no one knows what to do with it, but that's part of my plan. Edward and I appealed to the state to look at the students' failing grades. It isn't fair. It's not the boys' fault. It never was. I still think of Jack after all these years, as I imagine Mercy does.

"To think these clues were hidden here all along," I said.

We re-shelved the diaries in the hidden cubby for the final time, closing the shelf to make sure they'd remain secret forever.

"Mercy never did read us the clock letter," Justin said. "The addendum to Katherine's will."

"It's not fair," I said. "Mercy should've let us see it."

"Maybe there's something legal with it, and she can't?" Kacey suggested.

"She could do whatever she wanted!" I said. "She just keeps hiding things from us, and I am sick and tired of it."

"Willa, don't be mad at Mercy," Justin said. "She isn't the bad guy. It's like what Katherine wrote: We live in an unjust world."

Justin sure knew how to burst my bubble.

"Sometimes I wish you weren't always right," I said.

We'd finished Katherine's diaries and had a slim notebook to show for it. We'd read every last word—except the ones in the missing diary—and I still had no idea what was happening with Midlands, or what had happened between Mercy and Jack.

I was feeling as hopeless as Katherine felt when she was dying.

Sometimes You Have to Be Nosy

WHEN I'M BEING A SNOOP, sometimes I pretend like I'm not being a snoop, to make myself feel better about snooping. That's what happened when I went to bed early after Mercy let us have a movie night in the library. She plays movies onto the back of the closed library door, with the DVD projector that was donated a long time ago. It whirs so loud you can't hear the movie. We have ten or so DVDs. Tonight, *The Little Mermaid* got the most votes. I hate *The Little Mermaid*. It's a little kid movie. Plus, I've seen it a billion times, so I told Mercy I'd go up early for bed. I used the back stairs to try to sneak a cookie, but Charlie and Emily were in the kitchen with their staff. They were cleaning up from dinner and already getting ready for breakfast.

"If it isn't the best Willa of all the Willas!" Charlie said. He always makes you feel like he was just waiting for you to walk into the room this whole time, so he could see you again.

"Hi, Willa," Emily said. She was wiping all the counters clean.

"Hi, Charlie. Hi, Emily. I'm going to bed early tonight."

"I won't let you walk through my kitchen without feeding you," Charlie said. "How much have you grown this year? You look like one of the pole beans in the garden."

I could tell I was growing because all my pajama pants were too short. I'd find out how much I'd been growing soon because our doctor day was coming up. I'd never had a yearly checkup until I came to the Southern Ohio Children's Home. I'd had so many vaccinations to get caught up on, I'm still catching up. My momma only ever took me to the doctor if I was real sick. She definitely couldn't keep track of vaccinations. She could barely keep track of my own birthday. She only remembered my birthday because Grammaw would come find us wherever we were. Grammaw and Pop-pop always had ways of finding us, even if Momma was "never speaking to those jerks again." They'd bring me a birthday cake and a present. For about a minute, my momma couldn't be mad at them. But, after that minute, she'd be real mad because *they* were the ones who'd remembered my birthday and not her. Then my momma would go through her purse, pull out an old nail polish or something, hand it to me, and say *Happy birthday*, which was fine by me because I loved all the secret things in Momma's purse. Then, she'd give me a hug and take me to the dollar store to buy me anything I wanted. I still love the dollar store.

"I think I'm growing a lot," I told Charlie. It was probably from all the milk I drink. I was thinking of asking Mercy if we should get our own cow, but cows cost money, and Mercy didn't have money to spend on a cow right now.

"You're going to be taller than me soon, Willa," Charlie said.

"She's already taller than me!" Emily said, standing close. Sure enough, I had an inch on Emily.

"Here, take these," Emily said, handing me not one but two

chocolate chip cookies from a fresh batch she'd made for the next day.

"We don't want anybody's tummy growling tonight," Charlie said.

I hugged Emily and Charlie. They are so full of love.

I walked by Mercy's bedroom on the way to The Fortress. Her bedroom door was cracked open, and it's never cracked even a little, trust me. I saw this as an invitation. The gap between the door and the doorframe was calling out to me: *I'm already open, might as well.*

What I'm trying to say is, I did not mean to go into Mercy's bedroom without permission.

But that's what I did.

I stood inside the doorway with one foot in the hall and my heart beating so hard. I was acting like Clover when she lies on the threshold, half in–half out of the closet. She knows if she crosses it, that *something*—who knows what, but *something*—will happen. I felt the same way. I was in a forbidden place. A shiver came over me, like someone walking on my grave. Or was a ghost walking through Mercy's doorway with me? If it was Katherine's ghost, I'd be okay with that.

It wasn't my first time in Mercy's bedroom, so it didn't feel so crazy for me to go inside.

I shoved the last bites of cookie in my mouth so I wouldn't get crumbs everywhere and stepped all the way into her room with both feet.

Mercy's bedroom looks out over the garden and chicken coop and fields that go on and on as far as your eyes can see. When I looked out her windows, I saw lengths of long grass and a glowing orange sun burning low in the sky.

Even though I'd been in Mercy's room before, I'd been

distracted by everyone else and all of us looking for the letter. This time, I noticed the details.

I saw her fireplace, just like the one in the dollhouse version of the Southern Ohio Children's Home. Instead of a fire in the fireplace, there's a cardboard box filled with dusty papers and files. In dollhouse Mercy's bedroom, there were chandeliers and vases and candlesticks and even a puppy dog. Everything was perfect and *rich*. There was even one of those tables where you sit down and brush your hair in front of a mirror.

Mercy's real bedroom is nothing like the dollhouse bedroom. The dark red wallpaper with roses and ribbons of gold has been painted white, but you can still see a raised pattern of the same roses and ribbons. The old wallpaper behind the paint is peeling down from the corners, next to hanging ferns with dry leaves littering the carpet. There's not a fancy piece of furniture in sight. Probably Katherine had gotten rid of it all. Even the chandeliers are gone, replaced by globe-shaped lights screwed into the ceiling.

The bed in Mercy's dollhouse bedroom was canopied. Mercy's real bed is half buried beneath clothes and newspapers. I don't know how she sleeps. I could hardly see the bedspread. I wondered how Meredith felt, staying in Mercy's messy bedroom.

How is it that Mercy keeps her bedroom so messy when she keeps the rest of the Southern Ohio Children's Home so clean? I looked across the piles of newspapers, rows of cardboard boxes and plastic bins filled with papers or donated clothing and the mounds of half-knit blankets and half-made quilts on a chair in the corner.

"Where will I find it in this mess?" I whispered to myself.

I knew what I was snooping for even though I hadn't planned

on snooping. I needed to read the grandfather clock letter. And I needed to get out of Mercy's room fast because *The Little Mermaid* would be over soon. I was afraid of how much trouble I'd be in if Mercy caught me doing something I wasn't supposed to be doing again.

I'm getting older and probably shouldn't still be doing things I'm not supposed to do, like having a secret cat or reading someone else's diaries. I try being "exemplary," but I have not figured out how to do that anywhere close to one hundred percent all the time.

The sun was going to bed, sinking into the covers of the horizon. I couldn't turn the lights on because that'd be a dead giveaway. I could still see what I was doing but wouldn't be able to for long.

I scanned the piles. Maybe Mercy had left the letter lying around on top of something. It didn't seem like her filing system made any kind of sense. I opened a couple drawers and looked in boxes. I even looked in her bathroom because you never know. Her private bathroom has an antique clawfoot tub, which is probably older than Mercy and is filled with dirty laundry.

I sometimes had to snoop around my momma's things to find money if we didn't have any food. That was easy, though, because my momma would not wake up when she was sleeping. All I had to do was be sure she was asleep, and I could snoop all I wanted. After I'd find some money, usually a dollar or maybe five if I was lucky, I'd ride my bike to the gas station, and I'd get something all by myself. There was this one gas station lady who had gray hair. She said her grandkids were my age, and wasn't I too young to be coming in by myself all the time, and where was my mom? She always gave me a piece of gum with my change. I'd ride my bike back to wherever we were staying, and Momma would still be out like a light. I'd eat a whole bag of Cheetos and drink a whole can of Sprite.

I was pretty good at snooping, even if I didn't like that I was. It's not the kind of thing you want to be good at, unless you're a detective on a TV show. Standing there in Mercy's bedroom, I swore to myself that this was going to be my last time snooping for anything.

When I could barely see anymore because the sunlight had turned from orange to gray, I knew it was time to give up and go get ready for bed. Ariel would be marrying Eric by now, and soon they'd be singing "Under the Sea" while the credits rolled, which meant Mercy and Meredith would be coming upstairs any minute.

I sat on Mercy's bed next to the piles to take one more look around. I put my feet up to try and figure out how Mercy slept there. Newspapers, books, and five pairs of reading glasses were piled all over the top of the pillow on the other side of her bed, as if she'd pushed them over just to squeeze herself in. Then I saw an envelope poking out of the top of the bedspread, like Mercy had tucked it in.

I pulled it out from under the covers. "Yes!" I screamed quietly. I'd found the grandfather clock letter. I couldn't wait one more second even though I knew Mercy might be coming. My hands were shaking as I opened the envelope and read:

September 15, 1998

I, Katherine Ann Rost Karr, a resident of the County of Scioto, State of Ohio, declare that this is the codicil to my last will and testament, which is dated September 15, 1998.

I change said last will in the following manner:

I bequest that no profit be made from sale of The Land whereby sits Midlands Christian Academy for Boys and that The Land and Midlands Christian Academy for Boys be used solely for nonprofit purposes to benefit the community.

Otherwise, I hereby confirm and republish my will dated January 10, 1998, in all respects other than those herein mentioned.

I subscribe my name to this codicil this 15th day of September, 1998, in the presence of Edward Montgomery Karr, who subscribes his name here in my presence.

Katherine Karr
____
Maker

ATTEST

On the date last above written, Katherine Rost Karr, known by us to be the person whose signature appears at the end of this codicil, declared to me, Edward Montgomery Karr, the undersigned, that the foregoing instrument, consisting of one (1) page was the codicil to the will dated January 10, 1998; who then signed the codicil in our presence, and now in the presence of each other, we now sign our names as witnesses.

Edward Karr
____
Witness

I didn't understand most of the words (especially "codicil"), but then and there it hit me: Selling the property with Midlands Academy was not an option for Mercy.

Mercy had been hiding a lot from us, but mostly she'd been hiding her worry. She needed money—*bad*—and if she didn't have land to sell, what was she going to do? What were *we* going to do?

"It's not fair," I whispered to myself.

I needed to do something to help her even though there was nothing I *could* do.

I dropped the letter on the pillow and suddenly saw through new eyes how Mercy gives everything to us kids and doesn't have anything left for herself. That's why her room is so messy. It must have been how she felt inside—crammed with the details of our little lives, but also neglected. I'd never noticed how Mercy was neglecting herself. I'm not sure I could have even understood it if Meredith hadn't come along, all nice and un-neglected.

"Willa? What are you doing in my bedroom?"

I about jumped so high my head hit the ceiling, I swear, Mercy scared me so bad. Her eyes landed on Katherine's letter on the pillow. I was so sad and caught up thinking about how neglected Mercy was, that all I could do was run and put my arms around her. I buried my head in her shoulder and cried, the way I used to when I was waist high.

Mercy hugged me back. She hugged me back hard.

Something changed right then. Something changed inside me, but also something changed between Mercy and me.

I wasn't a little girl anymore. Mercy knew it, and so did I.

"I'm sad and scared about all of this, too, Willa," she said.

For the first time in my life, Mercy showed me her fears.

"I've been so scared you were going to get rid of me," I confessed.

"Why on earth—?"

"Because you ran out of cribs, and you never have any money," I said.

Mercy pulled out of our huggy-hug and looked me dead in the eye.

"Willa, I am not going to 'get rid' of you. Whatever happens, we'll be together. We'll be okay. *You're* going to be okay," she said.

"But how?" I couldn't see how we'd be okay if Mercy didn't have any money. Tears streamed down my cheeks steady as the leaky faucet in the basement laundry room.

"Because I said so," Mercy said.

I didn't believe her. She didn't believe herself, either. *Because I said so* is one of those things adults say when they're not telling you everything and they don't know what else to say.

I almost spilled it all right then—about Katherine's diaries and Jack and even Clover, but all my secret knowledge wouldn't do anything to help Mercy or me.

"It's time to go to bed, Willa." Mercy marched me out of her room, conversation over.

Everything Katherine had hidden had been found. And now, because of that, the Southern Ohio Children's Home and everyone in it might end up abandoned, same as Midlands Academy.

I still found myself crawling up to Kacey's bunk after lights out, even though we'd finished the diaries. We needed the company. That night, Kacey was crying again.

"What's wrong?" I whispered.

"I got a letter from my dad." Kacey rubbed their eyes and sat up to make room for me. They pulled a letter from under their pillow.

"What'd he say?" I asked. I tried reading in the moonlight, but his handwriting was chicken scratch.

"He says my mom still wants me to go to a conversion camp, and that if I ever want to come back to live with them, they'll be sending me there first."

"That's cruel," I said. I was so mad every time I thought about Kacey's mom wanting to change them from who they are. I couldn't understand why it mattered to her so much, why she couldn't let Kacey *be*.

"My mom is dead set on 'fixing' me," Kacey said, wiping away tears with their sheet. "My dad says he doesn't agree with it. He also said he's been taking care of Domino."

"That's good news about your cat at least," I said.

"I wish I could cut myself off from my mom, the way Mercy did with Eleanor," they said.

Clover could tell Kacey was upset. She climbed all the way up to their shoulder and nuzzled their neck, purring like a highway motorcycle.

"What are you going to do?" I asked.

"If my mom wants to send me away, there's only one thing I can do."

"What's that?"

"Run away," Kacey said.

"I am not letting you run away so long as I'm alive, Kacey Springdale. No way." I was already picturing Kacey getting hooked on drugs. That's how long it takes to start using drugs if you're a runaway: one second.

I tried reading their dad's chicken scratch again.

"Your dad also says he's sorry, Kacey. And that he loves you." I tried not to think about all the unanswered letters I'd written to my momma.

Kacey kept wiping fresh tears from their cheeks.

"He calls me Kacey in the letter." They pointed to where it said *Dear Kacey*.

"What else would he call you?" I asked.

"The name they gave me when I was born," Kacey said. "I haven't used it for three years at school, but my mom and dad kept using it at home, no matter how many times I told them it wasn't my name anymore."

I couldn't imagine Kacey having any other name except Kacey.

"But if my dad is really sorry," they said, "and if he really loves me, he'd tell my mom she's wrong. He'd let me come home."

I wanted Kacey to stay at the Southern Ohio Children's Home with me, but I didn't tell them that, because what they wanted was to be accepted at their *own* home.

I didn't leave Kacey's bunk that night. Somehow all three of us—me, Kacey, and Clover—found a way to sleep in the twin bunk.

We all needed each other for any chance of sweet dreams.

Curling Up With the Moon

WHEN THE MOON IS FULL and shines through the circle window across my pillow and bedspread, I imagine it is shining just for me. I feel peace inside when there's moonlight on my face. It's soft and harmless, unlike the sun, which burns my skin after ten seconds and gives me more freckles than I already have. I can lie in the moonlight all night and feel protected.

Momma used to sing me that song from *It's a Wonderful Life*, the movie on TV at Christmastime that we watched together a lot. It was her favorite. The song went:

Buffalo gals, won't you come out tonight?
Come out tonight,
Come out tonight?
Buffalo gals, won't you come out tonight,
And dance by the light of the moon?

A fat full moon was hanging in the sky the night after I went to Finn's house again. That day, Finn and me had been at All Creatures helping Moe with kittens. Thankfully, kitten season was winding down. We got Clover in with a bunch of other cats who were going to the vet for their low-cost spay and neuter surgeries. Even though we get them fixed, somehow, there are other cats who keep having more kittens (I do know *how*, of course). There are a lot of barn cats and trailer cats in our county, the ones who live outside and have humans who feed them sometimes, but most of the time not, so they eat rodents and birds. Moe puts pictures of the kittens online, and rescues from all over Ohio come to adopt them or take them to bigger shelters in Cincinnati or Columbus or someplace where there are more people who have enough money to take care of pets.

I imagine every single cat and dog getting adopted and living in homes where their new families brush them and feed them, and where they have a nice window to look out of without a care in the world. I make sure the cats at All Creatures are as well-groomed and cared for as possible, so when we take their adoption photos for the website, you can see their potential.

After finishing with the kittens, Finn and me each took three dogs out for our usual walk. We were headed down to the park by the river, past Courthouse Square, when I saw Meredith coming out of the courthouse building. She was wearing her high heels and those sunglasses. She did not look like a single other person in Courthouse Square, I can tell you that much.

"Who's that?" Finn couldn't help noticing her because that's how different she looked.

"That is Meredith Karr, Mercy's cousin-lawyer," I explained.

I waved at Meredith as she got into her black rental car, but I don't think she saw me. Or maybe she didn't recognize me because she wouldn't expect to see me anywhere but at the Southern Ohio Children's Home. Or maybe she just couldn't see anything with those sunglasses on.

"Mercy found out she can't make any money off the land with Midlands Academy, even though the property technically belongs to her," I said.

"Why not?" Finn asked.

"That's what the secret extra part to the will from her Aunt Katherine said," I explained. "Katherine changed it to make sure that Midlands Christian Academy for Boys would be used only for purposes to help the community. A 'not-profit,' they call it."

"Purposes to help the community? What does that mean?" Finn asked.

"I don't know. I hope Meredith will know what to do," I said.

There is something about people who walk around all confident, the way Meredith does, that makes you feel like they can handle anything. In Meredith's case, I was hoping my feeling was right.

"I'm really scared though, Finn." I hadn't talked to anybody about my new fears, the ones that boiled up when I laid my own eyes on Katherine's letter with her signature on it.

"What are you scared of?" he asked.

"I had been scared Mercy was going to get rid of me," I confessed.

"Mercy would never do that!" Finn said.

"I know! I know." My original fear seemed silly the more I said it out loud. "Now I'm scared the Southern Ohio Children's Home will close for real," I said. "Mercy really is running out of money, and now her plan won't work."

We sat on a park bench in the shade of a buckeye tree near the water, to give the panting dogs a break from the blazing sun.

"I'm scared for Justin, too," I said. "He's worried that if the Southern Ohio Children's Home closes, he'll end up somewhere like Midlands Academy."

"That could never happen," Finn said, but I knew he was only saying that to make me feel better.

"How do you know?" I asked.

"I guess I don't." Finn hadn't ever thought about it before, about what could happen to a kid who didn't have any family to take care of them. "Mercy wouldn't *let* it happen," he said. "Besides, Justin is the last kid who needs a reformatory school."

Even with his hopeful words, worry lines pinched Finn's brow.

"And then there's Kacey." I went on listing my fears.

"What about Kacey?" Finn asked.

"They're already thinking about running away. Their mom wants to send them to a conversion camp where they read the Bible all day and make you 'regular,' whatever that is."

"A senior at Shawneeville Central committed suicide after going to one of those places," Finn said.

"Oh my gosh, Finn. That is so sad. Everyone knows those places don't work. And why would anyone want them to work, anyway? Kacey would rather run away than try and be someone they're not. You know what happens to kids who run away and are homeless around here?"

Finn nodded. "Drugs."

He might live in a nice house and get good grades and have a mom and dad who love him, but Finn knows like everyone else that drugs take hold of people whether they want them to or not. He also knows that certain situations are riskier, like being a runaway or being without a job or getting hurt real bad where you need painkillers.

"Can't Mercy do a fundraiser?" Finn asked. "Like you do every year, but bigger?"

"That's what I was thinking, too," I said. "But will that be enough?"

"My mom will have some ideas. Why don't you come over today, before you go back?" he said.

Mrs. Harbour used to be in charge of our yearly fundraiser before she got Parkinson's. She'd raise thousands and thousands of dollars. Mercy said Mrs. Harbour was her fairy godmother. Mercy always needed the money when it came in, and she never had time to run her own fundraiser.

Of course I wanted to go to Finn's house. I was already hungry for whatever treat Mrs. Harbour was probably baking.

We walked the dogs back and said goodbye to Moe.

"Thank you again for helping me and Clover out," I told him, but he waved us out the door and brushed me away like an annoying gnat. Like he was saying, *As if I'd do anything else.*

Riding our bikes to Finn's house, I felt like a little kid next to him. Was I a little kid? Sometimes I didn't even know myself. Finn was going to be a junior in high school and I was only going into sixth grade. Most boys his age wouldn't be so nice to younger kids. Maybe it's easier to be nice when you've never had anything bad happen to you.

Finn's house smelled like a fresh-baked blueberry pie. Mrs. Harbour cut us each a slice without asking if we wanted any.

"Thank you, Mrs. Harbour," I said.

"You're the reason I bake pies, Willa."

"What about me, Mom?" Finn said.

"Stop it, Finn." She likes teasing Finn and Mr. Harbour about the sweet treats they eat. Baking is Mrs. Harbour's true passion, and I missed having her cookies more often. Now she saves up her baking for her "men," who do eat a lot. Mr. Harbour has a belly like Santa Claus.

After only a few bites of pie and a few sips of lemonade, my tummy felt squishy and tight at the same time. Something was not right.

"Excuse me," I said and took myself to the bathroom in the front hallway.

I about screamed when I saw the red splotch on my underwear. It had even leaked onto my jean shorts. My pee wasn't yellow but bright red. The insides of my legs had red on them, too.

I had been wondering when I was going to get my period since I'd turned ten years old. That's when Miss Samantha starts teaching us the things we need to know about our bodies, including menstruating. She gives us a Human Growth and Development lesson with everyone together, and then separately, for privacy and to make sure we wouldn't be scared to ask questions.

I'm thankful Miss Samantha teaches us Human Growth and Development, because can you imagine getting your period and not having anybody tell you about it first? You might think you were dying, because usually when your body is bleeding, it's because you've injured yourself, and you might need to go to the doctor or get stitches. If you are bleeding from your period and don't know what it is, you would probably be scared.

Some girls my age have already got their periods, but I only have stories to go by, no actual friends or family who can tell me about it.

I stayed for extra on the toilet, taking deep breaths. When I wiped, I had to wipe and wipe and wipe, because it was like I had a leak that leaked red paint and wouldn't stop leaking. I was afraid everyone in the kitchen could hear me flush again and again.

Finally, Mrs. Harbour knocked on the bathroom door.

"Are you okay in there, honey?" I like it how Mrs. Harbour calls me honey or pumpkin, like I am her own sweet thing.

"I'm not really okay, no. I mean, I'm okay but—" I had to tell Mrs. Harbour what had happened. Even though I was embarrassed, I knew I didn't need to be embarrassed, because it is something that happens to every girl. I mean woman, because that's what I was now. And if anyone would understand, it would be Mrs. Harbour. "I got my period."

"Oh! Okay, that's just fine." Her voice sounded strange. Maybe because she was excited. Or nervous. Or sad.

I felt bad because I didn't want her Parkinson's to flare up because of me. This seemed like a shaky time for Mrs. Harbour, so I tried staying as calm as possible for her. I thought I should act mature, because I was no longer a girl but a woman.

"Do you have anything I could use? Like—a pad?" I figured I should ask for a pad because I didn't know how to use a tampon, even though Miss Samantha had already told me about tampons and how weird they are.

"Yes, oh yes. I'll be right back."

I sat on the toilet with my red leak and waited for Mrs. Harbour to come back. I wondered if anyone would notice the red that had bled to the outside of my jean shorts.

There was no way I was riding my bike back to the Southern Ohio Children's Home.

"Here you go—" Mrs. Harbour knocked softly on the door. I opened it so she could hand me a pad. She'd gotten a warm washcloth for me, too.

"Thank you," I said.

"I sent Finn out to water the garden," she said. "Come meet me in the kitchen when you're ready."

I was grateful I wouldn't have to come out of the bathroom

with Finn being there. This was a private moment that he didn't need to know about, even though I'm sure he knew about menstruation. He just didn't need to know about *my* menstruation.

In the kitchen, Mrs. Harbour handed me a paper lunch sack.

"Here are more supplies for you," she said.

"Thank you." I did feel shy right then, I don't know why. Maybe because Mrs. Harbour accidentally knew a secret about me.

"There's chocolate in there, too," she whispered and rubbed my arm.

I was glad she said she gave me chocolate instead of saying *congratulations*, which is sometimes what people say when a girl gets her period and becomes a woman. I don't understand what there is to congratulate anyone about. It's not like you *did* anything. And it's not like becoming a woman is *that* great. I would be happier to stay a kid always and live with Mercy forever, but that dream of mine would never come true. All I could think about now was how the Southern Ohio Children's Home was going to close. The Black Hole of My Future was gaping and was even darker now that Mercy couldn't save us the way she'd thought she could.

I didn't want to cry in front of Mrs. Harbour, but I was noticing how true it is that you do feel more emotions when you get your period. Miss Samantha always lets us "have" our emotions, so I let myself have my emotions right then. I took some deep breaths, opened the brown bag, and ate some chocolate. I didn't think Mrs. Harbour would mind if I did not wait.

She pushed herself up and grabbed her cane and walked to her cookie cupboard to get me more. I was right, she didn't mind. It turns out she has a secret supply of miniature chocolate bars all the time, not just at Halloween.

"If you ever need anything else or anything more, let me

know," she said. "I know Mercy keeps her cupboards stocked, so I imagine she has what you need back at the house."

I honestly had no idea if Mercy had what I needed. I might have been the only resident living there for a long time who was menstruating. I didn't know about Kacey, and I didn't feel like it was respectful for me to ask, so I'd have to talk to Mercy or Miss Samantha about it.

What I did know was that Mercy did not have extra money to spend on me.

"Mrs. Harbour, I was wondering, since you used to be in charge of organizing our fundraisers, maybe could you help us with another big event?"

"I am happy to do anything you need, Willa."

"I think Mercy could use some help," I said.

"Then I will call Mercy first thing tomorrow," Mrs. Harbour said.

"Thank you so much, Mrs. Harbour. For everything."

I ate one more mini chocolate bar to keep myself from crying.

I knew Mrs. Harbour meant what she said. If I did most of the work with the other kids and Miss Samantha, Mrs. Harbour could give us all her knowledge about the best ways to make the most money. The community *needed* to support us, for its own good. But how could the community do that when it was the one having a crisis? The Black Hole kept finding ways to expand.

Mrs. Harbour gave me a lopsided hug and walked me out to get Finn. The sun was all the way to bed because it was dark now, the full moon bright in the sky. It was going to shine on me through my window, which made me feel hopeful.

"Do you mind driving Willa back, Finn?" Mrs. Harbour asked.

"Heck no, I don't mind," he said.

Now that Finn finally got his license for real, he loves driving more than anything, even though his old Chevrolet barely goes faster than 30 miles per hour. It has a huge trunk, so Finn tossed my bike in. I gave Mrs. Harbour one more hug.

I prayed I wouldn't leak on the short drive to the Southern Ohio Children's Home.

Finn turned on the radio and opened the windows. Suddenly, I felt like a regular almost-teenager who did regular almost-teenager stuff.

"Are you okay?" Finn asked.

"I'm fine." I let my hand fly out the window. I didn't want to talk.

Finn driving the car with his knees knocking the bottom of the steering wheel was giving me butterflies. Finn is special because of the kind way he talks and the honest way he listens, and because he is there for me. He is special for being himself.

Moonbeams sparkled on my skin. I closed my eyes and pictured moonlight fighting the Black Hole. In that moment, I had a feeling like the moonbeams could win.

Past Meets Present

No one was more secret about his life before the Southern Ohio Children's Home than Justin. He used to wear his headphones everywhere when he was little: in the dining room, in Miss Samantha's classroom (she made him take them off for lessons), and even outside while he was playing. Starting when he was ten, he'd take his headphones off more and more each day, until he only needed them at bedtime.

I used to think something loud had happened to Justin, and that's why he needed quiet. Now I know it wasn't like that. You could say what happened to Justin was quiet, and he'd been searching for that same peace and quiet ever since.

I asked him about it one day in the library when he was reading a book called *Locomotion*, which isn't from our shelves. It was all beat up, the cover hanging on by two strings.

"Justin, did your momma give you that book?" I asked.

He had started wearing his headphones during the daytime again. He took them off and nodded. "It has her handwriting inside. See?" He held up the inside cover, where his own mother had written him a note saying how much she loved him.

"You're so lucky," I said. "I don't have anything like that from my momma. You're going to love the cover right off if you keep reading it like that. Did your mom ever do drugs?" The question popped out of my mouth before I could stop it. I hoped Justin wouldn't mind me asking about his *before*.

"No. My mom had cancer," he said.

I learned then that unlike a lot of us kids at the home, Justin's family did not do drugs. He told me his dad had died from a heart attack, when Justin was too young to remember. Before his mom died from cancer, she had arranged for Justin to come to Mercy. She'd got in touch with Mercy because she didn't have family who could take her son. That's all Justin knew. Either that, or it's all he would say, and I don't blame him for not wanting to talk about it. Justin put his headphones back on and went back to *Locomotion*.

We were spending a lot of too-hot afternoons reading together, with Kacey, too. Three peas in a pod, all wanting the peace that comes with a good book and quiet company.

Justin kept wanting to tell Mercy about Jack, but he was not as experienced at being in trouble as I was.

"It's better to wait," I had explained to him. "Mercy might find out on her own anyway. Besides, if we wait until later, we won't have to get in trouble now."

Miss Samantha says that Justin is an "old soul," and I believe her. Justin was frustrated and scared. The fear that comes with not knowing what your own future holds was settling inside him, the same way my Black Hole was a part of me.

I first noticed Justin wearing his headphones during the daytime again when we were making crafts for the fundraiser.

I'd convinced Miss Samantha that we should set up her classroom for making homemade things we could sell—soaps, candles, herb sachets, hand-painted flowerpots, greeting cards—so *all* the kids could make stuff, even the toddlers. I love helping the toddlers with their crafts. Justin's specialty is making notepads from recycled paper. Elizabeth makes toys for dogs and cats. Roy doesn't have just one thing he is good at, so he bounces around and does everything.

Kacey's painted flowerpots had professional-looking designs on them, and everyone who saw them—Mercy and Charlie and Emily and Miss Samantha and Miss Lupe and even Meredith—said the same thing, which is that they wanted one. Kacey was proud about their contribution to the fundraiser. As for me, I was planting fresh herbs in their pots, picking the best basil, lavender, and mint.

The classroom looked like Santa's workshop with elves working hard everywhere. The younger kids take their jobs seriously, because they see us big kids doing important jobs all the time, like preparing food for cooking, taking care of the garden, feeding and watering the chickens, folding laundry, and sweeping floors. It's all fun to the little ones. When they get a "job" of soap-maker or card-drawer, they feel like a big kid. The best part is that even if a soap is cracked or a card is lopsided, we can sell it anyway, because anyone buying it would be reminded who made it and why.

Within days, we had boxes of crafts we could sell. Emily was baking extra cookies and putting them in the freezer. Mercy got help from the nuns at the Ministry of Hopelessness to post signs to get the word out, even beyond our community. Finn and me were going to plaster Courthouse Square with flyers. Meredith and Miss Samantha set up a new online store and created advertising for social media. The Southern Ohio Children's Home already has a website, but it is nothing much. Mercy says she is not "tech-savvy," because who has time for computers when there are dozens of children who need you to take care of them every day.

Even though us kids felt hopeful with our fundraising plan, I could tell the grown-ups did not. They were fighting over where the fundraiser would happen, because Meredith insisted we have it at Midlands Academy, and Mercy hated anything having to do with Midlands Academy.

"I found the keys." Meredith swooped in and dropped a giant cardboard box on the table where I was pulling tapered candles out of a crockpot full of hot wax. (The toddlers aren't allowed anywhere near the candle table.)

Meredith was still wearing her sunglasses even though it was storming outside. I love stormy days, same as my momma did. She used to pull up a garden chair and watch storms roll over, washing the sky. Storms never scared her the way they do some people. They don't scare me neither.

"What keys?" Mercy looked up from the inventory sheet where she was keeping track of everything we were making and the price of each item and how much money we could raise if we sold it all, which we wouldn't, but it was nice to think about anyway. It made us want to keep making more and more things.

If we made a million candles and sold them all, we'd have a million dollars, and the Southern Ohio Children's Home could keep going along like it always did, and Mercy wouldn't have to worry anymore and neither would I. But there was no way we were going to make a million candles, much less sell a million candles.

"The keys to Midlands," Meredith said. "They were in my dad's desk at his house."

Meredith had been talking to Mercy about how she had not had the "fortitude" to clean out her dad's house after he'd died a couple years ago. He'd been a widower for nearly twenty years before that. He and Meredith were close after her mom died, even though Meredith lived in New York City and had avoided Shawneeville like the plague.

"I'm regretting not cleaning the house out sooner," Meredith said. "Mom was nonstop, always donating her time or money or writing letters to senators or registering people to vote. Dad always joked how he couldn't keep up with her. She left behind a *lot* to go through. Apparently, he didn't have the energy to deal with it, either."

"Maybe he liked keeping her things with him," Elizabeth said.

"That's what my Pop-pop did with my Grammaw's stuff," I said. "I'd catch him smelling the clothes in her closet, even after it'd been a long time since she'd died."

"I am sure you are both right about that." Meredith flung off her giant sunglasses. It had gotten so I hardly noticed them anymore, even when she was wearing them inside during a thunderstorm. "How'd you get so smart?" she asked us.

"Miss Samantha," we said together. I was glad Miss Samantha was there to hear it so she could have a proud feeling for herself, which was clear she did from the smile on her face and the pink on her cheeks.

"Here is everything from his desk drawers." Meredith took things out of the box and made a messy pile on our worktable. "Look at these old photographs. More papers. A diary. A picture I drew when I was in kindergarten—"

Mercy put down her inventory sheet and reached across the table for the diary. Me, Justin, and Kacey dropped what we were doing and crowded around Mercy.

"A diary?" Justin said.

"Does it say when the diary is from?" I asked. It looked just like Katherine's other secret diaries from the library: black, hard covered, with a metal plate that had the year etched on it.

"1976," Mercy said as she flipped through the pages.

"1976?" Kacey repeated, even though they'd heard Mercy just fine. Justin pulled off his headphones. I had to stop myself from grabbing the missing diary out of Mercy's hands.

Mercy was standing right next to us, but I could tell her mind was going back someplace else as she looked at the diary. A red piece of tape stuck out from one of the pages.

"It's strange," Meredith said as she unloaded other small items from the box. "There's only the one diary. I wonder where the others are. My mom was never *not* writing in a diary. I can't imagine my dad would have lost track of those."

"Maybe she hid them, like she hid that letter," Elizabeth said while she focused on painting a flowerpot. Hers weren't as nice as Kacey's, but once you plant something inside a flowerpot, it looks pretty no matter what.

"As a matter of fact—" Justin started.

"You're right, Elizabeth!" I blurted, cutting Justin off. I did not want him to reveal our secret about Katherine's diaries. I suddenly realized Kacey, Justin, and me would have to tell Meredith and Mercy about them eventually, but not then—not in front of everyone. How could we explain that we hadn't known what we were reading when we'd started, and then we couldn't stop? Maybe Elizabeth was making it so we wouldn't have to confess, because she was going to figure it out herself.

"Do you think she hid them?" I asked, playing innocent and hoping Justin would "catch my drift," as Miss Samantha says to us when she's teaching.

"That does sound like something my mother would do," Meredith said. "Are you okay, Mercy?"

Worry had spread across Mercy's whole face, pinching her forehead, her eyes, her mouth, and even her neck. She clutched the diary to her chest.

"Where did you say you found this, Meredith?" she asked.

"In my dad's desk drawer. The keys to the school were lying right on top of it."

Watching Meredith and Mercy, I thought about how there are mysteries inside every family.

"Should we have another scavenger hunt for her diaries?" Meredith asked.

"Yes! I'm going to win this time!" Roy said.

I wanted to punch Roy and tell him Kacey had already won, but that'd definitely get me in trouble. This wasn't about winning, anyway.

Mercy nodded silently, still in some faraway place, probably in 1976. Probably remembering the night that, according to Katherine, her and Jack's lives had changed forever.

"Could we see the diary?" I asked, already knowing the answer. I figured if we got permission now, what we'd already done wouldn't seem so bad.

"I don't mind," Meredith said.

"No!" Mercy shouted. Her harsh tone surprised Meredith.

Justin, Kacey, and me were stuck between them, looking back and forth at Mercy and Meredith looking at each other. I had the feeling like I'd said a swear word and was about to get in trouble from Mercy, but Meredith is the kind of person who wouldn't care about saying swears. The two of them had to figure it out between themselves. I tried not to say any more words, because I was sure that if I did, it'd just make things worse.

"I mean …" Mercy said in a quieter voice. "I mean, maybe there are things in Katherine's diaries that should remain private."

"But when you think about it," Meredith said, nodding her head real slow, the way she does when she's having an idea. "What's the point of keeping diaries all your life if no one ever reads them? My mom's diaries are part of her legacy. A record of a different time."

"We might be able to learn something by reading them," I suggested, acting like we hadn't already read all her other diaries.

"Like something about history. Right, Justin?" Kacey nudged Justin's arm, but he was now frozen from realizing he was so close to getting in trouble. I can count on one finger the number of times Justin has been in trouble. And that was Roy's fault.

"I love that you all want to read Miss Katherine's diary to learn," Miss Samantha chimed in, "but remember, this is a private family history."

"'Private' being the key word," Mercy said, holding on to the diary for dear life.

"I guess I'd better read it myself first," Meredith said. "Sorry, Willa."

Meredith took the diary back from Mercy.

I pretended like it was no big deal, but I swore to myself right then and there that I was going to read that diary. Just the kind of thought that gets me in trouble. One look at Kacey told me they were having the same thought in their inmost soul. Justin, on the other hand, was trying to be invisible.

None of these secrets were doing anybody any good. Sometimes adults say *no* because it's easier, and kids have to "learn how to take *no* for an answer," even though children might know better. There's an X-ray vision that comes from being a kid, because our truth and justice filter is not clouded yet. That is something I've heard Justin say before. I understand it part of the way, like when my gut tells me what is true and what is not. I know my gut instinct is right, despite getting in trouble for following it sometimes.

Meredith put the entire mess of papers and photographs and the diary back into the box again. Everything except the keys, which she gave to Mercy.

"It's time to go back to Midlands Christian Academy," Meredith told her.

Mercy took the keys and put them on her key ring with shaking fingers.

"I can't go over there by myself," Mercy said.

"I'll go!" Kacey and me volunteered at the same time.

"What about me and Justin?" Roy said.

"I don't want to," Justin said.

"Aw, come on!" Roy nudged Justin in the arm. Justin ignored him and put his headphones on again.

"I'm definitely not going," Elizabeth said, turning her back to us while she painted.

"I'll call Deputy Bell and see when she's available," Mercy said, ignoring us all. "I need reassurance that no one has been trespassing."

"Mercy, please?" I didn't like to beg, but it seemed like Mercy needed us.

"I'll think about it." Mercy picked up her inventory list and walked to the other side of the classroom to check on the toddlers and their painted greeting cards.

"I'll take that as a 'maybe,'" I said.

Mercy gave me a sideways glance, telling me with one look that I'd better behave if I had any hope of going to Midlands Academy with her.

And somehow, I did behave. Well ... *almost.*

Mercy had been talking to Deputy Bell about making sure Midlands Christian Academy for Boys was "safe." Deputy Bell had told her, "Everything is fine, Mercy. You've got nothing to worry about." By "safe," I knew that Mercy meant "No Trespassers." No Jack.

But I also knew that by "safe," Deputy Bell meant there *was* a trespasser. Jack.

Mercy and Deputy Bell thought they were saying the same thing, but they actually were saying opposite things.

Kacey and me were hoping Jack wouldn't be there for Mercy's visit, otherwise she was going to be in for a big surprise. I knew eventually she'd have to find out about him. Somehow.

What would Jack think about a big fundraiser happening at Midlands Academy, where he'd been watching over ghost boys all by himself? Only Jack and Benji had been visiting those forgotten trees and buildings. I pictured having a ceremony in his sanctuary, like a real Forgetting Ceremony. How would he feel with everyone stomping around out there, trying to turn the old reformatory school into something new, because a woman who died a long time ago wrote a secret letter with a secret wish?

Maybe he would finally get help planting his garden.

"I'll put this in the library for now," Meredith said when she picked up the box of stuff from her dad's house. She looked right at me when she said it, too, I swear. She was telling me to read the diary. My gut told me that's what Meredith wanted me to do, despite what Mercy had said.

Maybe Meredith was tired of secrets, too. Maybe secrets were what made her move to New York City in the first place.

Kacey and me pretended like we weren't paying any attention to where Meredith was going with that box.

As soon as afternoon quiet time arrived, me and Kacey, along with Justin, met up in the library to read as fast as we could.

"What if Mercy catches us?" Justin asked.

"Don't worry! She won't," I said, even though I knew we were taking a big risk.

But the risk was worth it.

<u>May 15, 1976</u>

Mercy visited us before the carnival at Midlands Academy tonight. She looked beautiful in her new skirt and blouse. Grown up. Meredith asked if she was a princess, and Mercy said she felt like one, even if only for one night. We gave her a wrist corsage from the flower shop in Courthouse Square—a red rose with a spray of baby's breath. There was excitement in her eyes. She deserves it. She works so hard, but still, nothing is good enough for her mother. Eleanor didn't want Mercy to go to the carnival. Imagine! I kid myself and think it wouldn't have been any different if Eleanor had had a son, but it would have been. Press would've molded a son to take over Rost Pharmaceuticals. Eleanor is waiting to see who Mercy marries, because heaven forbid there's a woman in charge.

This carnival is the only attempt I've seen in my life for Midlands Academy to connect with the community. Mr. Winter, stubborn as

Kacey ran up to The Fortress to get our notebook from under their covers, so we could write down two important diary entries from 1976. I loved the part about Mrs. Harbour's cookies. And I imagined Katherine taking a picture of Mercy on the princess staircase.

<u>May 20, 1976</u>

Mercy came to babysit Meredith tonight. As soon as I saw her, I knew something was wrong. I told Edward our plans had changed and took Mercy into the kitchen while Edward watched Meredith. Mercy didn't tell me what was eating at her, but I know something happened at the carnival, and now Mercy doesn't feel safe at home. But she won't tell me why. I suppose I need to pay Press and Eleanor a visit to find out for myself what is going on. <u>The only thing Mercy would say was that she met a young man named Jack and that he didn't do anything wrong, no matter what anybody says.</u>

For now, I've asked Mercy to stay with us. God knows we have the room. I called Eleanor and Press and lied. I told them we needed extra help with Meredith and insisted Mercy stay for the weekend. I've seen Eleanor operate over the years. I know Mercy can't ever attain her mother's unreasonable standards, whether for appearances or achievements. Mercy doesn't have to explain it to me.

But I've never seen Mercy scared. She's always managed the situation at home remarkably well. I figured once she graduated high school, she would fly far away from her mother and father. It's easier for a young woman to do that these days than it was even ten years ago.

"It sounds like Jack got in trouble for something he didn't do," Kacey said.

The part of the diary we'd noticed earlier with the red flag was on the page with the underlined words: _The only thing Mercy would say was that she met a young man named Jack and that he didn't do anything wrong, no matter what anybody says._ I had a feeling that single line was the reason why this diary was separate from all the others. This diary proved that Jack hadn't done whatever it was people thought he'd done.

"Now we know why he ran away," I said.

"But we still don't know what happened, or what he was blamed for," Justin said.

There were only two people who could explain it to us: Jack and Mercy.

"I don't think we're ever going to find out the truth," I said.

As soon as we finished reading, Meredith walked by. I closed the diary as fast as I could. A piece of paper fluttered down to the floor. I grabbed it and put the diary back in the box.

"What's everyone up to in here?" Meredith asked. She came in from the foyer, red-faced and wearing her running clothes.

"Nothing!" we all said together, blocking the box from

Meredith's view, even though she knew what was on her mother's desk. She was the one who put it there, after all.

"See you at dinner." Meredith winked and walked away. She was in on our secret.

I quickly unfolded the piece of paper I'd picked up from the floor.

"What is it?" Justin asked.

"It looks like a letter," Kacey said.

"It is," I said. I read the words:

Dear Mercy,

It might not come as a big surprise that I have to leave Shawneeville. It's better if I disappear. I want you to know I am not sorry for meeting you. I'm pinning my hope on seeing you again someday. You are the only good thing that happened to me here.

Love,

Jack

"It's *the* letter!" Kacey said.

"The one Jack left in his library books!" I said.

"What's going on?" Mercy snuck up on us, as Justin had feared, and she spied the box on the desk.

I crammed the letter into my pocket.

"Give me that box. Now, please," Mercy said.

"Yes, ma'am." Justin practically threw the box at Mercy.

"Why did Meredith leave her mother's private things lying around?" Mercy asked.

"We didn't read anything," I lied. Again. A BIG lie, because now we'd read *everything*.

I could have kicked myself, giving us away like that, but the lie came out of my mouth before I could stop it. I swear, Mercy knew I was lying, the way she looked straight into my soul.

"I hope you're telling me the truth, Willa Johnson." Mercy took the box and swooped out of the library and up the princess staircase.

Kacey, Justin, and me collapsed onto the red couch.

"She knew you were lying," Kacey said.

"I know," I said.

"If she knew Willa was lying, why didn't we get in trouble?" Justin asked.

"Sometimes getting in trouble is more trouble than it's worth," I explained.

"You have a lot to learn about getting in trouble, don't you?" Kacey asked.

Justin shrugged. Getting in trouble was the only subject he *wasn't* an expert on.

I pulled Jack's letter out of my pocket so we could read it again.

"Mercy may have took Katherine's diary," I said, "but she doesn't know we have Jack's letter."

The School Revisited

I WAS ALWAYS WORRIED ABOUT leaking now that I had my period, and having extra pads seemed extra important, but also extra expensive. Mrs. Harbour had been right about Mercy having menstruation supplies, but they were running low.

Kacey came into the bathroom when I was searching the storage wardrobe.

"What are you looking for?" they asked.

"Nothing." I closed the wardrobe behind me, then realized it was silly to pretend like I hadn't got my period, especially in front of Kacey. "I got my period."

Kacey opened a bottom cupboard and pulled out a square basket with a lid. They opened it to reveal pads and tampons.

"Here you go," they said.

"Thank you." I took one, and Kacey put the basket back.

"Getting your period sucks," they said. "Miss Samantha has ibuprofen if you need it."

"Thanks for not congratulating me." I laughed, thinking about how I hadn't wanted to say anything, when Kacey is someone who understands me best of all.

Kacey closed the bathroom door and turned the lock. Usually, when the two of us are in the bathroom together with the door locked, we are playing with Clover. But today, I'd just left Clover to take a nap under Kacey's bed cover.

"Willa, I know you're good at keeping secrets," Kacey said.

"You know practically all the secrets I'm trying to keep," I said. The only secret I hadn't told Kacey was that I might have a crush on Finn, but I hadn't decided that for certain yet.

"I want to ask Miss Samantha to take me to a doctor, so I can find out about not getting my period anymore," Kacey said.

"You can do that?" I asked.

"Before my parents kicked me out, I was reading online how some birth control pills can stop your period."

"I thought birth control pills were for making it so you can't get pregnant when you're 'sexually active,'" I said. I confess, I didn't understand what Kacey was trying to tell me. The look on my face probably said it all.

"Listen," Kacey went on. "All I'm talking about is having a conversation—like a basic conversation. I've never had the chance to talk with anyone about anything about *me*. I want to talk to a doctor. I'd like to get some information, that's all. I've been thinking about it a lot since I've been away from my mom and dad."

"You couldn't exactly think about it when you were under their roof," I said.

"No, I couldn't. It's just …" Kacey was having a hard time finding their words. "This might be my only chance, Willa. I need to go with a parent, and mine won't take me."

"But Miss Samantha isn't your parent," I said.

"I know," Kacey said. "But she could be my guardian, just for seeing the doctor. The problem is, I'm scared to ask."

"I'll ask!" I said. "Miss Samantha always says we can ask her anything."

"Even this?" Kacey said.

"Especially this," I said.

"I don't know." Kacey's eyebrows bent. "Do you think Mercy would let her take me?"

"Yes, I do," I said. "She wants you to be who you are, Kacey. So do I. You being who you are is important. Because it's *you*."

"Thank you, Willa." Kacey hugged me hard. I could tell they needed to get that conversation out. I'd never had such a good friend as Kacey, maybe because I could feel how much they were relying on me for my friendship in return.

"I'm glad I get to be your friend, Kacey."

"Me too," they said.

They smiled and unlocked the bathroom door.

"We should go find Mercy," I said. "She's going to Midlands Academy soon."

"I'll meet you downstairs," Kacey said.

Mercy had finally told us we could come with her to Midlands Academy if we wanted, saying she could use the "moral support."

After finishing in the bathroom, I slid down the princess staircase railing, which is something I usually do when no one is watching. It turns out you can still slide down railings when you're wearing a "sanitary napkin," which is what the box calls it, even though they do not look like napkins, and why would anyone put a napkin in their underwear?

Mercy pulled the van into the driveway. It was funny seeing Mercy behind the wheel, because she doesn't get out much. Mostly, Mercy stays at the home, except for when she gets her hair cut, which is hardly ever. And sometimes she drives to the

Ministry of Hopelessness to return supplies like Calamity's baby carrier, or extra blankets. She also drives to the United Church of Christ, where the rummage sale ladies set aside the best items for Mercy to rummage through before everyone else. Other times, Mercy might drive to visit a family who wants to adopt a child, to make sure their home is appropriate, and that the parents are loving and kind. A kid hasn't been adopted in a long time, because there aren't many families in the community who can take one. I hate thinking about getting adopted or going to a foster family, but now I am thinking about it more. Will we all have to find foster families if the Southern Ohio Children's Home closes?

I wished Meredith would figure out a way to sell the reformatory school property, even though it would be against her mom's wishes. I'm certain Katherine *never* would have changed her will if she'd known it would have put a new generation of kids at risk of abandonment.

I hopped in the front seat next to Mercy instead of climbing in back with Kacey. She looked at me for a minute like, *What are you doing, Willa Johnson?*

"What?" I said. "You don't think I sit in the front seat when Finn drives me home?"

"I guess I'm just not used to you sitting in front," Mercy said.

"I'm not a little kid anymore," I said, even though Mercy didn't know about my period yet.

"I call shotgun on the way back," Kacey said.

"No fair!" I said.

"It's totally fair." Kacey smiled.

"Fine," I agreed.

Mercy shook her head as she pulled down the pebble driveway.

We could have walked to Midlands Christian Academy faster than we could drive if we cut across the field as the crow flies, but Mercy would never hike through the field, cross a muddy ravine, and trek through the woods.

I was nervous about going to Midlands with Mercy. I tried to keep quiet about everything I knew Mercy didn't know I knew, like Jack's letter in my front pocket. And Jack himself. And everything in Katherine's diaries. My skin tingled underneath Jack's letter, as if his words were burning through the fabric, reminding me of secrets.

"Do you have the key?" I asked her.

"I do," she said.

There was a lot going through my mind as Mercy turned onto County Highway J. I thought about my momma, because when she was alive, I was in the car with her every day driving all over town. I don't know why we drove so much. Her car always broke down and Pop-pop would come get us. I loved when that happened because sometimes we'd have no choice but to go to Grammaw and Pop-pop's house, where I would eat a cookie and take a nap on their bed, which had fifty pillows and smelled like cinnamon. When Grammaw was still alive, they had a dog named Bo. He was a Chihuahua-terrier combo who weighed eight pounds and was elderly and loved to curl up on the bed with me. Their trailer was a peaceful place. Momma never could create that peace for the two of us. I knew this even when I was only little. When we'd leave their house after Pop-pop had fixed the car, I'd cry and cry, and Momma would yell at me to cut it out. Who would want to leave such a peaceful home as that? My momma, that's who.

"What are you thinking about?" Mercy asked.

"My momma," I said.

Mercy nodded. I don't talk about my momma much, but Mercy knows I think about her every day. All the time. I knew Mercy wouldn't ask me any questions about Momma. There isn't anything about that story she doesn't already know. Mercy would always let me have my thoughts, the same way she and Miss Samantha let me have my feelings. We drove in silence.

After a few minutes, we slowed down, and Mercy turned onto the hidden, wooded driveway of Midlands Academy. I'd only ever seen the school by coming in sideways from the ravine, where there are ten million mosquitos. I was glad to be in the van and not in the woods.

The reformatory school looked more like a regular school from the driveway, and not some disorganized set of rundown buildings. I could picture an entrance and even where a parking lot might have been. We saw Deputy Bell's car already parked in what could have been a parking spot if there weren't weeds growing everywhere. Deputy Bell was meeting us there so we could have backup in case anything went wrong. I didn't know what could go wrong, except seeing ghosts. I also didn't know what would happen if Jack was there.

"I got my period," I blurted out to Mercy all of a sudden. My mouth has a habit of saying things my brain did not prepare it for. Maybe I was thinking I might as well get it out, since Kacey already knew, and Mercy needed to know because we were almost out of sanitary napkins. And maybe I did need to tell Mercy I was growing up, even though I was scared to.

"You what?" Mercy said.

"Willa got her period." Kacey piped up from the backseat.

Mercy looked shocked.

"Did you forget I was growing up?" I asked.

"Of course not!" she said.

I didn't know how to tell her that I did not want to grow up, and I did not want to have my period. I felt like she was mad at me.

"I'm sorry." I apologized, even though apologizing for menstruating doesn't make any sense. Maybe I was apologizing for growing up. "I'd rather I didn't grow up, if you want to know the truth," I said.

I waited for Mercy to say something, but she was speechless, which is not like her. Usually, if Mercy is not talking, it's because she doesn't want to. In this instance, Mercy didn't know what to say. She finally pulled herself together and spoke, to my relief.

"*I'm* sorry, Willa," she said. "You took me by surprise is all."

Those weren't the words I was expecting.

Mercy turned off the van and faced me. "Maybe I don't want to admit you're growing up, Willa. None of us can help it, even if we'd rather childhood lasted forever."

Mercy hugged me, which was nice, because when you get a hug from a person who is not a hugger, it feels more important than other hugs. I almost cried, and then my mouth kept blurting out words.

"I don't want to ever not live with you, Mercy," I said.

Then I *did* cry, and Mercy cried, too. I heard her sniffling and felt her hand move to wipe her cheek. Mercy doesn't cry much, even with all the sad-sadness because of the crisis in our community.

"You won't ever have to not live with me, Willa. I promise," Mercy said. She might have been making one of those hopeful promises that maybe you can't keep, like when I tell Clover she'll be my sweet kitty forever and will never ever have to live with anybody else—I want that to be true more than anything, but how do I know for certain?

It made me feel better hearing Mercy say it, anyway. I *needed* to hear Mercy say those words, because even if they didn't make my fear go all the way away, I could inhale and breathe again, at least for that minute, and smell Mercy's lavender perfume and feel safe.

"Are y'all done crying yet?" Kacey said. I wiped my tears away and laughed, because I think Mercy and me had practically forgot Kacey was there with us. "Deputy Bell is waiting," they said, opening the back door.

Deputy Bell was sitting inside her police car with the AC running, saving herself from the mosquitos. She got out and took off her hat, then wiped her brow with a tissue from her back pocket, moving her body in that precise way she does. Her hair was braided into two thick plaits on either side of her head. I never would want to be on Deputy Bell's bad side. I have no plans to ever get in trouble with the law. That is a promise I will keep. The only problem is, I know my momma never had plans to get in trouble with the law neither, but the police showed up looking for her enough times that it felt regular. Maybe promising to yourself not to have any run-ins with the law is another hopeful promise. Maybe all promises are hopeful promises.

"Here they are." Mercy held up the keys.

"Mercy." Deputy Bell nodded, officially saying hello.

"I brought Kacey and Willa along," Mercy said.

"For her 'moral support,'" I explained.

"How are you, Kacey?" Concern crossed Deputy Bell's face, like she'd been worrying over Kacey since the day she'd dropped them off.

"Better than last time I saw you," Kacey said.

Deputy Bell smiled, but her eyes were sad. I figured she

might still be sad about Kacey's own mom and dad not being able to see how amazing their kid is.

We walked toward the main entrance of Midlands. Mercy looked up and all around.

"You okay?" Deputy Bell is not as tall as Mercy, but Mercy suddenly looked like she had shrunk two inches.

"I haven't been here in a long time," Mercy said.

When Mercy said *long*, she said it like she meant a hundred years. And it did look like no one had been there for a hundred years. If you give nature a chance to take over, you will have plants growing in your basement in no time. Vines reached through the windows. Spiderwebs hung from every corner. When I peeked inside the window of what looked like an office to the right of the front door, I saw black mold growing across the walls. The desks and chairs were still there, with papers on top and everything, like everyone had up and walked away from Midlands Christian Academy and hadn't bothered cleaning or packing or taking anything with them. I wondered if they'd left the boys there, too. I half expected to find them still sitting in their classroom, I swear. Or at least their ghosts, since Jack seemed to be in regular conversation with them.

Mercy put the key in the lock and jingled it around but couldn't make it turn.

"I got this." Deputy Bell went to her car and pulled a crowbar out of the trunk. I supposed this is another reason why she was there with us, in case we needed to break in, or in case we'd find anything unsafe. Truly, it looked like all the buildings could come crumbling down any second, with the vines and mold and bugs crawling on every surface.

Deputy Bell stuck the crowbar in between the door and doorframe and jimmied it open without much trouble. We caught a smell right away of musty wetness. Mice scattered like we'd interrupted a party. Once we were a few steps inside, a fat raccoon from some room somewhere waddled by and squeezed out through a hole in the back wall.

"Ha! Don't mind us!" Mercy laughed at that raccoon, which startled me because she almost sounded like an animal herself, like how a raccoon might screech if you scared it right. There could be a dozen more raccoons for all we knew.

"I'm supposed to make this building functional again?" Mercy asked. It was a "rhetorical" question, and you're not supposed to answer those. "Rise up from the ashes like a phoenix?" Mercy asked rhetorically again. "Katherine never let big ideas stop her, but this is ridiculous. This building needs to be condemned, torn down, and erased from everyone's memories for good. Forgotten, once and for all."

Mercy got angrier and angrier, but Deputy Bell didn't say anything. She let Mercy have her feelings. Still, she raised her eyebrows and gave Mercy a look like *maybe yes, maybe no*—like maybe there was more to the story. We all knew we couldn't make an entire school disappear, even one that had already been invisible for so long.

"Let's go outside. In the back," I said. Honestly, I wanted to get out of the building. It was creepy and infested and smelled not-so-good, and now I was thinking that maybe there really *were* ghosts. The outside was more promising as a venue, especially because Jack had made it beautiful with his tree sanctuary. Maybe Mercy might feel more hopeful that Midlands could host a fundraiser outside. Because how could we host people inside buildings fit to be torn down?

I walked across the creaky wood floor and tried opening the back door. It was locked, but I kept trying anyway, since

I've always been good at figuring out how to open doors that don't open. Usually, it's because their locks don't line up right or the handle needs a special touch or the knob doesn't turn the way it's supposed to. Staying in other people's trailers helps you learn these things. I kicked the door with my foot after fiddling with the stuck locks, and it popped open onto a back porch that had fallen off on one side.

"Lord, have mercy," Mercy said.

Deputy Bell let out her own laugh now, but Mercy gave her a sideways glance to let her know she was *not* trying to be funny.

"Look!" I said and pointed to the perfect rows of aspen trees with their branches leafing out in July glory and stretching toward the sky on their tippy-toes to touch heaven. I imagined their roots below the dirt, intertwined fingers cradling the earth like a baby.

"Let me go check something here—" Deputy Bell said. She carefully stepped off the porch on the side that hadn't fallen off yet. I wondered if she might be looking for Jack.

Kacey and me looked at each other, holding our breaths, unsure if Mercy was about to get the surprise of her life or not.

Deputy Bell didn't have to go far. Jack came out of the creaky-doored shed, with Benji trotting happily by his side. Jack was carrying a pot of mulch and some seedlings. The light shone down on him, and suddenly, the forsaken place was no longer forsaken, but magical.

"Welcome back," Jack said to Deputy Bell.

"Why is there somebody here?" Mercy asked, but it was a whisper, like she could see Jack was king of these woods.

I held one of Mercy's elbows and Kacey held the other. We stepped down off the rickety porch next to her and walked to the tree sanctuary. Jack took a step toward us, and then Mercy leaned on us harder, like she was going to fall. We propped her up best we could.

"Mercy?" Kacey said.

"Are you okay?" I asked.

"Jack." Mercy said his name.

I didn't know if she'd recognize him. I regretted not warning her, even if it would have meant getting in trouble, because next thing you know, Mercy fainted.

Deputy Bell ran to help us catch Mercy's body, which was limp and heavy—like her spirit had gone away to have a visit with the spirits of the dead schoolboys in the trees. Jack and Benji ran to help, too. We set her down gentle and safe on a carpet of pine needles and leaves. We looked over Mercy, who was now queen of the woods with a pine needle crown. Benji whimpered and licked her hand.

"Mercy?" Jack said.

I'd been so caught up thinking about Mercy's big surprise that I hadn't figured it out the other way around.

Benji whined and nudged Jack's hand and then licked Mercy's cheek before Jack could brush him away. Benji was as worried as the rest of us.

"You know Mercy?" Deputy Bell asked. She was probably wondering why Mercy had kept asking to kick Jack off the property if they knew each other.

"We go back," Jack said. "But I didn't know she lived in town anymore. I assumed she left. Like I did."

Jack let Benji lick Mercy's face one more time. That did the trick. Mercy's hand shot up and touched her cheek at the tickle of Benji's soft tongue. We helped her sit up, where she could get a good close look at Jack.

You could see on Jack's face that the thing he'd been hoping

for every day of his life since he was seventeen years old had
finally happened. He stared and stared at Mercy, smiling, making sure she was real. Here was a piece of Jack's past that was
not a ghost.

"Is it really you?" he asked.

Mercy nodded, and after a minute, she smiled back.

Then, for the second time that day, Mercy cried.

What We Don't Talk About

EVERYONE'S SECRETS WERE HIDDEN LIKE BURROWED ticks, filled with blood, and ready to explode.

Moe once found a dog in a shoebox outside All Creatures, a tiny mutt covered in matted brown fur. That dog was not right. Its head flopped like a marionette puppet on strings.

"Tick paralysis," Moe had said when he found six engorged ticks on its body. He removed them with tweezers, picking off fleas as he went—there were about a million of them. It was the first time he had let me help in the clinic, probably because he'd needed it so bad. I thought he might cry, taking off all those ticks and fleas. Turns out some ticks have a poison that goes into your brain and makes it so your brain won't let your body move. On top of being paralyzed, that dog was also starving.

"How could anyone do this to an animal, Moe?" I had asked.

"I like to think they didn't mean no harm, Willa-chinchilla. Maybe they didn't have enough money, or they just didn't know how to take care of a dog."

Moe had shaved its mats and treated it for fleas and heart-worms until the pathetic creature was running like new. That dog was stronger than tick venom, and the paralysis went away after a couple days. Moe named him Samson and adopted him. Samson is the happiest shaggy dog you've ever seen and never leaves Moe's side. He knows how bad life can be if it wants.

Samson needed to trust Moe, same as how I need to trust adults to take care of me. I trust Mercy more than anyone, but I also know adults can screw things up. My momma showed me that. I know we all make mistakes. When you're a kid, grown-ups try to tell you they're always right and they know every-thing. But sometimes, they are *not* people you should trust.

Deputy Bell sat next to Mercy and rubbed her back on the falling-down porch. I sat on Mercy's other side. Kacey and Jack pulled up log stools, and Benji laid down in the middle of every-one. As Mercy shared her story, I had a feeling like the Earth was falling out of space.

"The last time I saw you, Jack, I was sixteen years old. 1976. We met at the first—and last—carnival at Midlands Christian Academy for Boys."

As Mercy talked, Jack nodded like he could remember that carnival clear as yesterday.

"My aunt Katherine was a champion of trying to fix Midlands Academy. To make it part of our community. It was always on the outskirts, branded as a bad school filled with troubled students. But Aunt Katherine never believed that. She helped arrange the car-nival. She had girls from IC attend—Immaculate Conception, the Catholic girls' school where my parents sent me. The carnival was open to the entire community. I was nervous. I didn't know who I'd talk to, or if I'd be a wallflower. I walked into the dining hall, and I saw you, Jack. And my nerves fell away."

A glimmer of light shined in Mercy's eyes.

"You smiled a great big smile at me and held out your arm

to dance. I took it. I had a feeling about you. I knew you were a 'nice boy,' as Aunt Katherine would say."

"I *told* you he was nice," I said. I couldn't help it. My gut had been right about Jack from the first time I'd met him.

Mercy ignored me and kept telling her story.

"Everyone was cautious about Midlands, as if the kids who went there deserved what they got. My own parents especially believed this. But that was never the case," Mercy said.

"You don't need to tell me," Jack said. Mercy was working her understanding magic on him.

Then, Mercy looked at the ground, and I swear she was trying to work her understanding magic on herself. Probably because she was finally telling a secret she'd been keeping her whole life, which is not an easy thing to do.

"You and I danced and danced. I even remember the songs … KC and the Sunshine Band, the Bee Gees, ABBA …"

"Don't forget The Eagles," Jack said. He looked like he might start dancing just thinking about it. Mercy laughed, and I felt like the world wasn't spinning off into space so much anymore.

"We went outside to play some games," Mercy continued. "That's when you met my aunt Katherine, who'd brought her daughter, Meredith, with her. Goodness, Meredith was only three at the time. I'd built that carnival up in my head for weeks, and when it turned out to be everything I'd hoped for—and more, because I met you—it felt like I was flying."

"Me too," Jack said. He couldn't stop smiling at Mercy.

"When we rode the rickety carnival Ferris wheel, we had some privacy. I suddenly felt so grown up. Some kind of courage came over me, because that's when I kissed you."

"You kissed?!" Kacey and me said together. Now we were the ones in shock. Mercy, Jack, and Deputy Bell all laughed.

"It's true!" Jack said, seeming happy and bashful.

"We were just children." Mercy smiled. "But then—" Her smile disappeared.

"'But then' is right," Jack said.

"But then, everything changed," Mercy finished, looking like she didn't want to talk anymore. Deputy Bell gave her some water, and Mercy went on.

"Midlands Academy had a young principal at the time. Mr. Winter," Mercy said.

I had to stop myself from nodding even though I knew exactly who Mercy was talking about from Katherine's diaries. Hearing her say Mr. Winter's name gave me a chill. Kacey and me gave each other a look.

"He wasn't that much older than us, I imagine," Mercy said. "I don't know what he thought the carnival was supposed to be, but he couldn't stand that all his students were having so much fun. Because for him, juvenile delinquents didn't deserve to have fun."

"Fun definitely was not allowed at Midlands," Jack agreed.

"Exactly," Mercy said. "Mr. Winter did not like that. 'Bad' kids shouldn't be rewarded with a carnival. Right?"

Jack watched Mercy with his eyebrows pulled down, like there was a lot he could say. Instead, he listened.

"Aunt Katherine came back to pick me up, and you and I said our goodbyes. We promised to see each other again soon. I thought I was falling in love. You know how it is when you're sixteen."

"Oh, yes, I do." Deputy Bell chimed in.

I did not know how it was when you are sixteen, but I could imagine Mercy had been having butterflies with Jack the same way I had been having butterflies with Finn.

"Then the rumors started," Mercy said.

"What rumors?" I asked.

"Mercy, you don't have to—" Jack said.

"No, I do," Mercy interrupted. "That is, unless you'd rather I stop."

"It's just … the kids—" Jack pointed his head toward Kacey and me.

"I can talk about it with Willa and Kacey," Mercy said. "They've discussed similar topics in the classroom. Besides, I need to let this go. It has eaten away at me every day of my life since it happened."

"Mine too," Jack said. He looked sad when he nodded at Mercy, like he understood they needed to talk about it, but also like he wished he could make the conversation disappear.

"I didn't mean …" Mercy's words trailed off.

"I know," Jack said. "It's okay."

"What happened?" Kacey asked.

Mercy took a deep breath before starting again.

"Mr. Winter called my mother and told her that Jack had assaulted me at the carnival," Mercy said. "He claimed that Jack had touched me inappropriately without my permission."

"Why am I not surprised?" Deputy Bell said in a sharp tone.

Kacey and me were definitely old enough to know what Mercy was talking about. Miss Samantha had been teaching us about consent in Human Growth and Development classes.

"That's when I started to become well acquainted with this shed," Jack said, pointing at his garden shed. "Mr. Winter sent me to spend the first of many nights out here. I didn't know why at the time. When I asked, the only explanation I got was, 'You know why, son.' I hated when he called me 'son.'"

"Was it cold?" Kacey asked.

"Thankfully, no," Jack said. "But cold weather never stopped him from using the shed. Boys died out here. Two while I was going to Midlands, and who knows how many others. We were all trapped. I remember hoping the carnival would create some change for good. That maybe we wouldn't be so alone anymore. But instead, things only got worse."

"It was as though the community was *waiting* for something terrible to happen at that carnival, to prove something about Midlands and the students who went there," Mercy said. "My mother gobbled up Mr. Winter's lie, as did many others."

Kacey and me looked at each other. We finally knew what had happened that night to change both Jack and Mercy's lives forever.

"It was all a lie," I said.

Mercy nodded. "Mr. Winter had made up a lie that Jack had somehow attacked me, without a shred of evidence—"

"Because there was none," Jack finished.

"There was none," Mercy said, repeating Jack's words. "Mr. Winter had given himself an excuse to be as tough on Jack as he wanted. My reputation was tarnished. No matter what I said, no one would listen. Not my parents. Not my teachers. I felt like my life was over."

"I'm confused," Kacey interrupted. "Even if the rumor had been true about what Jack did to you, why was your reputation ruined?"

"Victim blaming," Deputy Bell explained angrily. "If an assault happens to a young woman, it must have been *her* fault. Or so the thinking goes."

"Neither Mercy nor I could escape being damaged by Mr. Winter's accusation," Jack said. "Especially because nobody would listen to us. I was so angry when I finally found out what he'd said. Which only got me into more trouble, because I tried speaking my truth. I was young and naïve enough to still think there might be some justice in this world."

Jack made me remember the last line Katherine ever wrote in her diaries: "… *there will never be a time when the world is just.*"

"I was so worried about you, Jack," Mercy said. "My mother forbade me from ever seeing you again. She said vile things about you, without ever even meeting you. But it gets worse than that …"

Deputy Bell kept offering Mercy sips of water, which is a helpful thing to do if you're with someone who is upset. Mercy pulled a tissue from her pocket and dabbed her eyes.

"I didn't *want* to see you," she said. "I was too afraid of what would happen. And not just to you, Jack, but to *me*. I was a coward."

I wanted to hold up Mercy's heart and tell her, *It's okay.*

"You were a kid," Jack said. "So was I."

"We were powerless," Mercy said.

Deputy Bell hugged Mercy. I bet Jack would have hugged Mercy, too, if it hadn't been forty years since he'd seen her. He had fire in his eyes and was balling his hand into a fist, pumping it like a beating heart. Benji sat up and pawed Jack, nudging his armpit and trying to hug him.

"I realized my mother would never believe me," Mercy said. "She didn't want to. She made the entire situation worse by spreading Mr. Winter's lie far and wide. She asked my father to sue the school, which caused a stir because my grandfather was on the board. I finally saw my parents for who they were. Cold, privileged people who were used to wielding their power to get whatever they wanted. It wasn't a big surprise. But after that, I grew up fast. And I left. I moved in with Aunt Katherine and Uncle Edward and never looked back.

Mother was so ashamed. It felt like she was glad to see me go. I was still only in high school, but that's when we stopped speaking to each other."

"Is that why you never had your own family?" I asked.

"That is just how my life ended up playing out," Mercy said, looking at Jack. "All you kids are my family now." She put her arm around me and reached for Kacey's hand.

Tears came to my eyes, because the Southern Ohio Children's Home was filled with kids whose mothers couldn't be a mother for one reason or another. And here was Mercy, who would've been the best mother on planet Earth, but maybe the wound in her heart—the scab from Mercy's *before*—was too deep.

"I feel like nothing makes any sense," I said.

There *had* been something Mercy wasn't telling me—I'd been right about that all along. Except I never could've imagined it was this giant secret from her past that had been haunting her all these years.

"Life often doesn't make sense, Willa." Mercy comforted me, which might have made her feel better, since that's the way it usually was—her comforting me and not the other way around. She looked off toward the shed like she was looking straight into the past.

"You know what really doesn't make sense?" she asked.

Deputy Bell, Kacey, Jack, and me shook our heads and listened hard.

"*I* kissed *you*!" Mercy said, smiling at Jack. "A sweet, innocent first kiss. I had the wonderful memory of you, Jack, for one night—*one night*—before it got twisted into something evil."

"Sometimes, that's how the story goes," Deputy Bell said. It seemed like she had known what the ending was going to be all along, and that ending made her mad. I could tell she had the same amount of madness as my sadness. "I'm sorry, Jack. I had no idea," she said.

"I moved on," Jack said. "I had no choice but to get out and get on with life."

"And to think you've been here, so close," Mercy said, light returning to her eyes.

"At least no one can touch us now," he said with a smile.

Jack took Mercy's hand in both of his, releasing the ghost of a secret big enough to change a life from what it might have been.

It was time for me to release my secrets, too.

"Mercy, there's something I have to show you." I pulled Jack's letter out of my pocket and gave it to her. Mercy unfolded it.

"What on earth?" I could tell she recognized it right away. "I haven't seen this letter in years! How did you get this, Willa?"

"Promise not to be mad?" I asked.

But Mercy was done making hopeful promises that day.

We said goodbye to Deputy Bell and Jack and Benji. Jack told Deputy Bell that he needed to show her some items he'd found—with Benji's help—while digging up the dirt and planting his garden. "There is truth in this ground," he'd told her.

Mercy, Kacey, and me got back in the van to return home. Mercy drove silently with Jack's letter safely in her lap. It was back with her for good. I looked at Mercy with new eyes, seeing her scared, brave self right up close. She had a *before* story too, same as every kid living under her roof.

"Mercy, I'm sorry I never told you about Jack." I felt my

sorry-ness in every bone of my body. I wished I could take all Mercy's hurt away.

"I'm sorry, too," Kacey said. They'd remembered our deal and were sitting shotgun.

"How much did you two know, if you knew about Jack?" Now Mercy was the one who needed information.

"We'll explain everything. I promise," I said, knowing it was a promise I would keep.

"I can't wait to hear this," Mercy said, letting out a small laugh. She could not believe the day she was having.

"Thank you both for being strong and brave," Mercy said. "You help me more than you'll ever know. All of you kids. You heal my heart every day."

My heart swelled at Mercy's words.

We pulled into the driveway, and Mercy dropped us at the front door. Kacey and me ran straight to The Fortress.

"Justin, come on! We have to tell Mercy about the diaries," I said.

Kacey jumped up to their bed to grab our notebook from under the covers.

"What diaries?" Elizabeth asked. She and Roy were playing War with his deck of cards, while Justin read at the throne-desk. Clover purred sweetly, curled up in a circle on my bed.

"Won't we get in trouble?" Justin asked.

"Are you in trouble again, Willa?" Elizabeth asked.

"No!" I yelled. Sometimes Elizabeth knows how to set me off.

"Trust us," Kacey said. "It's now or never."

"Mercy knows about Jack," I explained.

"She does?" Justin looked scared. He closed his book.

Elizabeth jumped up from the card game and grabbed Lovey-Pup.

"But I was winning!" Roy threw his cards across the floor and followed us downstairs.

"Are we in trouble?" Justin asked again.

I was keeping all my fingers and toes crossed that Mercy would have sympathy on us.

"I don't know yet," I said.

By the time we got ourselves down to the library, Mercy was sitting on the red couch with Meredith by her side.

"So, Willa, tell me about Jack's letter." Mercy held it in her hand.

"We found it in Miss Katherine's diary from 1976," I said.

"Which I told you not to read," Mercy said.

"I know, but—" I started to protest.

"I led them to it, Mercy," Meredith admitted. "I didn't know there was anything personal in there about you."

"There's more," Justin said, relieved to finally fess up to our crimes. He, Kacey, and me looked at each other, daring anyone to go first.

Kacey walked to the secret shelf.

"This is where Katherine kept her diaries." Kacey pushed the latch, which popped the shelf out.

"Fun fact," Justin said. "Your grandfather had this made during Prohibition. For hiding alcohol."

"Wow!" Roy said, bouncing on his toes to see better.

Meredith jumped from the couch to see for herself. "Mom *did* keep them!" She saw all Katherine's diaries on the shelf, just how we'd left them. "I've been looking for years! Did you know about this shelf, Mercy?"

"I certainly did not. I thought Grandfather was a teetotaler."

"What's a teetotaler?" Elizabeth asked.

"Someone who doesn't drink alcohol," Meredith explained.

Mercy was so surprised. I was feeling bad for giving her so many surprises in one day.

And we weren't done yet.

"There's something else we should tell you," I said.

"There's more?" I could tell Mercy was fearful of what would come out of my mouth next.

I shut my eyes and confessed. "We read them all."

"You what?" Mercy said.

"*All* of them?" Meredith asked.

"All of them," I confirmed. I kept my eyes on the floor. If we were going to get in trouble, now was the time.

"Here's the good stuff," Kacey said, handing our notebook to Meredith.

"We needed information!" I said.

"What did you possibly need 'information' for?" Mercy asked.

Justin stepped forward and cleared his throat. "Mercy?"

"Yes, Justin?" She seemed surprised that Justin was also in on our secret.

"No one ever says anything about Midlands Christian Academy," he said. "No one ever talks about what happened there. Not then, and not now. Everyone pretends it never existed."

Mercy nodded her head in agreement and sighed. She was glued to her spot on the couch, her energy tank low from having so many emotions in one day.

Meanwhile, Meredith was taking her mother's diaries out of their secret hiding place. There was no need to keep them hidden anymore. Elizabeth put Lovey-Pup in the now-empty cubbyhole, playing hide-and-seek.

"Can you show us again, Kacey?" she asked.

"Sure." Kacey showed Elizabeth where the latch was.

Elizabeth squealed when the shelf opened again, even though she already knew it would and that she'd find her stuffed dog inside.

"Why do there have to be so many secrets, Mercy?" I asked.

"Good question," Meredith said.

"You're right," Mercy said. "The kids are right. Why must we have secrets? We've had so many. And for what? To protect ourselves and each other? Secrets only end up causing harm. Prolonging harm. They make us hang on to our heartache for longer than necessary. From now on, let's not keep any more secrets. Our lives will be better that way."

"Amen," Meredith said.

"No more secrets!" I said.

I breathed a sigh of relief—about the secrets, but also about not getting in trouble. After all, everyone had been guilty of keeping secrets. Even Katherine.

There was only one problem: I still had my secret cat.

Changing a System

LIBRARIES ARE SACRED, MAGICAL SPACES. Walking through the door of a library fills you with power.

The red couch in the Southern Ohio Children's Home library is the most magical spot in the entire house, because you can sink into it forever. Add a good book, and you will be swallowed up inside the safest hug you ever felt. There are the tall windows and quiet curtains, endless books, and of course, a secret bookshelf. Libraries give you a feeling there is always more to discover. If you read all those books, there is nothing in this world you cannot know.

Katherine knew the power of libraries. That's why she started one for Midlands Academy. The quote she'd inscribed on our library wall had a whole new meaning to me now:

You think your pain and your heartbreak are unprecedented in the history of the world, but then you read.

I understand now why Katherine loved James Baldwin's words so much that she put them on her wall for everyone to see, even after she was gone from this world.

Katherine's legacy breathes through the library walls and bookshelves. She feels alive to me, as if she's been sitting at her desk guiding me this whole time. A gentle spirit and protector of Mercy, Meredith, me, Kacey, Justin, and the Southern Ohio Children's Home. Knowing how much she loved Mercy makes me love Katherine. It's because of her that I am safe and cared for now.

But it's also because of her that the Southern Ohio Children's Home might close.

I must have been crying while rereading all her diaries out in the open. I was cuddled deep into the couch with that sad-happy feeling you get when you're reading a story where something bad happens, but you know there's going to be a happy ending.

I don't know if there will be a happy ending to *my* story.

I was thinking a lot about the boys from Midlands Christian Academy and how they were abused, and how some of them had even died. How many had died? What happened to them when the reformatory school closed? What would happen to me if *my* home closed? Where would I go? I couldn't picture my life without the Southern Ohio Children's Home.

The Black Hole of My Future blanketed my safe space in a choking darkness. I got a feeling like I might disappear from this life if the home went away.

These thoughts were heavy in my mind when Miss Samantha and Kacey came and found me. I had been making so many soaps and candles and bracelets and herb sachets that they noticed when I up and stopped coming to our craft table one day. I'd been focused on creating items to save our home because it was the only thing to keep my mind off my fear. That, and taking care of Clover, who'd been sleeping real close in my bed each night. She'd been nuzzling and purring into my neck extra after having her spaying surgery. She is a good cat. They are secretive creatures, and Clover is *definitely* in on being a secret.

But I needed a break.

"Where you at, Willa?" Miss Samantha asked. She meant "where you at," like my head and my heart, wondering what my feelings were doing. Mercy had trained her with the listening power where she gets close and looks you in the eye, so you know she wants to find out exactly what is happening inside your brain, as if she needs to know that in order to continue living on this Earth.

"I've reread all Miss Katherine's diaries." I held up the one I'd just finished. It was the most recent diary, the one she wrote leading up to the days when she was dying.

"That couldn't have been easy. She wrote a *lot*," Kacey said, pulling up a chair.

"What'd you learn from them?" Miss Samantha asked.

"That there is a lot of injustice in this world."

"That's true," Miss Samantha said. "Some days, I think it will always be true. But other days, I think we really can make a change."

"Miss Katherine tried and tried," I said, "but nothing ever changed. She got Midlands shut down, but what happened after that? What has changed?"

"She helped create a better school right here," Miss Samantha said.

"What about all the students who were at Midlands? What happened to them?" I asked.

"Do you think any of them came here?" Kacey asked.

"That would have been long before I started teaching," Miss Samantha said. "I was still a little girl myself. All those boys are grown men by now."

"At least the ones who survived," I said.

I put the diary back on the desk next to all the other diaries, which were no longer hidden in the cubbyhole. Then I returned to the couch and curled up in a Mrs. Harbour blanket. It was a hot day, but the new AC blasted freezing air.

Miss Samantha grabbed the other half of the blanket and covered her legs. "I've been thinking about how to fix things," she said. "There's no easy way to undo what's been done."

"It's like the whole world is built to help some people but hurt others," Kacey said.

"Yeah, like how it hurt the boys at Midlands, because everyone thought they were bad. And like how it hurt my mom," I said. "No one cares about people who get hooked on drugs—even if they didn't ever want to. They're 'no good' because they use drugs."

"You're not wrong, Willa," said Miss Samantha. "I saw it with my sister. There's little empathy for addicts. Many people consider it a moral failure. Not many people stop to think about how, or why, addicts got there in the first place."

"Or how to help them," Kacey said. They put their feet up on the couch so they could get a few inches of blanket. "My mom says I'm 'no good' because I'm different."

"It's not right, Kacey," Miss Samantha said. "If your mom was looking with clear eyes, she'd see we're *all* different from each other. You, me, Willa … every child who lives here."

"And everyone who works here," I added. I thought about Emily having Down syndrome and how that makes her different, but it's also what makes her special. "Being different from each other is what makes each of us special for being who we are."

We sat under the blanket and stared out the tall windows, our thoughts stuck inside a hurt so big you can't do anything about it.

"Sometimes, I think about the messiness of it all in terms of roads and cars," Miss Samantha said.

I did not want to embarrass Miss Samantha, but I had no idea what she was talking about. She must have seen that on my face and Kacey's, too.

"All the roads in Ohio, and in the entire United States, are a system," Miss Samantha clarified. "Roads are built for cars and trucks, right? But sometimes, other things are on the road."

"Like bikes," I said.

"Yes, bikes," Miss Samantha nodded. "Or pedestrians."

"Or turtles," Kacey said.

"I hadn't thought of that, but—yes—turtles," Miss Samantha agreed.

"Or a helpless little kitten," I added.

"How does it feel riding your bike on County Highway J, Willa?" Miss Samantha asked.

I shrugged. "Fine, I guess. I feel free when I ride my bike. Until a car goes by real fast and doesn't get over to the other side of the road, even when there aren't any other cars."

"The driver might not want you riding your bike on 'their' road," Miss Samantha said. "They might not notice you because they're more concerned about getting where they need to go."

I nodded. "They won't even stop if they hit a deer, I swear."

"Changing systems is hard," Miss Samantha said. "Because even if there are flaws, there is a tendency to accept or overlook them."

"Like roadkill," Kacey said.

I have seen plenty of dead animals along that highway, and it makes me sad every single time.

"Listen," Miss Samantha made sure we were paying attention. "Schools are part of a system. So is government. And hospitals. Systems are everywhere, in every institution you can think of. They feel normal, but they do not work for everybody. For example, the highway system works if you have a car. And education works great for kids at schools with plenty of resources."

"Everything works better for people who have money," I said, thinking about my family, who was always struggling.

"Are bathrooms a system?" Kacey asked. "Because if they are, boy bathrooms and girl bathrooms don't work for me."

"Yes, Kacey," said Miss Samantha. "Being nonbinary doesn't work with the system in place for bathrooms, and I'm sure you've noticed how hard it is to make change."

I was starting to understand why all our problems felt so big. They weren't just problems about boys at Midlands Academy, or drug users causing a crisis in our community, or Kacey's mom not accepting them for who they are. "The problem is everything!" I said, panicked.

"Let's be more specific," Miss Samantha said. "The education system did not work for students at Midlands. And our healthcare system is not working for addicts. It's not the students or the addicts who are broken; it's the systems. And *those* are what's hard to fix."

I felt so hopeless, I wanted to jump headfirst into the Black Hole.

"Willa, Kacey, this is your chance to make a difference." Miss Samantha pulled me back from the edge of the Black Hole. "If the community shows up how we need it to at our fundraiser, it's an opportunity to do something about a faulty system that has been in place since way before we were born. It's what Miss Katherine was fighting for her whole life. Her legacy is for the fight to continue."

Miss Samantha's voice was soft, but it burned.

"Mercy's Aunt Katherine would be surprised by how the world has changed since she died," Miss Samantha said. "She hadn't even known if anyone would find her letter, but she hoped. She never stopped hoping. You embody her hope, and if each of you tells your story, *that* is what will make people listen. Telling our stories can change systems."

There was nothing scarier in the world to me than telling my story. I'd rather ride my bike down the middle of an actual highway with six lanes of speeding cars.

My story is what I try to forget at our Forgetting Ceremonies with my Forgetting Letter buried in a box inside the earth, so earthworms can eat it and make it part of the earth again.

But the earth has a memory, even though we pretend it doesn't. You can't ever get rid of memories all the way, can you? No matter how hard you try. Somewhere, there are still memories of everything that had happened at Midlands Christian Academy for Boys. Jack and Benji had already found some.

I knew Miss Samantha was right. I knew it deep in my chest, which felt tight but also full of power. Even though it was scary, I knew I had to do it, because if I didn't, I wouldn't find out what would happen with all the power inside of me.

That feeling was telling me I had to write my story, not to *forget* it, but to make it so everyone else could *remember*.

I didn't know what would happen after I did that, but I did know I trusted Miss Samantha, and that telling my story was something both Kacey and me needed to do. And so did

Justin and Roy and Elizabeth, and every child at the Southern Ohio Children's Home. All of us had a story, and our stories put together could help fix a broken system.

"If a system isn't working for everyone, it's failing," Miss Samantha went on. "People get so comfortable driving in their cars, they forget about bikers or animals using the road. They forget that not everyone has a car. You can help them remember."

"I'm going to need your help," I told Miss Samantha.

"Me too," Kacey said.

Kacey felt a special bond with Miss Samantha now. She had taken them to talk to a doctor about making it so they wouldn't have to get their period anymore. Kacey had the biggest smile on their face when they told me, like they had a new discovery about the kind of person they are. If it hadn't been for that doctor's office visit, I don't know if Kacey would have agreed to tell anybody anything about their story.

"Of course I'll help," Miss Samantha said.

I was proud of both Kacey and me for asking Miss Samantha for help. That was something Mercy was always teaching us—to ask for help when we need it. She says it is something she herself has a hard time doing. And she isn't talking about help like feeding the chickens or making your bed (although it is okay to ask for help for those things, too).

She's talking about asking for help those times when you do not *want* to ask for help, either because you are being stubborn or because you want to show you don't need anybody's help. (Like how Roy will shout, *Leave me alone, I can do it myself!* and we leave him alone for five minutes until he shouts, *I need help!* like we weren't there all along.) Mercy was always telling us, in all capital letters, *IT IS OKAY TO ASK FOR HELP.* Maybe partly because she was always telling herself it is okay to ask for help. I understand why it is hard. It was hard for me now because I was asking for help for something I did not want to do but knew I had to.

Asking for Miss Samantha's help was admitting to myself that I was going to tell my story and there was no backing out, even if the thought of sharing made me want to disappear and run away from the problem, which I knew I couldn't do. Grammaw was always saying that to Momma: *You can't run away from your problems forever.* My momma ran and ran and ran.

Miss Samantha gave me and Kacey each a hug. She told us in her syrupy voice that she loves us, and that she was so proud of us she could cry.

I did cry. When someone tells you they are proud of you just for being who you are, it's magic.

The Remembering Ceremony

SUDDENLY, WE WERE BUSY REMEMBERING our *befores*—the exact *opposite* of what we'd been doing all along. Our *befores* are why we had Forgetting Ceremonies, to forget the time in our lives when things went so wrong, our families couldn't keep us. We were used to not talking about *before*, but now, here we were, spilling our guts.

I didn't want to share what I was writing. I don't want anyone to know the bad stuff from *before*, but the point of the essay is to read it in front of the entire community—the outside community—so they'll all know. I'm most afraid that people will feel sorry for me. I don't want anyone thinking anything about me, good or bad, because of something my momma did. I'd rather they see me, Willa Johnson, and not a drug addict's daughter. By writing my story, I'm also learning to see myself in a certain way—as my*self*.

All our stories have sad parts. But it's not all sad-sadness. There *is* a happiness part, too, because now we're with Mercy and with each other, but I wasn't writing about the happy parts in my essay.

We switched from making crafts in Miss Samantha's classroom (we'd made enough, I promise you) to writing essays in the library or The Fortress or at the kitchen table, when Charlie and Emily didn't mind the extra company.

To make it safe for people to be at Midlands Academy, Deputy Bell brought over an army of police officers and volunteers from the United Church of Christ to help clean up a small part of the forgotten place. She had roped off parts of the woods, to keep the fundraiser within a designated area—for safety, I figured.

Sisters Hazel and Constance, along with other nuns from the mission, came to help, too. They weeded and hacked at vines and repaired the porch and painted where mold had taken over. After a few weekends, the Midlands property was transformed. It surprised Mercy.

"Maybe this *is* possible after all," she'd said when we went to take a peek.

Mr. Harbour had managed to get some tents that Shawneeville Central used at their football games, to put over the tables that were full of our handmade goods. We had ten craft tables in all, with extra inventory boxes nearby. We were going to give out flyers with every purchase, explaining how Midlands Academy needed to reopen as a community center.

Jack finally had help making a community garden. His friend at the nursery donated some end-of-season plants, along with some volunteers to plant them. Jack told them what to put where, and we watched as his vision for the garden came to life.

We put out 150 folding chairs in rows, which looked like pews for parishioners. The sanctuary looked more real than ever.

Miss Samantha printed our essays and posted them on the aspen trees, up and down the sanctuary aisle. It helped knowing my words were already out there.

The fundraiser started at 9:00 a.m. on Saturday morning. I got real nervous when no one except Finn and Mr. and Mrs. Harbour showed up until 9:30. Each of us was reading at the top of the hour, and Meredith was making announcements every half-hour about what to buy and how to help our community. When Meredith talks, you feel like you have to do what she's asking. She is never not in charge.

Before it was my turn to read, I looked around at the medium-sized crowd and had a sinking feeling that even though we were doing everything we could, it still would not be enough.

"How could we have ever thought selling a few candles would save us?" I said to Kacey.

Their dad had called Mercy to let her know he'd be there—without Kacey's mother. Kacey scanned the crowd, looking for him. They were wearing nice blue jeans, a buttoned shirt, and a striped tie.

"You look handsome," I said. I admit, we did seem grown up with our dress clothes on.

"Thanks, so do you," they said, even though I'd never imagined myself as being "handsome," but it sounded better to my ears than "pretty" or "cute." Wearing a dress made me more nervous because I never wear dresses.

"Your dad is going to be so proud of you," I said.

We'd been practicing reading our essays to each other, but that was nothing compared to reading in front of perfect strangers. The outside community was starting to show up, but the crowd was sparse and spread out in clumps, like the coat of a mangy dog. Even Moe had stepped away from All Creatures. He brought Samson and introduced him to Benji. They were both happy to make a new friend. Deputy Bell came with her family, looking like a different person because she was wearing a dress, not a police uniform.

When Miss Samantha introduced me at the podium, on top of being nervous, I was sad. I looked at my feet, which is something Miss Samantha had told me not to do. Meredith had rented a microphone and a speaker, so even if I was looking down, everyone would be able to hear my voice. I smelled the bug spray I'd sprayed all over my body. Charlie had lit citronella torches for the mosquitos, but those do not work, and I was afraid they'd start a fire.

Kacey sat close by and gave me a thumbs-up, which provided the ounce of courage I needed to begin.

"My name is Willa Johnson, and I am 11 years old. The first time I saw my mom die, I was four years old. She'd sent me into the Family Dollar to buy my favorite cereal, while she waited in the car. I loved when she let me do that because it made me feel grown up, which is a good way to feel when you're four. They have all the marshmallow cereals right there on the bottom shelf so you can grab them even if you're a little kid. I got a box of Lucky Charms. It might have been the kind with just the marshmallows, or maybe I wish it was the kind with just the marshmallows, because the cereal with just the marshmallows would make the memory less bad. How many times have you ever had a box of cereal where you got just the marshmallows? I think you'd remember it, too."

People came over to the podium when I started reading my story. By the time I got to the part about the marshmallows, they laughed, and I felt a little better about saying my story out loud.

"I grabbed the cereal and gave the checkout lady my five-dol-lar bill, then held my hand out for the change. I went back outside to where my mom had pulled the car up to wait for me, but when I opened the front door to give her the change, she was slumped over the steering wheel. Her drugs were still in her arm, and her face was turning blue. I thought for sure she wasn't breathing, and I started screaming and crying so loud. Her cheek was smooshed against the top of the steering wheel, and something foamy was coming out of her mouth."

At this part of my story, anyone who was listening was shaking their head and looking worried. It's the part I hate most, but I looked at Miss Samantha, who promised to be right by my side—by all of us while we read our stories. She nodded at me, which told me I was doing good, and that I should keep going like we'd practiced.

"I shoved my mom to get her to wake up from being dead. I hugged her and held her cheeks the way we did when we were snuggling when she'd tuck me in at night. But she wasn't moving, and her body was heavy and not right. I kept screaming and crying and eventually somebody came. And then more people came, and suddenly all these grown-ups surrounded my mom and pushed me away. They tried dragging her out of the car. I was crying more and more. 'Inconsolable' is what you'd call it. I've seen toddlers get that way at the Southern Ohio Children's Home. It is not pretty, trust me."

I heard people laugh at this part, too, even though it was scary and I was being serious.

It was strange then during my reading, because everyone seemed to take a few steps closer, same as the people at the Family Dollar did, like they wanted to get right in and help take care of me. That is an overwhelming feeling, everyone crowding you like that.

I looked at Miss Samantha again. She nodded, and I looked across to the other side of the podium and saw Jack and Benji and Moe and Samson. Jack also nodded at me to tell me to keep going, and so did Moe. I looked at my feet again to try and get up some more courage.

are some of my happiest memories. I love cookies almost as much as I loved my momma. We couldn't make a batch of cookies without eating half right away. I remember she was so happy, too. She hugged me hard and told me how much she loved me. She said she was sorry. I didn't care, though. I thought I'd never be sad ever again for the rest of my life, because of how lucky I was. Who ever gets their momma back after she died?"

The crowd was real quiet now. Everyone looked at me, waiting for me to say more words, which usually is an easy thing for me, to blurt words out. But I didn't expect to see people wiping their eyes and crying, and I didn't want anyone feeling sorry for me.

That's what made me keep going.

"The rest of my story isn't hard to figure out. My momma was a drug addict who eventually died for real from an overdose. I am an orphan now, living here at the Southern Ohio Children's Home. I have lived my life knowing about the crisis in our community because of opioid addiction, and I have only seen the problem get worse. Over the past several years, there have been more and more orphans because of the crisis. If the other parents who became lost to their children were anything like my mom, I know they would not choose this. They would not choose to have an addiction to drugs. But there is nothing in our community to help them stop being addicted to drugs. Getting arrested and going to jail doesn't help them. Spending a couple nights at the hospital after having an overdose like my momma did doesn't help them. Judging them does not help them. I have been ashamed for my mom, but I know in my heart I don't need to be. I

miss her more than anything. She wasn't a perfect mom, but she loved me. I know that for sure, and that's why I know her problems were too much for her to fix by herself, even though she tried. She would have fixed them if she could have, because my momma loved me.

"I am grateful for the Southern Ohio Children's Home, for Mercy, for Miss Samantha, for Charlie and Emily—for everyone who takes care of us every day. The home is my home. It is my community. This school that used to be for boys who people said were 'bad' is going to be a new part of our community now, where people who are like my momma was can come and get help. Because I don't think there's any such thing as a 'bad' person."

I was done then. I didn't have a big flashy ending to my story, but when I stepped away from the podium, everybody clapped real hard. I'd done a good job.

I was relieved because it was over, but also because now everyone knew where I'd come from, and why. I didn't have that big secret about my momma anymore. The strange thing was that after I got my story out, it felt like it hadn't ever been such a big secret in the first place. Everyone at the fundraiser had someone they knew—a friend or neighbor or coworker or family—who had the same kinds of problems as my momma did.

"Willa, I am proud of you," Mrs. Harbour said when I walked by her. "Your momma would be so proud of you." She was sitting in a folding chair toward the back. I had to bend down to wrap my arms around her skinny shoulders when she reached up to give me a hug.

Finn was standing there, too. I smiled kind of shy at him, because he hadn't ever heard me talk about Momma being a drug addict, and I don't know if his mom or dad ever talk to him about why I am at the Southern Ohio Children's Home. He surprised me by giving me a hug right there in front of his parents, which is not a big deal except my stomach had a thousand butterflies flying all around. I was worried I might hug him back too tight or for too long because that's what I wanted to do. I hugged him back, but maybe I didn't hug him enough to make up for wanting to hug him real tight, or maybe I still hugged him too hard. I don't know. I do know that I feel like fainting when I think about hugging Finn. Good fainting, not bad fainting like what Mercy did from nearly having a heart attack when she saw Jack.

"You were brave to read your story, Willa." Mr. Harbour gave me a nice strong thump on my back. I was glad I didn't have to figure out how to hug him, too.

"I need to talk to Mercy about her plans for Midlands." Mr. Harbour surveyed the land and buildings like he was remembering how it looked years ago, when he'd taught English here.

"Helping Mercy will keep you from going stir-crazy after you retire," Mrs. Harbour said to Mr. Harbour, then turned toward me. "Otherwise, he might hover in the kitchen all day, eating pies and what-not."

"Mr. Harbour?" Jack joined our little group, along with Benji.

Mr. Harbour held out his hand, and he and Jack shook in that strong way you're taught to when you learn how to give a handshake.

"I'm Jack Thompson. You taught my English class."

"That's right … Jack Thompson." *Now* Mr. Harbour remembered Jack, just like I knew he probably did all along, because he remembers every last one of his students. Maybe I could forgive him for lying when I had asked him about Jack at dinner that night. Maybe he had just wanted to protect me because of stories he'd heard about Jack Thompson and Mercy after the carnival.

"How's life been treating you, Jack?" Mr. Harbour asked.

"Good! Life's good," Jack said. "I joined the Army after leaving Shawneeville. Wasn't sure what else I should do. And good thing I did, because I sang in the Soldiers' Chorus for 25 years. I'm a music teacher over in Virginia now." Jack smiled telling his story, which had turned out to have a lot of happiness.

"What brings you back?" Mr. Harbour asked him.

"I guess you could say I couldn't shake my memories of this place."

Mr. Harbour looked away and rubbed the back of his neck, which made me wonder again if he knew the whole story, the one I finally knew, about Jack and Mercy and Mr. Winter.

"Jack planted these aspen trees," I blurted out. I wanted everyone to know it was Jack's garden.

"There were times I thought nobody would ever come see these woods or this school again," Jack said. "Back when I was gathering up aspen saplings and planting them in their new home. There were times I was so angry, I couldn't picture how those saplings would grow into something so majestic, even though I must have dreamed it. I also couldn't picture how this school could be redeemed. But I feel different about that today."

"Thank you, Jack." Mr. Harbour surprised Jack by hugging him. They shared a new common purpose: to help Mercy bring Katherine's dying wish to life.

Mercy walked by us and up the aisle to the podium, where Meredith held the microphone.

"… we've just received a generous donation from Ian and Maria Banks!" Meredith was saying to a round of applause.

"Thank you! Please be sure to check out all the fine handmade goods for sale today. And ask any of us how you can donate to the Southern Ohio Children's Home and the new community center. For the next hour, I personally will match all donations!"

Meredith took off her sunglasses and curtsied as the crowd clapped and whooped. Then she passed the microphone to Mercy.

"Thank you all for being here today." Mercy fiddled with the microphone until she was sure she had it on. Her hands shook with a case of nerves. She wore her favorite lavender scarf, and I could tell she'd washed her hair that morning because her long gray curls were extra soft.

"It pains me to think that the Southern Ohio Children's Home might not be able to serve our community much longer, but thanks to donations and support from you, we have a chance. As happens to me every day, I am inspired by the children who live here. I am inspired by the teachers and assistants. By Miss Samantha, who encouraged our students to write and share their stories. I'm reminded today just how important each and every story is."

The crowd grew quiet listening to Mercy. Jack, Mr. Harbour, Finn, and me all sat down in chairs near Mrs. Harbour. Jack caught Justin's eye and waved him over. Justin smiled and took a seat next to Jack; he'd been keeping close to him all day, headphones snug around his neck (they'd moved down off his ears). Roy and Elizabeth sat in front, near Miss Samantha. Kacey stood off to the side, pretending like they weren't searching everywhere for their dad. They'd asked Miss Samantha if they could tell their remembering story last, because Kacey was afraid their dad might miss it if they read too early.

"I would like to use this opportunity to share *my* story,"

Mercy said. "I am also good at forgetting. But the children's bravery—I am so proud of you all—their bravery reminds me that it is by *remembering* that we ensure past mistakes are not repeated."

Jack looked at Mercy with so much love in his eyes. It felt like we were at church and Mercy was our minister, giving us a sermon.

"My story is about motherhood and orphans. I never became a mother myself. My own experiences instead set me on my path to help children who need a home. I am fortunate to have mothered hundreds of children. All of us were children once. It's an identity everyone shares. In fact, it's the *only* identity we *all* share. Childhood. Can you remember what it was like? The magic? The fear? When I was sixteen, my childhood ended abruptly. In a sense, I became an orphan. To be clear, it was by choice, because I left my family. I'd attended a carnival, right here at Midlands Christian Academy, where I met a nice young gentleman named Jack Thompson."

Mercy raised her hand toward Jack, and he gave a sad nod, knowing what came next.

"After the carnival, the director of the school, a man named Floyd Winter, made a false accusation about Jack. He made up a lie that everyone believed, including my own mother and father. What I couldn't tell my mother was that I believed I was falling in love!"

Mercy smiled when she said this, and Jack smiled back. Everyone listening smiled too, relieved to hear the happy beneath the sad.

"A young woman from the richest family in town, 'attacked' by an impoverished young man with no family. A 'juvenile delin-quent,' as everyone called the children who attended Midlands

Christian Academy for Boys," Mercy said, serious again. "Children who were treated like criminals—like prisoners—before they'd even had a chance to grow up. It didn't take much for Mr. Winter to convince people of his lie. The lie that forced Jack to flee our town. I knew I could no longer live with my family, because my own mother and father would never believe *my* story. Most of you are probably familiar with my family. The Rost family. There is a wing named for them at the Cincinnati Art Museum. A pediatric hospital in Cleveland. A beautiful park in Columbus, where you might have seen the statue of my grandfather, Prescott Rost. All of this charity is possible because of my family's fortune, made with the profits from Rost Pharmaceuticals. Profits from an opioid drug that *created* the epidemic ravaging this community and so many others across the country."

Mercy paused to let her words sink in. People dabbed at tears in their eyes.

"My suffering is nothing compared to those battling addiction," Mercy continued. "Unfortunately, our community is failing to help those who need it. My suffering also does not compare to the abuse and neglect the students at Midlands Academy endured when it was open. Our community failed to help the boys who were abused here, some of whom did not make it out alive."

Mercy looked to Deputy Bell across the silent crowd while Miss Samantha stood up beside Mercy to offer her support.

"Our community has never come to terms with what happened at Midlands Academy," Mercy pushed on. "We've simply accepted it as part of our history. It's the silence of privilege. The ability to look away. The refusal to name broken systems. Not examining our past creates a powerlessness."

Mercy paused to look out at each of our faces, which were all sending our love to her.

"I will no longer simply move on," she stated, "and I invite you to do the same. As a community, we can do better. We must make a change, and I believe it starts with remembering. I want to take a moment now to remember the students who attended Midlands Academy."

Mercy bowed her head as if in prayer, and we followed. I closed my eyes and heard the wind in the leaves and the buzzing of insects and a quiet cough and feet rearranging under chairs. I pictured the Midlands boys, as if they were there with us.

"They were children, and they were forgotten. By reopening this school as a community center, they will be forgotten no more. They will have a legacy. It gives me great satisfaction to announce that Deputy Belinda Bell will lead a criminal investigation of Midlands Academy, so we may finally know the full truth. The voices of the most vulnerable will guide us."

The wind whipped through the trees as Mercy finished speaking, making branches sway side to side. Jack looked up, like he was looking for the boys. They had always been real to him. He'd been the only one remembering them all these years. Now, because of Mercy—and Katherine—we would all remember and work toward justice.

Deputy Bell approached Mercy and asked if she could have the microphone.

"The families of the students who attended this school have a right to know what happened to their sons," Deputy Bell began. "A team of forensic archaeologists and I are embarking on a special investigation that will involve ground-truthing and restorative justice. So that we *all* may heal."

The crowd clapped hard. Deputy Bell handed the microphone

back to Mercy. Now I knew why she had roped off the woods. She was digging for the truth.

Jack walked to the podium and gave Mercy a hug. He took his spot behind the microphone and waved Justin and Roy up to stand by his side. Justin shuffled through the leaves, while Roy bounded up from his seat. From one of the craft tents, Benji let out a single bark, but Moe shushed him with a dog treat.

"Hi, everyone," Jack started. "I'll keep this brief. I'm Jack. Like Mercy said, I attended Midlands Christian Academy for Boys." He paused for a long time before starting again, his words tangled up inside his heart.

"We stand on unmarked graves," he said. "I am grateful, though, because I will no longer be remembering these lives alone. We've been talking a lot about remembering today. It's important to remember, for our community to heal. So kids like Justin and Roy and everyone in Mercy's care can witness reconciliation. So they don't have to be afraid. So they know we have their backs. Thank you for coming today. And thank you for supporting the children."

It felt like a new beginning, even though the Southern Ohio Children's Home was coming to an end.

Hope Isn't Always Enough

SOME OF THE DESCENDANTS OF the Shawnee Tribe live not far from the Southern Ohio Children's Home, the ones whose ancestors escaped the great removal. They're the ones our town is named after. How does anyone get away with naming a place after the people you just kicked out? And why would anyone do that anyway? Naming their land after them like you're doing them some big favor, then making them disappear. It doesn't make sense, but it is "status quo," as Miss Samantha says. Something we live with without noticing. We say their tribe's name every day and go to Shawneeville Central, home of the Redskins, but you can only find a couple families in town whose ancestors were here first.

Reading through Katherine's diaries again made me think more and more about injustice, and how we have a history of injustice going back to the start. Here we all were, swimming around in that injustice like fish in the sea, trying to figure out why life gets sideways. Why sometimes kids don't feel safe. Why some people are "have-nots" and other people are "haves." *I'd like to know what a fish calls water*, Miss Samantha sometimes says, and I *finally* understand what she means. The fish swim in water every day, so do they even know what it is?

I was having a hard time picturing Mercy being one of the "haves." I wished nobody needed to be a "have-not." We think of "haves" as being fine citizens, but members of the Rost family were not. They were show-offy rich people who were cruel to their daughter and let her go because of a lie that made their family look bad. Then, they gave everything to their son, who ran their pharmaceutical company that makes the drugs everyone is addicted to.

What I was seeing more than anything was how complicated life is, and how there are no easy answers or explanations, and that means that sometimes, nothing makes sense.

Like what happened after the fundraiser. More people from our sad community showed up than we ever imagined would. And we did sell a million candles, I swear, and everything else too—the soaps and cards and Kacey's flowerpots and Emily's cookies. People came and went all day, buying things and listening to our remembering stories and staring up at Jack's tree sanctuary like it was the most magical church they'd ever seen.

But we still did not raise nearly enough money—not even close—for Mercy to continue operations on a daily basis at the Southern Ohio Children's Home. We were looking to a broken community to save us, and it couldn't.

That's why we were all making preparations to move on to whatever was next, which was my Black Hole in a blank sky. Elizabeth and Justin and Roy were helping Miss Samantha pack up the supplies in her classroom. She was going to keep everything in storage bins at her house and was swearing up and down she'd still be our teacher no matter what, she'd figure out a way. Elizabeth was crying a lot. I was real sad too, and when you're that sad, you're allowed to drop whatever it is you're doing and come to The Fortress and have some time with your emotions. Having a cat in your bedroom is also helpful if you are in that situation. I was more grateful than ever for Clover and her soft purrs.

The only one of us who was not facing unknown-ness was Kacey. Their dad had ended up coming to the Remembering Ceremony like he'd said he would, but not until the end, so it was a good thing Kacey had asked Miss Samantha to go last. They were so nervous with him showing up late like that, fearing maybe he'd changed his mind.

Kacey's dad had had a long talk with Mercy after buying three of Kacey's painted pots and two bags of Emily's chocolate chip cookies. He wanted to take Kacey back home with him. Mercy reminded him about how we are all different from each other. She loves Kacey same as the rest of us, and Mercy needed guarantees that Kacey's dad was planning on doing right by them. She told him about Kacey going to see the doctor with Miss Samantha, and Kacey's dad promised to take them back to that same doctor, so Kacey can get whatever care they need.

When Kacey read their remembering story, their dad cried. A *big* cry, like the toddler kind where they go over. I've never seen a grown adult blubber like that, but it showed how much he was hurting with Kacey being away, and how much he loves Kacey, who said this:

"Cultures around the world have a name for those who are nonbinary, for those who shift and change and represent a gender spectrum. You have probably heard of Two Spirit. In Hawai'i, they are called māhū—*third-gender people. The word used by the Mohave people is* hwame. *The Diné people have ancient words,* nadleehi *and* dilbaa, *to describe a third*

and a fourth gender. In Indonesia, the Buginese use the term calalai *and recognize five separate genders. These words exist in different cultures for people who are like me. Because people like me exist, and we exist all around the world."*

Miss Samantha stood by Kacey's side, same as she had for the rest of us. She was especially proud of how hard Kacey had worked on their gender research. Kacey had been hungry to do it.

"In my culture, which I'll call 'American,' we have words for people like me, too. My mother has said them to me. Words like 'abnormal,' 'wrong,' 'different,' 'not right,' and worse. With a better name, maybe I won't be seen as something that needs to be fixed.

"Today, I give myself my own names.

"I am Kacey the Immeasurable.

"I am Kacey the Limitless.

"I am Kacey the Untold.

"I am Kacey the Transcendent.

"When you think of me, use these words. You will be helping me love myself for who I am, and you will see that I am worthy of being loved. Some would have me believe I am alone in this world, but I am not. At the Southern Ohio Children's Home, everyone accepts you no matter what, because what we know at the Southern Ohio Children's Home is that we can't help certain things—like being a child, or being an orphan, or being who we are. I love my Southern Ohio Children's Home family."

Kacey had us all crying, but their dad's shoulders were heaving up and down like he might fall out of his chair.

He'd made arrangements to come pick up Kacey after he got an apartment where him and Kacey could live, giving Kacey time to pack their things and say a long goodbye. Kacey's mom was going to keep their regular house for herself. She'd rather live alone with her fears than have her family, and that was fine by Kacey. And now, it was fine by their dad, too.

"You're the bravest person I know," I told Kacey after they were done reading their remembering story.

"It's easier to be brave when I have a friend like you," they said.

Kacey had practiced and practiced the name part, so they'd have buckets of courage for the real presentation. They didn't even cry like the rest of us, they were so proud to say who they are out loud.

If I was Kacey, I'd be looking forward to seeing Domino, and being with one of my own parents again. But Kacey's dad was going to have to prove to them he's changed and that he won't kick them out again. Especially if Kacey's mom shows up to say anything about it. He wouldn't be able to send them back to the Southern Ohio Children's Home because it was closing, and Kacey had already told their dad about running away if talk of a conversion camp ever started up again. That scared him good.

I was excited that Kacey was preparing for a new life at a new home with their dad, but I didn't want them to go. I didn't want anyone to go. How would we keep connected to each other if we were not all living in The Fortress?

Everyone else was downstairs helping Miss Samantha pack, but I needed a break. I was lying up in Kacey's bunk petting Clover, contemplating.

I heard footsteps coming down the hall, interrupting my thoughts. I scrambled down off Kacey's bunk, scooping up Clover and putting her in the closet. Her cat bed is so nice, and she has her water and a litter box right there, too. Plus, I always give her treats when I have to close the closet door on her, so she doesn't mind it. Usually, she curls up and goes to sleep because she feels safe in there, and she needs her twenty hours.

Meredith poked her head inside the doorway of The Fortress, which was surprising to me because she didn't normally come upstairs anymore. Not since she'd moved back to her dad's house, which was finally almost cleared out of all his and her mom's things. She must have gotten tired of staying in Mercy's messy bedroom.

"Mind if I come in?" Meredith asked.

I shook my head—I didn't mind. I just hoped Clover wouldn't meow.

I sat on my bunk and pointed to the chair at the desk. Meredith looked out of place sitting in our small chair with her long legs and high heels. Her hair was shiny and her nails were long and pink, but she was wearing less makeup than when she had first came back to Shawneeville.

"I decided I'm not going back to New York," Meredith said.

"You're staying in Shawneeville?" I hadn't been thinking about where Meredith was going to live, because I'd been too busy thinking about where *I* was going to live.

"I had thought I'd wanted to follow in my mom's footsteps," she said, "but I'd wanted to do it better. I left Shawneeville to find bigger problems to fix, problems that quote-unquote mattered. I needed to one-up my mom, who was stuck being a housewife. I was frustrated by how ineffective and powerless she was."

"Your mom seemed powerful to me," I said. I was trying to figure out what Meredith meant by problems that "quote-unquote mattered." Had she thought that New York City problems were more important than Shawneeville problems? Maybe they'd made her feel more important. And more rich. Is that what Meredith meant?

"I hated Shawneeville when I was growing up here," she said.

"Why did you hate it?" I asked.

"You really don't hate it?" she asked back. Meredith has a way of shining a spotlight on you when she asks questions, like there is only one right answer, and if you don't give it, something is seriously wrong with you. Maybe it's a trick she learned from being a lawyer.

"It's where I'm from," I said. "It's where my momma is from, and my Grammaw and Pop-pop. I like being here because I can see places where my family has been, and places my family has seen. I like seeing those places because it reminds me of them. I know our community is having its crisis and all, but I haven't ever thought about living anywhere else, because I can't."

Meredith rubbed her temples.

"I'm such a jerk," she said.

Just then, Clover started meowing and I about started having a heart attack.

"No, you're not!" I almost screamed it so she wouldn't hear Clover.

"There's a lifetime's worth of work for me to do right here in Shawneeville. I see now what my mom wanted for me. She knew she couldn't force me though. I had to figure it out on my own."

"Maybe we should go help pack downstairs," I said, getting

off my bed and walking to the bedroom door. Clover was meowing real loud now. Meredith did not budge. She still had some things she needed to get off her chest.

"My mom knew I'd figure it out," Meredith said. "That's the thing. She was clever and patient. Her will lured me back. Helping Mercy lured me back. And for my mom, helping Mercy was part of her mission, because helping Mercy means making a difference for our community."

"Yes, it does!" I agreed, waiting by the door for Meredith to follow me, but she still didn't. She was too busy making her speech.

"I want to make a difference with *this* community," she went on. "Where *I'm* from. Unlike you, though, I'm not so appreciative of seeing the places my family has been and seen. I have shame. My family is a *big* part of the problem. ... Am I listening to a cat meowing right now?"

Meredith finally looked at me standing in the doorway, halfway in, halfway out, like how Clover does when she can't decide if she wants to stay safe in her closet or be out in The Fortress, which has "scary" things, like kids.

I came back inside The Fortress and shut the door behind me, which we are not allowed to do. Bedroom doors always have to be open (except Mercy's), but Meredith didn't know this rule. She hopefully didn't know the "No Pets" rule either.

"That's just my cat. Clover." I said it all natural, like it was perfectly normal I had my own cat. I opened the closet door and pulled out Clover.

"Oh! She's so sweet! Is it a she?" Meredith said.

I nodded and handed Clover to Meredith. Clover purred and purred.

"She's spayed," I said. I didn't want Meredith to think I was an irresponsible pet owner.

"She's gorgeous, but I'm allergic to cats." Meredith held Clover away from her face and gave her back to me. Now that she was "out of the bag," I put Clover on my bed. That must have been where she wanted to go because she curled up on my pillow and squinted her eyes at me (that's how a cat says "I love you"). She looked out the circle window at the fields and the black oak tree, past the ravine toward Midlands Academy, which we couldn't see, but now I knew it was there. No longer invisible. Clover's head darted from side to side whenever a sparrow flew by.

"Can you please do me a favor and don't tell Mercy I have a cat?" I said.

"You bet." Meredith looked like she was trying not to smile. She was a person who probably didn't follow the rules all the time either. "I kept a bunny in my closet once," she said. "They poop a lot. Oh, and a frog. Turns out my mom didn't care, but it made me feel good to have something of my own to take care of."

I felt a kinship with Meredith then, like we both had more words to say that didn't need saying because she and I were both thinking those same words. We saw it in each other's eyes. Meredith reached over to pet Clover once more, and I smelled her sweet perfume, which probably cost a thousand dollars.

"Willa, I want you to know that whatever happens, you and the rest of the kids are going to be okay. I am going to make sure of that."

It was yet another hopeful promise. I didn't know how Meredith could keep that promise unless she made money fall from the sky. She came from a rich family, and she donated as much of her own money as she could at the fundraiser, but she herself could not fix Mercy's situation.

"When the reform school closed, what happened to all the boys who were living there?" I asked. That's what worried me when I thought about if I'd be okay. Because while I had Meredith and Mercy and Miss Samantha and Mr. and Mrs. Harbour to help me, I couldn't stop wondering whether the boys at Midlands had had anybody at all looking out for them.

"We don't have a record of what happened," Meredith said. "It's part of the history of Midlands that we need to work to discover, to help set things right. Jack and I are going to track down every student we can. And Deputy Bell has her forensics team to uncover every shred of evidence they can find. We have the Attorney General's official blessing."

"Mr. Harbour can help with the history stuff," I said. "He knows more than you might think."

"That's a good idea, Willa. I'll talk to him."

"Can I help?" I asked.

"Of course, you can!" Meredith said.

I was back where I'd started, petting Clover on my bed, but now Meredith was with me. Each of us knew about all the secrets, except for the one about what happened to the boys when Midlands got shut down. Soon, we'd figure out those secrets, too. I believed that with all my heart. If there was one thing I'd learned, it's that secrets make the world an even more mixed-up place.

Suddenly, an idea popped into my head.

"Meredith, if the Rost family has so much money from making and selling all the opioid drugs, why can't some of it be used for us and the new community center?"

"You're reading my mind, Willa. Unfortunately, as you know,

Mercy has been on the outs with her family for decades now. The Rost Pharmaceutical money is locked up tight."

"Can't a fancy lawyer from New York City figure out how to get some?" I asked.

Meredith smiled like we were about to cause some trouble.

"I've said it before, and I'll say it again, Willa: How'd you get so smart?"

How Do You Say Goodbye?

I CAN RIDE MY BIKE from one side of Shawneeville to the other and never really be lost, but I don't ever do it, because that'd get me in trouble. I have my route—to All Creatures, to Finn's, and back to the Southern Ohio Children's Home. Now I had a strong desire to ride my bike all around town, to get a look at my community after the fundraiser couldn't save Mercy or us.

Soon I'd have a new route—to Kacey's apartment. We'd started another notebook, the kind where you write thoughts from your inmost soul and pass it back and forth with your kindred spirit. The notebook is better than putting letters in the mail because our thoughts will all be together in one place forever. We are planning to visit each other every week for as long as I am still living at the Southern Ohio Children's Home. After that, we don't know.

There is no way I am going to bring myself to say goodbye to Kacey. Ever. Miss Samantha says instead of saying goodbye, you can say, *Until we meet again.* I like that better.

Maybe the fundraiser had only been a hopeful promise all along. Faced with its broken promise and its hope gone, I finally had to accept that my life was about to change for the first time in the four years since I'd showed up on Mercy's porch steps and walked through her front door.

I was saying goodbye to my life as I know it.

I got on my bike and rode to All Creatures, like I always did and like I'd been doing a lot lately, to see if Finn was there and to take care of helpless creatures besides myself. Fall hadn't arrived yet and it was still too hot outside, but some leaves had already curled brown at the edges.

When I got to the tiny All Creatures building across from the proud courthouse, I did not stop. Could I even get in trouble anymore? I rode three circles around Courthouse Square, keeping my bike smack in the middle of the street. It was Monday morning, and there wasn't a single car.

This town feels so empty, I thought.

Next, I took the path down to the water's edge, where Finn and me walk happy dogs who wag their tails at butterflies. The water flowed fast and full since we'd had a lot of downpour rain. An old fisherman stood lonely on the riverbank, trying to hook a catfish. Pop-pop had been big-time into fishing before he got sick. He didn't mind giving it up, though. *You can't hardly walk the riverbank without stepping on a needle no more,* is what he'd said.

I decided to take Highway 157, in the other direction from where I typically ride, toward the places I thought I remembered from when I was little. I wasn't exactly sure where those places were because I was always stuck in the backseat of the car, craning my neck to look out the window. Momma had spilled a beer on my booster seat once and had to take it out of the car to clean it. After that, she never put the booster back in. Instead, it sat on the crooked porch of her friend's house, until the feral cats peed on it, and that was that.

I didn't feel scared riding my bike, knowing kind of where I was going but not really knowing at all.

The only time I felt scared was when the cars drove by and wouldn't make way for me, even though the other side of the road was empty, which is nothing new. One car even honked at me. I remembered Miss Samantha's talk about the highway system. I felt it then, riding my bike on a system made for cars, and people driving their cars not appreciating me being on my bike, like I'm messing it up for them, even though I'm just a kid, and even though it is not hard for them to get around me. But they don't want to have to move for me.

All I can do is keep riding.

I am happy about the drivers who go slow and don't mind giving me space. It doesn't seem like it'd be so hard. One lady even smiled and waved at me, and it didn't hurt her one bit. Maybe everything is hard for people who are living inside a crisis. I don't know. Maybe I'll understand better when I get my driver's license.

My community is not scary to me, despite it being in its crisis that only ever seems to be getting worse. I noticed how raggedy all the houses look, with their beat-down cars in their weedy driveways. One of the streets is called Hardscrabble Ridge, I am not kidding. Even though it was hot outside, we were well past the "dog days of summer," and every last garden was either dead or overgrown from not being cared for. The town is dying, along with the addicts dying from overdosing on drugs. Soon, there'll be nothing but ghosts around here, haunting a ghost town.

I eventually found Grammaw and Pop-pop's trailer home. My internal compass must have been pointing me there, homing in like a pigeon. I had a feeling I might be riding in their neighborhood because it was the only home I'd been to on a regular basis when I was little, when Momma and me could not ever stay put. Grammaw and Pop-pop's trailer beckoned to me from all the other sad houses. I felt that same loved and cared for feeling I got whenever I used to go there.

I braked on the gravel and stared. The brown heart woven from grapevines still hung on the side of the trailer where Grammaw had it, except it wasn't decorated with flowers and lights anymore. Just naked vines. The ugly statue of St. Francis still blessed the front yard. It was strange, staring at this home that had been here the whole time when I'd only been keeping it alive in my memory. I could almost smell Grammaw's cinnamon heart candles.

The front door slammed open. A man with tattoos on his neck and forehead stormed out and got into the beat-up car parked in the grass. He seemed older than Finn, but maybe only by a little. And he was angry. He turned his radio up to blaring and peeled out of there, his tires shredding dirt stripes on the lawn. I was afraid he'd hit me—I could tell he was seeing red and not much else.

A scared looking woman in a green bathrobe inched outside onto the porch. Then she closed the front door real slow, like she didn't want anyone to see her.

I got so mad then. Out of nowhere, I don't know why. It must've been from seeing these different, mean people living in *my* Pop-pop and Grammaw's house. Before I knew what I was doing, I threw my bike on the dirt yard and marched up to the trailer. The grapevine wreath hung just above my head. I had to jump to reach it. I tried a few times, and finally I jumped high enough to grab Grammaw's wreath and yank it right off the side of the trailer home.

The woman came out again. I didn't care if I'd been caught. That's how mad I was.

"What do you think you're doing?" she yelled, not seeming scared anymore.

"This is my Grammaw and Pop-pop's!" I screamed from the top of my lungs.

"Give that back! It's *mine!*" she said.

"It is *not!* This is *not* your house!" I stomped to my bike and put the wreath around my handlebars. Blood boiled hot in my veins, and my heart thumped loud in my ears. I couldn't get my bike standing up straight.

"You little piece of trash—" the woman said.

"*You're* who's trash!" I yelled.

"I'm calling the cops!" she shouted, but I knew she wouldn't. A police officer was the last person she wanted to see.

I pedaled out of there so fast. I felt my skin turn red as Roy's as I rode my bike harder than ever. The streets were a blur from the tears stinging my eyes. All I knew is that the heart wreath was *not* hers. That trailer home was *not* theirs. They were strangers in Pop-pop's house, and there were probably needles all over the floor.

I didn't know what home was anymore.

I let myself think about a life that I could have had if things hadn't turned out the way they did—if there hadn't been a crisis in our community. Maybe I could have had a whole different, happy-happiness kind of life, filled with nothing but love. With Grammaw and Pop-pop. Or even with Momma, if she'd never started doing drugs.

I'd met my biological father once when I was a baby, but I don't remember. He died from his drug overdose after that. Momma never had a good thing to say about my dad, other than he was cute in high school. She'd warn me to stay away from cute boys because they're trouble. (But Finn is not trouble and he is a cute boy, so I don't believe Momma was one hundred percent right about that.) The man who was my father, and the rest of his family, had stayed away from Momma and me. They are complete strangers to me. It is a funny thing not to have a single feeling in your heart about the man who is your daddy. But there it is—I don't. Miss Samantha warns me that someday I might. I hope she's wrong, because it's easier not having those feelings.

I still didn't know where I was going on my bike, and now I had Grammaw's heart-wreath on my handlebars. I needed to cool down and catch my breath and make it so my heart wasn't pumping so fast. I followed my sense of direction and found myself passing the hidden drive to Midlands Academy. Deflated balloons left over from the fundraiser fluttered in the trees.

I turned up the drive, hoping I might see Jack in his garden.

A breeze caught the high tree branches, and they waved hello. I parked my bike and grabbed Grammaw's wreath.

"Jack? Benji?" I called out.

I did not hear the creaking door of the shed. Jack had been spending all his spare time with Mercy before heading back to Virginia. He'd even taken her out to dinner at Café Scarpucci, Shawneeville's only nice restaurant. (It's actually one town over.)

The woods looked wild again with the tents and chairs gone. Deputy Bell's police tape told you someone had been out here, finally paying attention to what had happened at the school for so-called juvenile delinquents. And Jack's garden told you some-one had given it some love.

Still, it needed more. A lot more.

I tiptoed toward the garden shed. Ghosts were watching me.

I needed to see inside the place where Jack had spent more than one scared, lonely night. Where other boys had been abused. Where at least two had died.

The only sound I heard as I opened the creaky shed door was my heart beating inside my ears. I stepped through the doorway and silence surrounded me. I let the door close behind me, even though I was scared. Inside, the shed was dark, and the walls felt close. A metal bed frame was being used as a storage bench. There was nothing more than pots and bags of dirt and mulch and lawn bags, which I was relieved for. I noticed scratches on the walls.

Jack's words echoed in my mind.

It's not safe for children here.

I got too scared and quick ran out of the shed, slamming the door behind me by accident. The sound flushed a flock of cedar waxwings from the black elderberry shrubs we'd planted. Waxwings are good luck, you know. At least that's what Momma said. I might as well believe her on that.

Rusty nails stuck out from the shed's walls. I found one I could reach near the middle of the side wall. I grabbed Grammaw's wreath off my bike and hung it on that nail.

"That's better." I gave the shed some love with Grammaw's heart.

I took one more look at the place, stood once more in the aspen tree cathedral, and said a prayer for the boys. I also said a prayer for myself. The aspens shivered and sent three leaves down.

I picked up my bike and went back to the Southern Ohio Children's Home. I didn't want to be out on the open road anymore, so I slow-walked through the woods, across the ravine, and across the field. I dropped my bike by the kitchen and gave the chickens food from their bin and fresh water from the hose, pretending like life wasn't turning upside-down.

I pretended everything was routine because I didn't know how to leave.

I don't know how Mercy is going to be with all of us gone, and her not knowing every day exactly how we're doing. You'd think she'd be busier than ever, but she seemed to disappear after the fundraiser, like she was hiding from the situation that was knocking at her front door.

I went in through the kitchen after petting Henrietta and found Mercy sitting at the table with Charlie and Emily. Each of them was drinking a beer, which was strange because alcohol is not allowed inside the Southern Ohio Children's Home. Mercy was breaking the rules and drinking beer, just like I had broke the rules and took my bike all over town.

"There she is!" Charlie gave me his big smile. I gave him a hug.

"Hi, Willa," Emily said. "I'm drinking a beer!" Emily was so proud to be drinking a beer. It must have been the first one she'd ever had.

"Hi, Emily," I said. I gave her a hug, too.

"Where have you been?" Mercy asked.

"On my bike." I didn't need to tell Mercy how much of a ride I'd had.

I heard a meow and a hiss, but I wasn't sure how that was possible. Maybe I was having ear ghosts from working at All Creatures. Then Clover ran into the kitchen, followed by Elizabeth and Roy and Justin.

"I'm sorry, Willa! I'm sorry! She escaped! I couldn't stop her!" Elizabeth was practically crying.

Justin and Roy were chasing Clover like they were on fire.

They were making her so scared, she ran faster and right into things, like the kitchen cabinets and the kitchen door. Finally, she jumped on top of the kitchen table, and I gently snatched her and held her the way she likes, to make her feel calm.

"Leave her alone!" I told them.

Their energy was too much for poor Clover. Roy and Justin were panting and laughing, all from chasing a six-pound kitten.

Kacey ran into the kitchen after the rest of them.

"I left The Fortress for five seconds to pack my bathroom stuff, and this is what happens?" Kacey looked like they didn't know if they should scream or laugh.

"I'm sorry, Willa!" Elizabeth seemed to think it was all her fault that Clover had escaped The Fortress, but I knew it had more to do with the boys wrestling than with her. Roy had been after Justin more than usual lately. Everyone was feeling extra anxious.

"It's okay, Elizabeth!" I said. "It's my fault for making you have to keep a secret."

We all looked at Mercy with guilty faces. Charlie was still as a statue, his eyebrows up on top of his head. Emily was more interested in taking another sip of her beer than she was interested in Clover. Mercy was calm, as if cats ran around her kitchen every day, but I knew she had a lot of words spinning around inside her head that she wasn't letting come out of her mouth. I tried to explain.

"I found a kitten in the ditch, and it's okay because she's already been spayed, and she uses the litter box fine and her name is Clover." I held Clover up, like she could speak for herself. All you had to do was look at her and see how cute she was to know you'd have done the same thing if you'd been the one who found her crying in a ditch on the side of the road.

Mercy did something that surprised me then: She burst out laughing. Charlie laughed too, and Emily laughed so hard beer came out her nose. Elizabeth switched from crying to laughing, and Roy and Justin laughed and punched each other, then started wrestling on the floor. Kacey almost doubled over from laughing. I try not to use swears, but I swear, all hell broke loose.

We had lost our minds.

We'd been so sad and scared about the Southern Ohio Children's Home stopping operations and us kids being homeless all of a sudden that maybe what we needed was a good laugh. It was sad-laughing and sad-happiness, but it still felt nice, because we were together. Plus, I wasn't getting in trouble over having a cat. Charlie even got out some milk for her and put it in a saucer on the floor. I let her lap it up, even though milk isn't good for cats—everyone thinks it is, but it gives them diarrhea. That's the kind of thing you learn working at an animal shelter, especially when you're the one cleaning the cages.

I felt so much relief that all of our secrets had finally been set free. I made a vow to myself to never have another secret for the rest of my life as long as I live, which might be hard because I already have another one I don't want to tell, but probably anyone could guess it anyway, which is that I *do* have a crush on Finn.

During all this commotion, Meredith walked into the kitchen. I laughed harder because her giant sunglasses finally got me. It had turned into a cloudy day, and I wondered if she ever wore those sunglasses on a sunny day. She whipped them off and looked around, trying to figure out why everyone was so happy, when we were supposed to be sad.

"Okay," she said, sizing up the situation and nodding her head. She held her sunglasses in one hand and a piece of paper in the other. She was wearing her high heels, looking fancy and important.

I couldn't stop giggling, no matter how I tried. Justin and Roy were still wrestling on the floor, and Mercy wasn't even stopping them. Emily had put the cookie jar in the middle of the table, and she and Elizabeth ate cookies straight from it.

"Okay," Meredith said again. "I'm glad to see you all are handling things all right."

"What else can we do?" Charlie said and got a bottle of beer for Meredith from the six-pack that had magically appeared in the fridge.

If the Southern Ohio Children's Home had ever had a party, this was it. I wondered if we would be able to have a party for Mercy turning 60 next year, like Charlie and Emily had been planning before everything had happened with losing the home.

Meredith raised her beer bottle up to the ceiling.

"Cheers!" We did cheers all around the room, holding up a drink or a cookie or nothing.

"It's going to be okay!" Meredith said.

Looking around at all the people I consider to be my family, I knew it *was* going to be okay. I felt so much love. I felt so proud. I wished my momma could see me now, so she could be proud of me, too. We might not have the Southern Ohio Children's Home, but we would always have each other. That would not change, not ever. I would still have friends and teachers who love me, and animals to care for.

"I mean it. Really. It's going to be okay," Meredith repeated.

"What do you mean, 'It's going to be okay'?" Mercy had stopped drinking her beer.

"I mean, it's really, really, really going to be okay, Mercy,"

Meredith said. "Willa gave me a great idea a couple weeks ago. Ever since, I have been working an Eleanor angle."

"Who's Eleanor?" Elizabeth asked.

Mercy had a mouthful of cookie, and I couldn't wait for her to finish chewing.

"Eleanor was Mercy's mother," I said.

"*Is* Mercy's mother," Meredith corrected me.

Everyone had been caught off guard when we'd learned about Mercy's father after discovering his name inside the grandfather clock. Now, we were surprised to hear Mercy still had a mother.

"She's alive?" I asked. Meredith nodded, surprised by my surprise.

"Alive and kicking. In fact, I just saw her with my own two eyes," Meredith said.

My own eyes were bugging out of my head. But I knew I needed to drop it, at least right then. Mercy's feelings for her mother lived inside a hole in her heart where she'd buried them over forty years ago, the scar over it too thick to ever heal right.

Mercy could not bring herself to admit her mother existed. Instead, she took another bite of cookie. I bet she'd eat the whole jar of cookies to avoid talking about Eleanor.

"I know this goes against your wishes, Mercy," Meredith said. "I didn't want to say anything until I won."

"Won what?" Roy asked.

I picked up Clover. "Come on, let's take Clover back to The Fortress," I said. I wanted to hear what Meredith had to say just as bad as anybody else, but I also knew that if Meredith had visited Mercy's alive-and-kicking mother, they needed to have their own private conversation about it.

"I want to hear how Meredith won!" Roy said.

"So do I," said Justin.

"Me three," said Elizabeth.

"Let's give Mercy her space," Kacey said. "Same way she gives you your space, right?"

Mercy nodded a *thank you* as we left. Meredith pulled a chair up to the table.

We retreated to The Fortress, curious and anxious. We hoped we'd hear about this final secret sooner, because there was no *way* we could wait until later.

Making the World Your Home as You Would Like to See It

PEOPLE MIGHT NOT KNOW IT by looking at me, but not a day goes by when I'm not thinking about my momma. Thinking of her is a regular thing, like an itch or a sore tooth or a bellyache.

I was wondering if Mercy had a bellyache for her own momma.

When I found out Mercy's mom is *not* dead—that Eleanor Rost lives in the Rost mansion in Cincinnati—I about dropped dead myself. You wouldn't know Eleanor was still breathing on this earth because Mercy hasn't spoken to her for more than forty years. I'd thought without thinking, having read Katherine's diaries from so long ago, that Eleanor and Prescot Jr. and everyone else was dead by now. Press really *was* dead, but there are other ways of being dead, like "writing someone out of your life" and pretending they do not exist.

I decided that Mercy did not have a bellyache for her own momma, because for Mercy, what her mother did was unforgivable. Still, that didn't stop her from needing to say *thank you* for all of a sudden receiving buckets of Rost family money.

"Willa … Justin … I have a favor to ask." Mercy stopped us in the dining room one day after lunch while Justin and me were having a table-wiping contest to see whose were cleaner.

"Yes, ma'am." We put our sponges down and sat at a table with Mercy.

"Jack is leaving for Virginia soon," Mercy said. "He has to prepare for his new music students."

"He's coming back though, right?" Justin asked.

Justin especially was bonding with Jack over setting things right at Midlands. We were all secretly hoping that Jack and Mercy would be going to more fancy dinners.

"He is," Mercy smiled. "The community center needs someone to run it, and I can't think of anyone better than Jack. It will be a big change for him. For both of us. There's something I need to do before he leaves. Something I need to do with him and with you. If you're willing."

"Sure," I agreed, before knowing what Mercy was asking. I would take any excuse to spend extra time with Jack and Benji.

"I'd like for you to come with me to see my mother," she said.

"You want to see Eleanor?" I asked.

Mercy nodded. "There is a tugging inside of me, telling me I need to try, at the very least, to say thank you for her generosity. Face to face. I have my trepidations, though."

"Are you happy about seeing your mom, or are you scared?" I asked, taking a guess about what "trepidations" meant. I was imagining how I'd feel if I could see my own momma again—happy-happiness for sure.

Mercy thought for a minute. "I'm nervous," she said. Mercy is atypical for adults because she doesn't act like she already knows everything. I'd never seen Mercy look more uncertain than when she was talking about her mother. "My heart is telling me that with such a generous endowment, the only way I'll feel right about it is by seeing her. And I think she should meet some of the children she's helping."

"Why do you want Jack to come?" Justin asked.

"Maybe to give her a chance to redeem herself," Mercy said. "It's probably foolish. I learned a long time ago not to get my hopes up. Meredith will be there, too. Honestly, I need all the support I can get, and you kids give me a *lot* of support."

"We'll be there, Mercy," I said.

"Yes, ma'am, we will," Justin said.

"Thank you both," Mercy said with a proud smile. She stood up and pointed to a piece of grated cheese on the table. "Missed a spot."

Justin and me picked up our sponges. I was lost in new thoughts about meeting Eleanor Rost. I'd be lying if I didn't tell you I was scared as heck.

We left the Southern Ohio Children's Home early the next morning. Meredith drove the van, with Mercy in front. Jack and Justin sat in the middle, and Benji and me piled into the rear. I was grateful for sitting in the back, so I could have my thoughts for myself while I looked out the window and petted Benji's head. His favorite thing is car rides.

I wanted to try and help take Mercy's mind off her worry, but I was nervous, same as her. Jack got a few smiles when he sang Mercy songs from his Soldiers' Chorus days. He even got Justin and Meredith to join in. I lost track of time during the two-hour drive because Benji and me kept falling asleep.

Momma always said I was a good car sleeper. I must've known it made her happy, but it's a sad memory, because she was using drugs while I slept in her car.

After catching the sunrise over farmland and driving past suburb after suburb, we finally arrived in Cincinnati. The sun shone yellow in a cloudless blue sky. The Ohio River in Cincinnati doesn't look anything like the Ohio River in Shawneeville, even though it's the same river. In Cincinnati, it's wide and low, with steel bridges and big shipping boats.

When the van finally slowed down, I thought Meredith had made a mistake and accidentally took a wrong turn into a museum. I kept looking for the parking lot.

"Geez," I said, my face pressed against the van window.

I've always known the Southern Ohio Children's Home is a mansion, but I did not know what a mansion really was until I saw Eleanor Rost's gray stone castle on a hill. It was about ten thousand times huger than the Southern Ohio Children's Home.

"Here's our stop!" Meredith announced like a tour bus driver. She buzzed a code into an iron gate. It rolled open, slow and heavy, to let us up the brick driveway. The entire property—at least what I could see—was enclosed by thick stone walls.

"This is a house?" Justin asked.

"Indeed," Meredith said.

"The house that Rost Pharmaceuticals built," Mercy said.

"Your mom lives *here*?" Justin asked again, but he already knew the answer.

Jack let out a laugh and gave Justin a pat on the back.

"Doesn't make much sense, does it?" Jack said. "How one person could need so much."

Meredith parked near the front door. I couldn't stop staring.

We got out to have a good look at where Mercy's mother was still alive and kicking. I realized that the mansion wasn't a house so much as a fortress, with fancy gardens rolling down green hills as far as your eye could see, plus a swimming pool and fountain and more gardens that overlooked both the Ohio River and the city.

"Life must be easy with a view like this," I said. "The world looking so pretty."

"Dang," Justin said. It was the closest he'd ever come to saying a swear.

Jack leashed Benji and took him for a pee. "Not on the bushes, Benji."

Mercy stared up at the palace. "I never imagined I'd set foot in this house again," she said.

Stone steps led to an oversized front door. I couldn't count all the windows, there were so many. Three of them went up the side of the house like stairs, leading to an actual turret. The only thing missing was guards in suits of armor.

Meredith stood next to Mercy. "Are you okay?" She touched Mercy's arm.

Mercy nodded. Then she looked at Justin, me, and Jack. "Are *you* okay?" she asked us.

"I'm fine," Justin and Jack said at the same time.

"Talk about a show-off house," I said.

Meredith laughed. Mercy was silent. I couldn't stand the way that house was looking down its nose at Mercy. At all of us. Eleanor Rost had no idea there even was a crisis in our community. How could she, sitting in her mansion looking at a picture-perfect world outside her windows? She had no idea her daughter was out here doing all she could to fix the mess that Rost Pharmaceuticals had made. All of a sudden, it felt like everything bad that had happened to me in my whole life was Eleanor's fault.

"I am *not* fine," I said, telling the truth for once. "My momma started off using a couple pain pills that her boyfriend gave her, but she wasn't in any pain. It was *not* her fault she got addicted to drugs!"

I hadn't even gone inside to meet Eleanor Rost, but I already hated her as much as I imagine Mercy had when she'd left her family. Tears creeped into the corners of my eyes, which made me more angry. I didn't want anyone to see me cry.

I looked up at Mercy. I knew her heart was aching as much as mine.

"It cost me everything," I said. Every bit of sad-sadness I'd been through my whole life came crashing down on me all at once. "It cost my momma everything." I was crying for real now, there was no hiding it. Mercy rubbed my back, letting me have my tears.

"The cost for my mother is nothing," Mercy said quietly. "She'll never pay for anything. Not really."

Mercy crouched down on one knee by my side, so I was taller than she was. She held my arms and looked up into my face.

I couldn't stop crying.

"I haven't been her daughter for a long time," Mercy explained. "I don't need to go inside. I'm not going in there, and neither are you. The endowment is all I need. It's all we need. I got what I needed. I can move on from my mother. I did it before, and I'll do it again."

I fell into Mercy's arms, my tears spilling onto her shoulders.

"I understand, Willa," Mercy whispered. "It's not fair."

"It's *not* fair," I bawled.

I needed Mercy's understanding magic to work on me because I was inconsolable. Just like a toddler. Mercy grabbed my shoulders and looked into my eyes. I saw her tears.

"I understand," she repeated. And I knew she did.

Jack and Justin stood by us, Justin holding Benji's leash. Jack put his hand on Mercy's shoulder. Benji tugged, trying to nudge my elbow—he hates when anyone gets upset. Meredith came closer and rubbed my back.

"Money is the only language Eleanor knows," Meredith said. "And you know what? We're going to take it. That's all the redemption we're going to get."

Mercy gave me another hug, and finally I was able to take a deep breath and breathe normally again.

"I don't blame you for not going in," Meredith said. "I can finish up our business over the phone. Let's get out of here."

Everyone was relieved to hear that the visit was over.

"I'm sorry for making you come all this way," Mercy said to us.

"Benji loves nothing more in this world than a car ride," Jack said with a shrug.

On cue, Benji barked.

Meredith unlocked the van. As soon as she slid open the side door, Benji jumped in. I followed. I wanted to make sure I got the back seat again. Meredith and Mercy had promised us lunch at a famous barbeque restaurant before returning to Shawneeville, but I wasn't hungry.

I couldn't wait to get home.

We'd already got Miss Samantha unpacked and back into her classroom. She says I am smart as a whip and that I'll find out just how smart I am when I'm "unleashed to full capacity" at Shawneeville Central High School in three years. I am glad I get to finish junior high in her classroom, though. She is the best teacher, and her classroom makes me feel safe.

By the time I'll be a freshman in high school, Finn will have graduated already, but I'll still have at least one friend there: Kacey. We'll probably have filled up a hundred notebooks with thoughts from our inmost souls by then.

Our new school year with Miss Samantha was going to start soon, but we had a few days to take a break. I enjoyed that worry-free time. Emily and me helped Charlie can tomatoes and make jams and jellies, just like he always does at the end of summer. I love making jelly because it reminds me of Grammaw. She used to have me listen for the lids to pop.

The extra work was making me tired enough to sleep in like a teenager most mornings, along with Clover. Mercy let her be our official house cat and gave her the entire run of the home. (I told Mercy how having pets actually *helps* allergies not be so bad. Moe had told me that was true, even though it seems backwards. It's called "exposure therapy.") Clover's favorite place to sleep is on the red couch in the library, which is also my favorite place to read and have peace. I think of Katherine every time I walk through the library doorway, feeling her power and anger and love and justice. Everything has turned out in a way that would make her feel something has changed. All because of her will.

Clover follows me upstairs from her spot on the red couch at bedtime. Even with having the run of the house, she knows where she sleeps at night, and it's my bed.

I've always loved cool, late-summer nights—the kind where you want to feel the air on you while you're sleeping. The circle window in The Fortress opens a crack if you tilt the bottom out so the top comes in. There's no screen, which is bad because of the bugs, but the breeze feels good on your face, and it makes Clover's whiskers twitch.

I was reading my book from the library. I'd decided to reread all the *Anne* books and was already almost done with *Anne of Avonlea*. Roy, Justin, and Elizabeth were doing their routines: brushing teeth, picking out books, fighting (in the case of Justin and Roy), and getting Lovey-Pup ready for bed (in the case of Elizabeth). I sure missed Kacey, but they were happy being with their dad. I switched to their top bunk, which helped them feel close to me.

I put my head near the open window, right next to Clover, and we listened to the black-capped chickadees and wrens and robins celebrating their last bugs of the day. I saw a family of deer in the moonlight, including a buck, across the field near the black oak tree.

Meredith and Mercy's conversation from outside drifted up to the window, like it wanted to get inside my ears. They were sitting in the rocking chairs on the front porch, drinking lemonade and watching the sky grow dark. My ears are still good at hearing things they shouldn't, but in this case, I knew most of it already. Mercy and Meredith were filling in the gaps.

"… it's finally catching up to them in the courts," Meredith was saying. "The overprescribing and selling is being scrutinized, and it does not look good. Not at all. It's infuriating, Mercy. So, I said to dear Aunt Eleanor, 'Wouldn't it be nice if one of those pharmaceutical companies had created an endowment to help the community recover? To care for its parentless children, and to care for the people who are addicted to their drugs?'"

"I still can't believe you convinced her, knowing it would help me," Mercy said.

"She's completely focused on the lawsuits," Meredith replied. "All I had to do was explain how it would help them in court. If she's already making amends and donating to the community, Rost Pharmaceuticals doesn't appear quite so heartless."

That's how Meredith had won. She had got Eleanor to fork over all that money—and I'm not talking about a million dollars. I'm talking about *a hundred million* dollars. I had not known the half of how rich the Rost family was. Suddenly, Mercy had a new problem: What was she going to do with all that money? It was a *good* problem she'd told me, but I didn't need convincing.

"I did tell her she owed you, Mercy," Meredith said. "At least that much."

Mercy laughed. "What on earth did she say when you told her she 'owed' me?"

"Nothing," Meredith said. "All she did was promise the money."

"The only way she knows how to communicate," Mercy said. "Thank you, Meredith."

"You should thank Willa. She's the one who inspired me to try."

Hearing Meredith's words, I had a moment of pride. My story alone might not have changed things, but stories like mine were piling up, and that was making a difference. Eleanor's big fat check was more than enough to keep both the Southern Ohio Children's Home and The Shawneeville Center for Hope, which is what we'd decided to name the community center, open for "perpetuity," which I know means forever. I didn't even have to look it up or ask Justin.

"Rost Pharmaceutical's fate is in the hands of the judicial system now," Meredith said.

I wondered if the judicial system was anything like the

highway system. I pictured Eleanor sitting in the back of the biggest limousine you ever saw, telling her chauffeur to run over anyone and anything standing in her way.

Before falling asleep, I said a prayer for my entire Southern Ohio Children's Home family, with a feeling for the first time like it might be answered.

On Indigenous Peoples' Day, Meredith hosted a party at the new Shawneeville Center for Hope. I thought we'd gone to some far away fantasyland, she had everything looking so nice. She'd put a long table covered in a white tablecloth down the middle of the aspen tree sanctuary. She'd ordered about a hundred pizzas because nearly everyone from the home was there. All except Miss Lupe and her helpers (Meredith had promised to bring them pizza) and the babies and toddlers, who needed to go to bed. Even the younger kids were there, running around with bug spray on, screaming and laughing. Us older kids were there too, of course. We practically felt like we'd discovered Midlands Academy all on our own. I was most excited to see Kacey, who'd come with their dad. We stuck to each other like glue. Jack and Benji came back for the party, too, and so did Deputy Bell.

"Do you think Mercy is going to kiss Jack again?" I asked Kacey.

"Probably," Kacey said, smiling. "Now they can't get in trouble from anyone."

Grammaw's heart wreath was still on the shed, decorated with flowers. Meredith had lit the table with candles that look real but run on a battery. She did not want to burn the whole forest and school down, which is what Mercy *had* wanted to do not that long ago. Now Mercy was grateful she'd followed Katherine's wishes from ghost-hood. I prayed the ghost boys would see us and see the work Deputy Bell was doing. Someday, we would hear their *befores.*

Meredith started off by reading a land acknowledgement. She was trying her hardest to get everything right, because so much wrong had happened.

"We are on the traditional lands of the Shawnee, Osage, Miami, and Wyandot Tribes. We commemorate the Indigenous peoples' kinship to the land, and honor those who have blood memory of this place. We are orphans of family, and we acknowledge current members of these Nations, who are orphans of land. We pay our respects to, and grieve for, all those who were forcibly removed from here with the passing of the 1830 Indian Removal Act. We remain connected to one another by ancestors past, present, and future."

Justin had helped Meredith to write it. He used to begin all our Forgetting Ceremonies with a land acknowledgment. Acknowledging and remembering was better than forgetting, I'd learned that much.

"I'd like to welcome you all to The Shawneeville Center for Hope," Jack said. His emotions welled up inside, catching in his throat.

Mercy stood by him, grinning ear to ear.

"And I'd like to introduce you to its new director," Mercy said. She gave Jack a real huggy-hug from deep down.

Mercy couldn't wait for Jack to move back full-time after he finished out his school year. Sometimes we caught them holding hands and acting like teenagers—how they would have been if Mr. Winter hadn't spread his lie. They were finally able to be happy together.

Jack put one arm around Mercy and raised a glass with his other. We all joined him. Mercy, Meredith, Miss Samantha, Charlie, Emily, Justin, Roy, Elizabeth (who had left her stuffed dog at home), the Harbours, and Finn—who was sitting by me and put his arm around my shoulder, which made me feel like a lighted-up firefly. Kacey and their dad sat across from me. Mercy had reminded them that they would always belong at the Southern Ohio Children's Home.

I'd learned I was strong enough, smart enough, and brave enough to leave Mercy if it came down to it. I'd also learned that Mercy needs me as bad as I need her, and I will always be there for her. I will also always have my Southern Ohio Children's Home family, no matter where I live.

When I imagine my future, I do not see a Black Hole anymore. I see my home, my community, and all the ways we help each other. I know how lucky we are that the Southern Ohio Children's Home is here. I am always happy when a new kid arrives, because they're coming to a special place. My life is still filled with sad-happiness, because I know the sad parts won't ever go away, but now I see the happiness clearly, shining bright as the full moon in a black sky.

Acknowledgments

For twenty years I worked as an editor for medical journals. Articles about patients (and doctors) abusing prescription opioid medication appeared starting in 2004, but it wasn't until 2012 that it was named an "epidemic." The journals published a steady stream of articles about the crisis, and I was struck by how the statistics only grew worse, year after year. One person's struggle was a family's struggle and, eventually, a community's and country's struggle. In *Orphanland*, Willa's story is the story of an entire community because that is how the opioid epidemic has played out.

I relied on several books for research. Sam Quinones's book *Dreamland: The True Tale of America's Opiate Epidemic* helped me understand the specific geographies associated with the sale of opioids and fentanyl. The book *Dopesick* by Beth Macy (and the subsequent TV series) was another valuable source of information. I also relied on a memoir by Richard McKenzie called *The Home: A Memoir of Growing Up in an Orphanage*. For Kacey's story, I used many resources available online at The Trevor Project and PFLAG. The animated short film *Kapaemahu*, directed by Hinaleimoana Wong-Kalu, was particularly inspiring. Reporting on the Florida School for Boys (also known as the Arthur G. Dozier School for Boys) by Ben Montgomery and Waveney Ann Moore ("For Their Own Good," *The St. Petersburg Times,* now available on *The Tampa Bay Times'* website) and the book *We Carry Their Bones: The Search for Justice at the Dozier School for Boys* by Erin Kimmerle were my sources for the fictional reformatory school Midlands Christian Academy for Boys. My inspiration for the fictional Southern Ohio Children's Home school is Near North Montessori School; thank you to NNMS for being such an important part of my family's community. Thank you to the school's librarian, Kevin Whiteneir Jr., for his generosity and for being the first librarian to put my book on a library shelf. My love for libraries and librarians runs deep!

I was spoiled by having many early readers for *Orphanland.* Thank you to the very earliest readers, dear friends Heba Kamel, Emily Makinson, and Shelly Shimon. I am grateful for having had a reading team of smart folks who generously donated their time and feedback. Thank you to Juliet Bradley, MD (who helped me with details about Jessica Johnson's overdose, as well as information about pharmaceutical companies), Lindsay Ditto, Amanda Elman-Kolb, Clothilde Ewing (whose moral support and friendship all along the [very long!] way kept me going), Diana Fischer-Woods, Ashley Hutti, Julie Nimesheim, Deborah Pugh (who helped with her lawyer's perspective), Kim Ruffer, Amy Segalla, and Jim Shapiro. Thank you to longtime readers and SCBWI friends Kelly Darke, Linda Elman (my high school speech coach), and Bernadette Golitz, as well as my sister-in-law Nancy Goodfellow, who has been by my side for this writing journey. Thank you to the younger readers—the most important kind!—including Mabel Buresh, Toby and Suhail Kuznetsov, and Jane Shapiro, along with my own kids, who helped me more than they'll ever know. Thank you to the readers who generously provided endorsements, including Juliet Bradley, MD, and Clothilde Ewing, as well as Sydney Dunlap, Rob Snow, and Lynn Leitch. Thank you to Three Avenues Bookshop for your excitement and energy for this debut author's manuscript.

Thank you to the folks at Mission Point Press for being a supportive and knowledgeable publishing team. I am especially grateful to Misha Neidorfler (fellow tuxedo cat mom) for her calm, flexible, and positive management of book production as well as guidance about marketing (along with Julie Hazlett) and distribution.

Thank you to my agent, David Dunton, who sent my manuscript out to publishers far and wide and never wavered in his support. He read early drafts and provided valuable feedback, as did his pre-teenager, who was another important early reader.

Thank you to my mom, Cathryn Bomberger, for being a supporter of this intergenerational women's story. Thank you to my dad, Peter Bomberger, whom I still feel encouraging me every day and who would be proud of me for putting my writing out into the world.

Thank you to my husband, Pat, for massive support and encouragement over the five years I spent writing this book. I wouldn't be here if you hadn't been there.

Mike the cat was with me every early morning writing session and insisted on sitting on my lap; I miss him.

As I've navigated the publication of *Orphanland*, I have stayed grounded by remembering my WHY: Kids—specifically, young readers ages 10 to 14. Kids who live in communities dealing with widespread problems stemming from the opioid crisis.

Readers who have a family member struggling with addiction. Nonbinary readers. LGBTQ readers and allies. Kids who need to feel safe, and kids who long to be seen. My hope is for my book to find its way into your hands. If *Orphanland* meant something to you and if you are able, please send me a letter or note through my website, www.laurenbfischer.com, or leave a review online. As an independent author, it would mean the world to me.

Discussion Questions

- Who can be considered an orphan in *Orphanland*? Why?
- What systems (for example, education, health care, religious) have affected the lives of the orphans living at the Southern Ohio Children's Home?
- What are some different examples of motherhood as portrayed in *Orphanland*?
- Name the different types of privilege that different characters have.
- What are some benefits of having privilege? What are some detriments of having privilege?
- What does Katherine do with her privilege? In what ways do her choices differ from choices made by her sister-in-law (Eleanor)? In what ways do Meredith's choices differ from Katherine's?
- Do you agree or disagree with Katherine's statement that *We live in a cruel and unjust world ... there will never be a time when the world is just*?
- List some of the different identities the characters have in *Orphanland*. Is there one identity that they've all had in common?

- Mercy says that Eleanor will "never have to pay" despite the fact that she donates a large sum of money. What does Mercy mean?
- Why does Meredith read a land acknowledgment? Is there anything that her land acknowledgment is missing, or that you would add?
- How do you see the depiction of a rural setting in this book? Is it a setting you are familiar with? Can you think of any stereotypes that might be associated with small towns?
- What role does community play in *Orphanland*?
- Willa says that she has learned that remembering and acknowledging is better than forgetting. What does she mean, and why does she feel this to be true?

Lauren Bomberger Fischer was born and raised in Indiana, graduated from Miami University in Oxford, Ohio, and lives in Chicago with her family and rescue cats. She edited many articles about the opioid epidemic while working as a science editor at The JAMA Network. To learn more and sign up for her newsletter, visit her website at www.laurenbfischer.com.